OTHER GUN PEDERSEN BOOKS
BY L. L. ENGER

SACRIFICE
STRIKE
COMEBACK
SWING

THE
SINNERS'
LEAGUE

A GUN PEDERSEN MYSTERY

L. L. ENGER

OTTO PENZLER BOOKS

NEW YORK

OTTO
PENZLER
BOOKS

Otto Penzler Books   Simon & Schuster Inc.
129 West 56th Street   Rockefeller Center
New York, NY 10019   1230 Avenue of the Americas
(Editorial offices only)   New York, NY 10020

Library of Congress Cataloging-in-Publication Data
Enger, L. L.
The sinners' league : a Gun Pedersen mystery / L.L. Enger.
        p.   cm.
ISBN 1-883402-64-6
1. Pedersen, Gun (Fictitious character)—Fiction. 2. Private investigators—
Minnesota—Fiction.   I. Title.
PS3555.N422S56   1994
813'.54—dc20   94-15996
CIP

1   3   5   7   9   10   8   6   4   2

Manufactured in the United States of America

To Dana Isaacson

THE
SINNERS' LEAGUE

CHAPTER ONE

The whore's trailer house sat rusted and cockeyed beneath a solid wall of venerable pines. Standing in a cool September drizzle, feet planted in the muddy yard, Gun Pedersen looked up toward the North Star, which winked like a yellow dog eye in the vaporous night. He heard his wife knock once more on the aluminum door.

"Not home," Gun told her. He turned away, hands in his pockets. Only a small clearing had been hacked out of the trees. Enough room for a tilting steel swing set, a large sandbox built of pine logs, and a makeshift carport whose corrugated plastic roof sheltered a curvacious silver Geo coupe and a squashed pickup truck. According to instructions, Gun and Carol had parked their own vehicle a quarter-mile to the west in a thicket of red willows.

"I think I hear something," Carol said, at the door. "Yes, here she is."

He saw the bare light bulb pop on above the trailer house door, saw Carol lean close to the window, saw her lift a hand in greeting. Selfish instinct told him to walk away, go back to the truck, find a country station on the radio, wait—this business was Carol's. Instead he mounted the sand-filled tire that served as a doorstep and followed his wife inside.

To the left was the kitchen, chaste white and spotless. To the right, the living room, seventies Mediterranean: dark paneling, heavy furniture, red shag carpeting. Everything in its place here, orderly. A magazine rack with *Travel and Leisure*, a coffee table with books opened to color photographs of splatter-art and minimalist sculpture. On the walls hung prints of mountains and islands under gaudy skies.

"So here we are," said the woman. She was dark, tall, and much too thin, shoulder bones spiky beneath a silk blouse. Her eyes worked Gun over, top to bottom, weighing, measuring. She zeroed in on his feet and her lips clamped in disapproval. His running shoes were caked with the fine sandy muck of her front yard.

"Do you mind?" she said.

"It wasn't my idea, walking in." Gun looked at her hard enough to communicate what he wanted her to know: *I'm not the one who wants the goods on your life.*

She blinked and glanced into the kitchen, where a Mr. Coffee groaned and spit. She crossed her arms and stepped backward. "Thanks for coming, Carol. And sorry about your feet. It's just, if my mother sees a car out front . . ."

"It's okay."

Carol had explained to Gun on the way out. Each night Loreen's mother watched the two kids until two-thirty A.M., then dropped them off on her way to the casino, where she worked the three-to-eleven shift. The clock in the kitchen said one-forty.

"Oh, and you two haven't met. Gun, this is Loreen Baxter. And Loreen, Gun. I hope you don't mind I brought him along. He still gets worried when I'm out late." Carol laughed, embarrassed.

"New husbands don't ever stay new," said Loreen.

• • •

In the living room they were offered a scarlet sofa that smelled strongly of vanilla. The cushions were flat and the springs shot. Loreen went into the kitchen for coffee.

"You did insist on coming," Carol whispered.

Gun looked at her. Her eyes were a lighter shade of green, cooler in this mood, and the few silver lines in her dark hair twisted and veered. Of course he'd insisted. You didn't let your wife go into the Reservation in the dead of night, even if your wife is a journalist. Even if the story is a big one. Even if your wife is a proud woman and doesn't want you along.

He smiled at her and reached into his pocket for tobacco and papers. Carol gave him an earnest frown which Gun ignored as he built a smoke against one knee.

"Here." Loreen had the fingers of her right hand laced through the handles of three steaming mugs. She handed them out. On the coffee table she placed a glass ashtray that advertised Hawk Lake Casino. Just ten months old, the Chippewa-owned casino had brought money and crime to a region not used to either.

"Thanks," Gun said, and lit up.

Loreen moved a rocking chair next to Carol's end of the couch and sat down. Lit her own cigarette, unfiltered. Her fingers—nails painted a surprising baby blue to match her eyelids—made the cigarette shake. Her face was gaunt, pretty. Good cheekbones, lustrous black hair that fell across both shoulders clear to her waist.

She said, "This is dumb."

"Having me here?" Carol asked.

Loreen nodded.

"Want us to leave?"

Loreen squinted, shook her head. She took a long draw on

the cigarette, pulling half an inch of paper to ash. "No. But it's still dumb."

Carol glanced at her wristwatch. "Your kids'll be here in forty-five minutes."

"Yes," said Loreen.

"I guess you understand it's not what you do that I'm interested in. It's who . . . arranges things. Who profits."

"Who pimps," Loreen said. Her eyes held fast to Carol's. "Not so easy, that one. It's not like there's anything set up." She smiled, showing a set of straight, long, unstained teeth. "There's not exactly a standard contract."

"They give you business, though."

"Put it like this. Somehow they know how to find me. First they lose, over there. Then they come over here and win. And mostly they know I'm finished at one. I don't get any coming around after that. They know."

"But you don't have any arrangements with the casino? With anyone connected to it? Nothing like that?"

"Nothing hard and fast." Loreen took a long satisfied pull on her cigarette, then coughed, and you could hear the years of heavy smoking. "Look, I'm not hurting. I do okay. But there's other girls . . ." she said, her eyes going dull. "Which is why you're sitting here. See, I didn't invite you over to cut my own throat." She ground her cigarette into the ashtray. Gun still had a good two inches left of the smoke he'd rolled.

"Go ahead," said Carol, glancing again at her watch. "The other girls."

Loreen pushed back in the rocker and crossed her legs. She looked away, into the kitchen, and started biting one of her baby-blue fingernails.

Gun looked at his watch. Five before two. He stood up

and said, "Think I'll go out for a walk," but he hadn't taken a step when he heard a car pull up outside. A loose-sounding car, low-pitched, like a large American-made.

Loreen sprang out of her rocking chair, saying, "That ain't Mama, shit," and ran to the door. She took one look out the window then ordered Gun to stay put, waving him away with an arm. "Now just be quiet," she whispered before slipping outside.

Gun moved to the wall next to the large picture window. Carefully he made a line of sight for himself at the edge of the drawn shades. He felt Carol at his elbow. "I thought she said they never showed up after one," she whispered.

Outside a tall man in a dark suit rose from an Olds Toronado. He was tieless, his white shirt open at the collar. He called out "Hi" to Loreen, who was standing on her front step, saying, "Do you know what time it is, sir?"

He walked around to the passenger door, stepping carefully in the mud, shaking his head.

"Sir?" said Loreen.

The man rapped at the passenger-door window. Inside the car, a girl was shaking her head. The man rapped again, jerked a thumb toward the trailer house. Through the thin metal wall, Gun heard Loreen's voice. "It's two o'clock, sir. I finish up at one. Sorry, but you'll have to leave."

"Oh, God," said Carol.

Gun saw the man twist his upper body around to face Loreen, heard him say, "You're not done, yet. Overtime, tonight."

"Hey—you heard me." Loreen's voice was harder now, and an octave lower.

"Time and a half," said the man. He worked his car key into the passenger door and swung it wide saying, "Let's go,

Dotty," then reached in for the girl. The car's interior light allowed Gun to see the girl pull free and scramble toward the backseat. The man leaned in and picked her out of his car by the waist, upside down, her legs kicking in the air as he straightened up. She had on tights, the kind all the girls wore now, pink ones, and high-heeled shoes. She was scrawny. The guy dropped her headfirst in the mud, then staggered backward, arms at his sides, hooting. Coming through the walls of the trailer it sounded like a cheap sitcom laugh track.

"I can't watch this," said Gun. He started for the door, but Carol held onto him.

"Please—not yet. I've got to hear this." She pressed a hand on the small of his back.

". . . and I didn't drive clear the hell out here to stand in this soup," the man was saying. "Now get your asses inside." He swung his pointing finger from Loreen to the girl in the pink tights, who'd managed to get to her knees. "Now get yourself up, Dotty." He reached down and grasped her shoulder.

"Leave her be!" snapped Loreen. "Girl, you get away now. Get away from him." But the girl was stiff as a garden saint, kneeling there in the mud at the man's feet.

The guy straighted up and laughed once more. He said, "Oh, shit," and his hand fell slapping to his thigh. "Loreen, Loreen, you misunderstand me. I'm not into resistance. No, no. Me, it's submission. And I'm gonna have the both of you submitting yourselves all over me. Now, come on." He lifted his hands palms up and wiggled his fingers.

"Leave, I'm saying. Get your shitty carcass off my property."

Gun could see Loreen's words working their way past the guy's narrowed eyes and into his head. He leaned down and slapped the girl hard across the face. Gun got out the door as fast as he could but was stopped short on the front step by the sight of Loreen, her skinny body moving in a violent, graceful dance, snapping the antenna off the Olds, testing its bite against the air, and closing on the man. She laid him out with a single arcing blow to the side of the head. He fell without sound or struggle, face down, his arms and legs forming a perfect X on the ground. The girl found her legs now and stood over him. She kicked him twice in the ribs with her sharp little shoes, then turned and gave herself up to Loreen's long arms.

Loreen looked from the man in the mud over to Gun, and her eyes caught his in a gaze he couldn't have held for long. then she dropped the antenna to the mud, saying, "It's getting late. Help me get this piece of shit out of my yard and down the road."

CHAPTER TWO

Gun turned him over and used a lapel from his dark suit jacket to wipe the mud from his face. A welt ran from the man's chin, across one cheek and disappeared into the hairline. He was bleeding from the outer corner of his left eye. His breathing and his heartbeat were strong.

"He'll survive," Gun said.

"Too bad," said Loreen. "Give me his wallet." She still held Dotty's face to her chest, but now the girl pulled away and looked at Gun. There was nothing but challenge in her face, no fear left, no pain or confusion. Her eyes were little black rocks, hard and flat.She looked about thirteen.

"My Lord, what's she doing here?" Gun said.

Loreen ignored him, and the girl broke free and walked over to the Oldsmobile and dropped herself into the passenger seat.

On the ground, the man sat up and looked around, rubbing the welt on his face. His focus came to rest on Gun's knees and traveled up. "Aw, damn it. Police?"

Gun laughed.

"Hold it, hold it. I know you. Shit. Baseball player. You're Gun Pedersen." He closed his eyes and worked his forehead with his fingers. "Heard you lived up around here somewhere. I don't believe this."

Gun walked over to the tire step and sat down on it next to Carol. Loreen squatted next to the man in the mud. She held his driver's license close to her eyes and read from it.

"James Eldon Swanson, Forty-five twenty Burke Avenue South, Minneapolis. Born nine twelve fifty-eight. Blue eyes. Six-two, two hundred and ten." She tossed the wallet back to him and stood up. Flexed the plastic card in her fingers. "James, that wife you told me about last time? Well I feel for her. And I feel for you, James. How she makes you pee sitting down, the other stuff you told me. But you don't want to hurt her, I know that. And you don't want to hurt your three little girls. So, if you forget about tonight, then so will I."

"Yeah, yeah." He rocked himself up to one knee. He couldn't keep his fingers off the welt on his face. "I'm out of here."

"We have a deal?" Loreen leaned over and pushed him back down on his butt.

"Yeah, I said. It's done. Forgotten, all right? Now let me have my license."

"Not till you've answered the lady's questions." Loreen motioned with her hand for Carol.

Gun felt his wife stiffen at his side, but she caught on quickly. "What we've got to know," Carol said, "is how you hooked up with Dotty here. Who set you up with her."

James Swanson jerked his head toward Carol and said to Loreen, "What is she, a cop?"

"She's a messenger of God, James—tell her what she wants to know."

Swanson stood and walked heavy-footed to the Toronado and leaned on the front right fender. He said, "Nobody. Least nobody I know of."

"What happened then? Where'd you find her?"

Swanson shrugged. "I was on the slots. She just came up and stood real close and said stuff. I mean, it was hard to ignore." He looked over at the girl, who was staring down at her hands, which were covered with rings, at least one on each finger, Gun noticed now. Mostly silver, some with big colored stones. Costume jewelry.

"Hey, I'd never go out and pick up a girl like that, a kid her age. I mean, she was painting herself all over me. And the mouth she's got on her, I figured this was like every night to her."

Carol said, "Was it like he says, Dotty?"

The girl didn't move or speak, but Gun saw Loreen catch Carol's eye and nod.

"Nobody at Hawk Lake set you up with her?" Carol asked Swanson.

The man held her eyes for a moment. "I honestly couldn't say."

"Honestly?" said Loreen.

"I swear it. I don't know."

"Then get the hell out of here, James."

Dotty lifted her feet and swung herself into the Olds.

"Where do you think *you're* off to?" Loreen asked.

"Going back with him. Let him drop me off."

"Drop you off where?"

"Wherever, it doesn't matter." Dotty pulled her door shut and locked it.

Loreen walked over to Swanson and asked for his car keys, which he handed over, groaning. He was draped across the front corner of his car like a depressed, oversized cat. Loreen used his key to open Dotty's door, then ordered the girl out. Dotty obeyed. She seemed resigned now. The whole night was getting slow and thick, the air denser, sounds and voices muffled by the wetness. The stars had gotten choked out completely. Gun looked again at his watch. Twenty past two.

Loreen returned the keys to Swanson, told him "Have a nice trip." He walked around the front of his car, moving so slowly it was painful to witness. Before he got in, he looked over the hood of his Olds and said, "Gun Pedersen. I'll be damned."

Gun nodded.

The man started his car, backed onto the gravel road, and headed south toward the casino. Loreen and Carol walked the girl to the front door of the trailer house. Gun stood, wiping the damp sand from the back of his trousers.

Loreen said, "What're we going to do with you, Dotty?"

"That ain't my real name," said the girl.

"Ain't it now," said Loreen.

The girl shrugged. "It's what I call myself."

"Well, we can't send you back where you came from," Loreen said. "Wherever that is. And you can't stay here."

Gun started off down the wet road toward his truck. "I'll be waiting," he called back to his wife.

The mist was turning to honest rain.

CHAPTER THREE

By morning the front had passed to the east and dissipated over Lake Superior. The first vague light, filtering like smoke through the high old white pines, woke Gun before six. He drew the heavy shades for Carol's sake and walked into the kitchen in his underwear and started coffee. Then, remembering they were not alone this morning, he retreated quietly into the bedroom and pulled on yesterday's chinos.

He did his push-ups on the kitchen floor, ninety-six of them, the formula being his age times two. At the table he rolled a cigarette, his eyes holding to the old familiar square of sky through the window above the sink. During these first minutes of a day, Gun did not allow himself to think, but tried simply to note the sensations of the cold floor beneath the soles of his feet, the clear northern air on his skin, the fresh tobacco and strong coffee on his tongue. By the time he went outside—a boxful of baseballs under an arm and a thirty-five-inch bat on his shoulder—he was ready to consider what the day might hold in the way of rewards and obligations.

A dozen balls came fast and true from the iron arm of his home-built pitching machine. Seven reached Stony Lake, home-run distance away, and this neither pleased nor displeased Gun, the motion of swinging a bat as natural to him as swinging a hammer was to a carpenter. It was the way he'd made a living, a life for himself.

• • •

He had known that Carol would bring the girl home last night. He'd known it immediately, even before Loreen's thrashing of the hapless Mr. Swanson. It was fine; it was Carol's way. Get involved, put yourself on the line. Yet Gun was afraid she might think she could write a story or two, direct her moral high beam into the appropriate crevices, then stand back and watch the big boots of justice march in and stomp the monsters. A pretty thought, and Gun knew Carol had more savvy than to subscribe to it completely. Still, he wondered if she had any sense of how deep and twisting those crevices might be, and how nasty the creatures therein. It was why Gun had insisted on going along last night, and why he half-expected surprise visitors today. Loreen might have intimidated James Swanson into silence, but the girl Dotty, whoever she was—if she represented somebody's investment, that somebody would be wondering what happened to her.

Gun walked down across the wide, unmown, heavily treed yard to Stony Lake, stripped to his underwear on the wooden dock, and dove in. The water, with just a memory of the summer sun left in it, was chilly enough to tighten his skin and make him stroke hard for warmth. He surfaced thirty yards out, turned onto his back, and aimed as he did every morning for the island a quarter-mile away.

Half an hour later, as he pulled himself back up on the dock, his heart was going good and strong, pulsing in every cell and fiber.

• • •

Walking up to the house he was surprised to see Carol through the kitchen window. She gave him a small, unconvincing wave, a stingy smile. It was seven o'clock, and this was normally her morning to sleep in. The *Journal* hit the stands on Thursdays, and Fridays she liked to get up at nine or ten, then make the phone calls necessary to get herself pointed toward next week's stories. Friday was also the day Gun breakfasted in town with his friend Jack LaSalle, though today Jack was in Duluth helping Stony's former priest move into a condominium for retired clerics.

Carol didn't turn as he entered the house. Arms plunged in dishwater, she stood facing the kitchen window through which Gun, alone, had watched the last decade of mornings come up.

"Thought you'd be asleep," he said.

She nodded but did not reply. He wondered from the slant of her shoulders whether she'd been crying.

Still wet from the swim, Gun crossed to the table in his towel and sat down to watch the new sun lay a silver edge on her black hair. How odd, he thought, yet how utterly natural to see Carol against this familiar pattern of trees and sky. He remembered his father saying once how women had a way of supplanting history with themselves, of making men forget everything but their scented necks and smart moves, their satiny voices. Of course, the old man was a romantic who had married just once, and married well at that.

Gun rose from his chair and stood close behind his wife, put his arms around her, his fingers on her flat belly. He spoke into the softness of her hair. "What's wrong?"

Carol turned and pressed her face to his chest. She shook her head and put her ear to his heart. "The girl," she said. "I feel so badly about her. Thirteen, and she's already used up. And that look she has, like there's nobody there at all. Have you seen that? Like whatever she had inside before just pulled out, left." Her voice stiffened. "And the people that used her, Gun—I can't tell you how much I hate them. I hate them." Gun felt Carol's arms tighten about him, pushing air from his lungs.

"You're doing what you can," he said. "Maybe you'll make the difference for her."

Carol inhaled deeply and blew out. "I'm scared, and that's not me. I don't get scared much."

"It's going to be all right."

"No, Gun, I don't think so. Sometimes I get a feeling, like something horrible's coming. Like it's on its way—I can't see it, but it can see me and there's nothing to be done. That's how I feel now. I woke up in the night and I knew it. Gun, we've got to be careful."

"We'll be careful."

"We've got to watch out for each other." Carol pulled away from him now and looked up. Her eyes were dry and solemn, and darker than he'd ever seen them.

He pulled her close again. Held her.

A quarter of an hour later, as they sat next to each other over coffee, Dotty appeared in the hallway wearing a bathrobe of Carol's. In response to Carol's "Good morning" she mumbled something unintelligible, then popped into the bathroom, which was adjacent to the kitchen.

Carol whispered, "Look, Gun, maybe you could go fishing or something."

"What?"

"I'd really like to talk with her alone for a while this morning. Besides, walleye for breakfast—that'd make a good impression."

In their bedroom Gun dressed for a cool morning on the lake, then took the plastic carton of leeches from the refrigerator and went down to the stone boathouse for his gear. The walleyes had gone into a sulk the past few weeks and he didn't expect success, but it was time on the water and that was enough.

Chapter Four

An hour later he pulled his laden stringer from the water, swung it flopping to the floor of the boat, threw the gear lever of the 25-horse Johnson into forward, and headed home. The walleyes had been fussy at first but he'd managed to squeeze more than a breakfast from the lake, and it wasn't nine o'clock yet. He cleaned the fish on the dock, then carried them up to the house, the stack of fillets glistening dully in the sun.

Carol opened the door for him, but her eyes didn't go to his catch. They stayed on his face.

He said, "What's wrong?" glancing past her to the girl, who sat sideways to the kitchen table, smoking, ignoring a bowl of uneaten Wheaties. Dotty's legs were crossed at the knees and again at the ankles in a way that made her look ten years older than she was.

"You got a phone call," said Carol. "Diane Apple. She's in Minneapolis."

"Oh."

"She wants you to call. I took her number."

Gun hefted the stack of fillets balanced on his palm and managed a smile. "Hope you're hungry."

"Go ahead. I had some cereal. Maybe Dotty wants some." Carol turned and briskly walked into the kitchen. "Dotty? You like walleye?"

"Naw. Too many bones."

"Oh—Gun?" Carol's voice was just the tiniest bit too intimate. "Diane mentioned the old-timers game tonight."

He opened the door to the basement and descended, punishing the stairs on his way down. Using bread bags he double-wrapped the walleye fillets, then dropped them in the freezer and spent the next fifteen minutes tying up months' worth of newspapers into bundles for recycling. It was a job he usually put off for as long as possible.

Diane Apple was a good friend who could have been much more. Gun had met her two years before in Florida, under difficult circumstances. Her brother Billy had been murdered in a case involving an old baseball friend of Gun's. For a couple of weeks Diane and Gun together had survived a variety of shit-storms and by the time it was all over, leaving her and heading back north had not been easy. Once or twice in passing he'd mentioned her to Carol, but he'd never seen the purpose in trying to explain to his wife the nature of his friendship with Diane—the connection he felt to her, the way she'd made herself available to him. The last time he'd seen her was three months ago, a few weeks before his marriage to Carol. It was a chance meeting, at which he'd made his choice clear to Diane. And now, though in truth he'd *not* had second thoughts, Gun couldn't help remembering the pang of losing her. Alongside which, Carol's jealousy—her suspicion, whatever it was—seemed especially hard to take. It was unwarranted, and the guilt she was apparently assigning him, undeserved.

As he stepped back into the kitchen, Carol was closing herself into the bathroom which adjoined it.

"Woman's in a great mood," said Dotty. She spoke without taking her eyes from the newspaper spread upon the table. The comic section. She traced the words with an index finger as she read.

Gun took the notepad from the kitchen phone and went into the bedroom. Using the old black rotary model on the nightstand, he dialed the number Carol had taken down in a hand sharper and more firmly pressed than usual.

The phone rang three times and then Diane's voice was there, as soft and deep as he remembered. More relaxed, though. Languid. He could see her stretched out on a huge bed, her auburn hair wet and turbaned in a towel. Her eyes closed.

"It's Gun."

"Gun, I was afraid . . . I don't know." She laughed quietly. "It's so good to hear you."

"You surprised me."

"I surprised your wife, too."

"Yes," Gun said, and let the silence ride for a moment. "My impression in Toronto was, you'd rather not have anything more to do with me."

"I'm a poor loser, no doubt about that. Then again, I get over things. When I get beat, I usually get up and fight again. Or I move on. In this case, I've moved on. No offense, Gun, but you're not hurting me anymore."

"What's in Minneapolis?" he asked.

"Business. A script-writing deal. I'm only here for a couple days." She told him about the project, writing a movie based on a legal thriller written by a Minneapolis attorney. "But why I called. I was reading the paper this morning, the sports page, and I guess you know what I saw."

As a benefit for disabled former big-leaguers, the Twins were sponsoring an old-timers game, scheduled for tonight, and Gun had agreed to be there. He'd be in the outfield with Oliva, Yastrzemski, and others, depending on how they were platooned. Respectable company, any way you cut it.

"Gun, are you there?"

"Yup."

"You *are* planning to be there tonight."

"Yeah."

"I was thinking we could meet for dinner, beforehand. Or for coffee afterwards. Whatever works for you. And if Carol's coming, great. I'd love to meet her."

"She's not," Gun said.

"Well, what do you think?"

"I'm not sure."

"Look, Gun. I'm not kidding when I say it's all right. I'm fine with this. I mean, as long as you are."

She made it sound so easy, so uncomplicated. Which it was. "I'd love to see you," he said, thinking, *Carol will just have to live with it.*

They agreed on coffee at a small restaurant near the Metrodome, a place called My Red Supper, for its ribs. After the game.

When the conversation was over, for no reason that made sense to Gun, he laid the receiver in its cradle carefully, so as to make no sound. Then he sat waiting for Carol in the rough-hewn cedar chair he'd built for his first wife Amanda twenty years ago. Outside the window a pair of jays squawked, fighting over the tough strap of bacon fat Gun had tacked to the birch tree. In the kitchen, the girl had evidently finished reading the comics. He heard her switch on the television, crank the volume, and go channel-hopping. She landed on a game show, the voices of young men and women shouting and laughing at each other. Some kind of dating program. Gun rolled a cigarette, smoked it. Rolled another.

Finally the shower went silent. Minutes later Carol entered the bedroom wrapped in a huge apricot towel. Her shoulders and feet were pink and steaming from the hot water. She closed the door behind her.

Gun drew on his cigarette. "Our guest seems to have made herself comfortable."

"I hope so."

"And you're lovely." He watched her move to the dresser and shake her damp head in front of the mirror. She brushed out her hair quickly, inspecting her face from various angles as she worked, and the impressions she made on herself seemed to register in the slight adjustments of her hips beneath the apricot towel.

"Did I just tell you I think you're lovely?" Gun asked.

"You did." Carol's green eyes found his in the mirror.

"I thought so."

Carol took a red lipstick from the top of the dresser and leaned close to the mirror. She performed a flat, lip-stretching smile, then puckered up. Lipstick was the only makeup Gun had ever seen her use. "I made a couple of calls this morning," she said, tracing her lips. "Sheriff Durkins, and Donna." Donna Wright was the head of Stony County Child Protection and a friend of Carol's.

"I suppose you talked them into letting us keep her."

"Sort of. Donna said as long as Dotty's willing, it's fine for now. There's that place over in Moose Creek where they keep juveniles until the courts decide where to put them. Durkins said he'd poke around and see if he can find who she belongs to, and if he doesn't have any luck in the next day or two, that's where Dotty'll go. In the meantime, we keep a close eye on her, feed her, let her relax. God, she's wound up."

"As we speak, she's probably halfway to town," said Gun, but just then he heard the sound of the shower starting up. He shrugged.

"Is it such a bother, having her around? Gun, she's a kid. She needs somebody to start treating her like one, take care of her. That's what I'm going to do. I don't know, make cookies, go shopping, buy some clothes."

"Get her talking. Get her to tell us her real name."

"That, too."

Carol turned and walked to the bed, on which she had laid out a clean pair of Levis and a gray sweatshirt. She unwrapped the apricot bath towel from around herself and let if fall to the floor. With a toe she hooked it and sent it away.

Gun admired her quietly, then said, "Fine."

Carol turned and faced him, her eyes level, her mouth contemplating a smile.

"Fine with me if Dotty sticks around." He looked at his wife and took a long breath, saw her do the same. He saw the deep color of her lips, the line of light at the curve of her waist. He cleared his throat and let his eyes wander to the closed door. "Do you suppose she takes long showers?"

Carol had picked up the sweatshirt, but now dropped it. "Probably not, but that's all right, isn't it?"

Glancing down at his cigarette hand, Gun saw an inch-long ash. He reached for the ashtray on the nightstand, and immediately felt the weight of the moment shift in the direction he was leaning. He looked up. Carol's eyes were fastened to the notepad next to the telephone.

"You called her already," she said.

Gun rubbed out his cigarette. He thought about saying, *I wouldn't have to go*. Then reconsidered. "Yes," he said.

Quickly, efficiently, Carol collected her bath towel from the floor and rewrapped herself in it. Her shoulders were no longer pink, but pale. Her feet looked white and blue-veined. She said, "Sometimes I'd rather be alone when I get dressed."

Gun rose from the chair and took his leave.

CHAPTER FIVE

He tried once to talk with her, more out of guilt than earnest hope, and expecting nothing. It was an hour later, and she and Dotty were back from town with a few groceries. Carol had the girl mixing chocolate-chip cookies in the kitchen. Baking wasn't an interest of Carol's, but at the moment she was holding forth like Mrs. Fields.

"You want to mix the eggs and shortening and sugar very well before adding the other ingredients. No, here. You want to hold the bowl like this, up close to you. That'll give you some leverage. Good. There."

Gun listened from the living room, pretending to read *Baseball Weekly*. When Carol walked past him saying, "Be right back, Dotty," he got up and followed her. She pushed through the screen door and outside. He caught up to her inside the garage where she was standing, hands on hips, surveying the large square pile of cardboard boxes she hadn't gotten around to unpacking yet. "I can't believe this. We don't have any cookie sheets inside."

"What about mine?"

"They were covered with mouse turds. I threw them out."

"And you've got some here?"

"Here somewhere, yes."

Gun started taking boxes from the top of the pile, shaking each one, and setting those that sounded promising on the concrete floor. Carol dug through them, working her shoulders and pumping her arms, putting her whole body into the effort.

Gun said, "I'm only having coffee with the woman, Carol."

"I hope it's good coffee."

"There's nothing to be upset about."

"No?"

"No."

"Then how come we're having this conversation?"

"Because you're overreacting."

Carol said, "Ah," and held up a shiny metal cookie sheet. She stood up and gave the box a shove with her foot. "I wish you could've seen your face react when I told you who called this morning." She straightened up and walked away, leaving Gun staring down into half a dozen boxes filled with the artifacts of the life Carol had left behind.

He was still in the garage when he heard the car turn into the driveway. Stepping into the sun, he saw a gleaming gold Range Rover emerge from the shade of the two fir trees standing like huge gateposts at the edge of the yard.

The vehicle stopped just short of where Gun stood. Men stepped out from both front doors, which had been painted with the words Hawk Lake Gaming Association. The men were dressed in blue suits, fashionably cut. They both had on Jack Nicholson–style sunglasses. The driver was blond, a healthy six-footer with a tightly set jawline. He looked about forty-five. The other man, red-haired, appeared younger than the driver by about ten years and still carried baby fat in his face and on his frame. He was smiling to himself, almost lewdly, as if he'd just remembered a dirty joke.

"Ronald Stanky," he said, stepping up and offering a hand. "And this is Rich Morton." The blond one nodded, kept his hand to himself. "And you're Gun Pedersen," added Stanky. "Good to meet you."

"What do you boys do for the casino?" Gun took a single step backward, straightened himself to his full height, and peered down at the men. There were advantages to being six and a half feet tall, and he'd learned how to use them.

The red-haired one, Stanky, nodded. "Head of media relations," he said. "And Rich here's security. Used to be with the Feds." Stanky lowered his voice and the point of his tongue appeared at the corner of his mouth. "FBI, don't tell," and he laughed.

Gun didn't smile. "How is the thievery trade? Still booming?"

"Legal, too." Stanky chuckled. "We're here to see your wife. Is she home?"

"What do you want Carol for?"

"Well—we understand she's doing a story."

"That's what journalists do for a living."

"Of course, and they want to get their facts straight, don't they? Frankly, Mr. Pedersen, we're out here because we thought we could be of some help to your wife."

"Carol will be so pleased."

"Do you mind if we come in?" asked Stanky, removing his glasses and nodding toward the house. Morton hadn't moved or spoken, though his impressive jaw muscles still ticked away. Maybe it was an old bureau trick.

"In fact, I'd rather you didn't come in. Maybe you want to leave a message for Carol. I'd pass it on dutifully."

"No, we've got to see the lady herself, if we're going to be of any help to her."

"She keeps office hours in town," Gun said. "Monday through Thursday, ten till four."

Now Morton too removed his sunglasses. His irises were a washed-out shade of blue, so pale it seemed almost possible to look straight through them into his skull. "This can't wait till Monday," he said, breaking his silence.

Gun heard the creaky spring of his front storm door. He said, "Maybe you won't have to." Carol let the door slam shut behind her and came forward across the lawn, propelled by her most aggressive gait, one Gun had seen her use only a few times. The two men drew back from Gun and shifted themselves stiffly to greet Carol.

"Ms. Long," said Stanky. "We're glad to find you home." He introduced himself and Morton, identified their employer.

"I offered to take a message," Gun said.

Carol didn't acknowledge him, and Stanky, smiling, said, "I'm sure you're accustomed to speaking for yourself, Ms. Long."

In his imagination, Gun took a grip on Stanky's wide face and squeezed until his fingers met in the center of the man's mouth cavity, above the back of his tongue.

Carol said, "State your business, Mr. Stanky."

"Let me be frank with you, Carol. Can I call you Carol? Truth is, the story you're doing on us—we're concerned about it. We're afraid you might not be finding the right angle. That's what you do, isn't it? Look for an angle?"

"Which story is it you're talking about? There are so many. Your check-kiting scandal? Your tax problem? Profit distribution?"

Stanky laughed. "I think even you would agree, Carol, there's been plenty written about those subjects already. And you've done your part, I might add."

"None of those, then."

"No. I'm talking about prostitution, of course. We know you're doing some research. We don't think you're talking to the right people."

"Who am I talking to?"

"That's not the point—"

"You just told me I've been talking to the wrong people."

"Hold it, hold it." Stanky lifted a hand. "It's not like we've been chasing after you, taking notes. We've heard things, is all. The grapevine, okay? And it looks to us like you should be going at things in a different way."

"You think I should've started with you, maybe?"

"Terrific idea, Carol."

"And you could've reassured me that everything at Hawk Lake is on the up-and-up, squeaky clean."

"Look, Carol, I said I'd be honest with you, and I will. But you've gotta be willing to hear me. Can we go inside?"

"I can hear you fine right here," said Carol.

"All right." Stanky took a deep breath and fished a pack of Camels and a lighter from the pocket of his suit jacket. He lit one and raised his eyebrows at Morton, who coughed and looked away toward the water. Morton made a show of taking in the wide yard and the sky above, but Gun saw his pale eyes sharpen as they passed across the house. Morton said, "Mind if I walk a little? Beautiful place you got out here."

"It is. And we mind," said Gun.

"Shit," said Morton, under his breath. He retreated to the Range Rover and got in behind the wheel, leaving the door open.

Stanky shook his head, spoke quietly. "One of these days, the poor bastard's just gonna snap. I keep telling him he's gotta learn to love life a little. Go fishing, I don't know." He sucked his Camel, blew smoke. "Anyway, prostitution." He sucked again, with resolve. "God no, we're not squeaky clean. A guy looking to buy himself some love is going to find somebody to take his money. Nothing we can do is gonna change that. There's plenty of girls in business for themselves and they'd say we're doing them a favor. But get me straight here. They do what they do on their own time, in their own place. We don't even want to know who they are. Do you understand me?"

"Yes," said Carol. "You came out here to say that?"

"Partly. I also came out to say things aren't always what they seem. I can tell you're a smart woman, Carol, and I don't want to talk down to you. But just because a whore's loitering someplace, it doesn't mean she's wanted there. We do our best, but they come around. Hey, we've had to throw some girls out — and I mean girls. There've been a couple that didn't look more than sixteen, seventeen. It's a problem. You know those little birds that eat lice off the backs of rhinos? It's sort of like that."

Gun and Carol stood and watched until the Range Rover rounded the curve in the driveway, disappearing in white birch and green fir. They listened until the engine wound out against the highway, faded, and was gone. Then Gun suggested they go inside and give Loreen a call.

From his wife's end of the conversation, he gathered that Loreen was fine; just now getting out of bed, in fact. No visitors. An uncomplicated morning.

Carol hung up the phone and said, simply, "She's fine. Nothing."

In the kitchen Gun threw together egg-salad sandwiches for lunch and listened as Carol attempted to draw Dotty into a conversation the girl wanted no part of. The three of them ate together in a silent, sun-drenched dining room, the girl smoking, Carol watching her, Gun watching Carol. The meal took all of ten minutes.

CHAPTER SIX

Gun left the house just before two o'clock. Dotty was still transfixed before the television; the soaps were on. Gun paused at the door to the room that was Carol's home office, seeing her there at her computer, working on next week's edition. Her hair was pulled into a ponytail fastened with a cherry-wood clip, the soap-smooth skin visible behind her ears. He leaned in the doorway with a folded windbreaker under his arm, waiting to see if she'd turn and speak. She didn't.

His retired Ford pickup rested these days beneath a maple tree behind the garage, inside which sat his new Ford pickup. He turned the familiar key and the Ford churned and shivered and finally woke with a burst of tail-pipe smoke that rose through foliage, rousting squirrels. He gave the engine a little time to remember itself, then eased out.

He hesitated at the highway. Closed his eyes; listened to the truck. Amanda had loved the old brute and so he'd kept it running; when he drove it, he did so out of a need beyond transportation. There were directions it seemed to take him—north, usually, but always away from confusion and noise.

Gun turned onto the highway. And yes, north. Not south toward Minneapolis. He accelerated hard, the drone of the road rising in pitch.

The old ball players, after all, would do very well without him tonight, and so would Diane. Her invitation had given him some harmless pleasure; let it stay that way. He thought of returning home, phoning Diane, calling it off. But he didn't wish to explain his decision to Carol—not at this moment. Anyway there was a pay phone twenty miles north, in the gravel parking lot of a tavern Gun knew. He'd drive there, call Diane. Then come back home.

He drove with the windows three-quarters down, the resulting breeze lifting gooseflesh on his arms. Miles wound away beneath him. A low gravel road arose on the left, and on impulse he took it, using the clutch respectfully; the Ford got grouchy in the lower gears. The road followed an obsolete fence line over a hump and down its back side, then curved and nearly disappeared along the edge of a dry swamp. Gun stayed with it until he found a patch smooth enough to turn around on, and there he stopped.

A great thing about Amanda's truck: It always took him to places that didn't need him.

A thin dirt trail crowded with deer tracks led him away from the swamp through stunted tamaracks which sub-sided to oaks as the elevation rose. The oaks in turn gave way to a clearing overgrown with scrub grass and aspen. It was a farmstead, or had been. He approached a dark mound, which became a house sunk into itself like a squash decaying. The T of a clothesline pole stood next to the mound, still planted eerily straight.

The barn was standing too, and in surprisingly good con-dition. Paintless, a little mule-backed, listing toward east. Still, Gun had seen many younger barns that looked worse. A section of the lower front barnyard wall was gone and he stepped through it. The vertical timbers were literally that: whole sections of trees, including the bark, which time had smoothed and which Gun judged to be oak. They supported a low ceiling of sawn planks. A ladder was built onto the nearest wall. He gave the boards a tug and they creaked but held. There was a boyish stir in his gut as he ascended to the haymow.

Up there it was twilight. Pale slanted ropes of sun came down from holes in the roof the size of bullets. At the back of the barn stood a large shape Gun almost recognized. Then his eyes fitted themselves to the light.

There was an airplane in the haymow.

Actually, only a fuselage. Gun walked the perimeter of the floor feeling oddly blessed, but he couldn't find the wings. A square hanging door faced the nose of the plane and he slid it open, the breeze entering recklessly, raising dust. The plane was painted a pale yellow which looked from the undersurface to have been orange once. It was a tiny two-passenger outfit, barely post-war, Gun guessed. Some land-bound farmer's dream, with stubby triangular legs, flat front tires, a minimal tail skid. It squatted at an angle, its windshield aimed at sky. He reached for the metal door handle and the latch clicked easily, the door opening without a sound. The whole thing wobbled as he climbed inside.

He sat in there thinking not of planes but of wives, one living, one dead, both of them still strong. Amanda had raised their daughter Mazy largely without his help, and now Carol was the one at home, doing the tough work: watchdogging the runaway, trying to help the girl while at the same time fighting those who'd made her what she was.

It occurred to Gun that he'd run from complications so long that resignation had nearly replaced regret. When playing for the Tigers he'd become overly impressed by his success and built for himself an admirable complication by betraying Amanda with a bad actress who admired his swing. A lot of ballplayers did that, and a lot of them lost their wives, but not the way Gun did. Amanda discovered the affair and boarded a flight for Minnesota, where the Tigers were playing the Twins. He hadn't even known she was on that plane, so when he first heard of the crash it was like all such far-off disasters, an awful shame but nothing you brooded about between innings.

Amanda had died on account of his mistakes, and Gun had coped by quitting baseball and going north. For more than a decade he'd pared his commitments: waking early, taking his swings, working it out with fear and trembling, and push-ups against bare wood. Praying for the sort of peace men had who hadn't killed their wives.

The plane's windshield was so fogged with age and dust that Gun couldn't see much from the cockpit. He stepped down, noticing a leather strap poking from beneath the seat. It was attached to a tan hard-shelled case. He pulled and brought out a pair of thick black-walled binoculars, Japanese make. From their weight alone he'd have guessed they were good ones, but it wasn't until he crouched in the sunlit opening of the sliding door and adjusted them to his eyes that he realized *how* good: no distortion, no pinch in his optic nerve. The glasses were so finely ground that they magnified not only objects but also light and the intensity of color, making the world almost too full to look at. Gun laid them down. He rolled a cigarette. Maybe he allowed Amanda's old pickup to whisk him away too often, but this time it had outdone itself.

He looked through the glasses once more. There was a narrow slough several hundred yards off with dry cattails along the edge and a thin stripe of green down the middle length. He caught movement among the trees at the far end of the slough. It wasn't much—a change of shadow from black to brown beneath the lacy webwork of low tamarack. He refocused the glasses and kept his eye on the spot. A minute later a white-tailed buck stepped out from the shade and pushed forward into dry cattails. It was a large deer with a black-hair yoke across its shoulders and a chest like an oil drum, and it ducked its wide antlers warily as it entered the swamp. The glasses brought the buck so close that it felt odd not to hear the brittle *schuss* of swamp grass as the animal surged forward. He had a moment to admire its caution and then it was gone, leaving nothing in the lenses but tan and shadows and one stark red-winged blackbird shifting on a cattail stem.

He tucked the glasses back into their case before leaving, and pushed the case back under the pilot's seat. Descending from the haymow he noticed how low the sun had fallen, and the lateness jolted him: He'd forgotten to call Diane.

Of course, there might still be time to catch her before she left the hotel.

He drove out along the tattered fence line, keeping his speed at the high end of sensible, reached the highway, and headed for the tavern known as Chippewa Corners. The Corners had the only public phone he knew of out here; he'd used it once, years before, when he'd come upon a one-car accident a mile or so north. It had been December, two days before Christmas, and the woman in the car had been drunk and almost frozen.

He reached Chippewa Corners as the sun flattened against the horizon. There were no cars in the lot; neon beer signs hung colorless in the windows. The place looked closed, and not just for the day. Gun parked next to the phone booth, reached into his pocket and came up with five quarters. He lifted the receiver. It was as dead as the tavern.

"Well . . ." Gun said, aloud. Diane was probably gone by now, anyhow—she certainly would be by the time he reached home. He'd have to call her tomorrow and explain. And Carol, Gun realized, disgusted with himself—Carol still thought he was down in the city, having dinner with Diane.

A misperception he'd be glad to put right.

She was cool but pleased when he drove in early, and they made love in whispers, the girl being in the next room. Afterward he didn't sleep as soon as Carol did, but it wasn't unpleasant to be awake. If he'd gone to the Cities, after all, he wouldn't be lying here with Carol's unbound hair drifting on his shoulder. He wouldn't even be back yet but driving still, drinking gas-station coffee from a styrofoam cup, anticipating home and a freezing reception.

His last waking thought was a confidence that he would not dream that night, and he didn't.

CHAPTER SEVEN

A dozen or so years ago when Gun's daughter Mazy had been thirteen, Dotty's age, he'd often found himself speechless in her presence. Dumb, in every sense of the word. Her woman's logic, arriving suddenly with a fullness all too significant, stymied him. Mazy required only a few words or that peculiar expression she'd perfected—haughty, yet kind—to make him understand and accept his limitations as the father of a daughter. He felt she alternately pitied him, loved him beyond deserving, put up with him. In light of this history, Gun saw no use this morning in trying to help Carol with her Dotty project. Smarter to stay out of the way, or better, out of sight.

So at nine o'clock he went out to the garage and sharpened the chain for his chain saw and went after a pair of old aspen trees, dead but still standing in the aging growth at the north edge of his land. At eleven o'clock Carol came out to say she and Dotty were driving over to Maddy Johnson's for eggs. When they left, Gun went inside to call Diane.

The phone rang several times and was finally picked up at the hotel desk. "Marriot." A chirpy female. Gun hung up. He didn't want to leave a message for Diane; it didn't seem right that *she* should have to call *him* to receive the apology she deserved.

Until noon Gun worked on the trees, cutting, hauling and stacking, adding to their winter mountain of wood fuel. He ate lunch with Carol and Dotty, then spent the afternoon on jobs he'd been saving for such a day: changing oil in his truck, fixing a roof leak in his boathouse, replacing some rotted dock planks. He tried to reach Diane two more times but she didn't answer, and that evening he went to bed with a vague concern that all night grew sharper in his dreams.

In the morning he and Carol woke early to radio news: The body of a screenwriter named Diane Leslie Apple had been found yesterday morning in a wooded Minneapolis park.

As an act of self-defense Gun started breakfast. But he found the motions and movements so habitual, so unrequiring of his concentration, that they offered no protection. It was too easy: slap bacon in a pan, crack eggs into another, adjust the flame, chop the onion, pop in the toast, hands working all by themselves—while in his mind, right there behind every door he tried, was Diane Apple, alive, a question on her face:

Where were you?

With my wife, where I was supposed to be. I tried to call—and at this, Diane would nod. That quality she had—to understand nearly everything, no matter how complex. Or, lacking understanding, the strength of character to try.

Gun smelled scorched eggs and reacted with the spatula. The eggs were fused to the bottom of the skillet, to which he'd forgotten to apply grease. He swore, shut off the burner, and dropped into one of the maple kitchen chairs. He lay his hands on the table and closed his eyes and felt the burning in his tear ducts. Then Carol was at his side, and he let her take his head and draw it close beneath her breasts. He felt her arms tighten about him, her hands cup gently over his ears, and he breathed in the smell of her—ocean, wilted flowers, cotton robe—and something inside him eased and warmed, if only slightly.

He let her hold him this way until the image of Diane began to clarify again in his brain. Then he touched his wife's hand and she released him. She went to the counter and poured a cup of coffee and set it on the table in front of him, then sat beside him, bringing his hand into her lap, her eyes so easy in how they regarded his.

"I love you," he said.

She nodded, accepting this, yet also radiating a love that somehow diminished his own for her. Gun was struck by this independence from language she'd achieved, and he felt compelled to say it again: "I love you."

Her eyes widened slightly, reciprocating. Quietly she said, "You've never said much about Diane."

"I didn't think there was much to tell."

"No?"

"We met in Florida, but you know that. Two winters ago. She had a brother, Billy."

"The reporter," Carol nodded. "The one who was killed."

"You could say it was a matter of my being there, and Diane needing somebody to be there. And we liked each other, too. Quite a bit. But nothing ever came of it."

"And now she just calls you up, out of the blue?" Carol spoke matter-of-factly, without accusation.

"Not quite." A dull guilt rose in Gun's chest. "Last summer when I went to Toronto—before the wedding—I ran into her. It was pure coincidence. They were filming a movie in the Sky Dome. We had dinner. Talked. We walked around for a couple of hours." Gun shrugged. "That was it."

"Why didn't you tell me?"

"There was nothing to tell, Carol. Nothing important enough to complicate things."

She shook her head. "What you're saying doesn't feel right, Gun. Not at all. It's like you haven't been honest with me. And you haven't, either, not completely." She still held his hand in her lap, but her fingers felt loose and dry.

"I didn't let anything happen, Carol. I'm telling you the truth."

"That's not the point. Something *could* have happened."

He laughed. What could he say? Of course something could have happened, but he'd made sure nothing did. He looked away from her and out the window, where he saw a line of geese in formation high above the pine trees.

"Gun, I believe you. But I'm wondering why you wanted to see her." Gun heard Carol take a breath. He felt the weight of her eyes on him. "Because you did, didn't you?"

"In a way, yes. But not in the way you think."

"I don't understand."

Gun didn't understand it himself. He hadn't wanted to start anything with Diane, or reclaim a lost opportunity. Nothing so simple. In a vague way Diane had offered a pleasing alternative to an already pleasing life—an alternative merely for contemplation. But more than that, Carol's reaction to Diane's phone call had irked him. The way she'd instantly put him on the defensive, ascribing him guilt he had not earned.

Carol said, "Don't take this on as yours, Gun. You're not responsible. Please."

"Of course I'm responsible."

She let go of his hand and stood, went to the sink, and

rinsed out her coffee cup. He watched her lay the cup aside and turn to him, hands on her waist, working up to something. Flecks of gold flashed in her green eyes.

Before she could speak Gun said, "If I'd gone down there like I said I would, Diane wouldn't be dead."

Carol groaned. "How can you say that, Gun? You were going to spend what, a couple of hours with her? Coffee, right? So the two of you have coffee. It's ten at night, eleven maybe when she leaves the restaurant. And then what happens? We don't know who killed her or where. We don't know anything. Let's say you'd gone down and seen her—we can't know what might've happened after you left. Can we?"

"No, we can't," Gun said.

"She's not your responsibility, Gun. It's simply not your fault."

"You might be right."

With soft finality Carol said, "Of course I'm right," smiling it seemed for his benefit. Gun felt grateful, and unconvinced.

He said, "I hope you are, Carol. But I need to find out. I need to know for sure. Please understand that."

Carol pressed her fingers to her brows. Her shoulders dropped and she leaned back against the kitchen counter. "Don't do this, Gun."

He reached forward and captured his wife's hands, which felt small and cool. "It's for me as much as for her," he said. He waited for Carol to ask, *What about me?* But she said nothing. Her eyes were closed.

"It seems wrong to you, I know," he said, "but it's necessary. For me, and for us. Will you try to believe that?"

For a long moment Carol didn't move. She might have been asleep, chin resting on her chest, her breath coming slowly. Then her eyes opened, shadow-green, and she looked at Gun carefully and without judgment. "All right," she said.

CHAPTER EIGHT

Harper LaMont, that was the name Diane had given him. In fact it was a name you couldn't escape lately. LaMont was the latest hot-rod attorney to decide he ought to write crime novels, and now he was on every wire rack in every grocery store you saw: *Harper LaMont,* his name in big foil letters, and *Time* magazine's assessment scripted below it, "The New Master of the Legal Thriller." Gun hadn't read them. None of the lawyer-writers reminded him of A. B. Guthrie and it was tough to be interested.

Now Gun drove through the midday streets of warehouse-district Minneapolis, looking for the building that housed the master's office. Diane had been working on a screen adaptation of LaMont's latest novel, *Hung Jury.* She'd written a few things that had gained some visibility, a movie of the week, and a baseball picture starring a former soap actor hoping to go legitimate. Nothing like *Hung Jury,* which—she'd said on the phone—had sold six hundred thousand in hardcover at $22.95 per. It was her big break all right.

Apparently they'd abducted her using a taxicab stolen from Metro Passage Inc. It wasn't known where she was picked up, but the cab hadn't taken her where she wanted to go. Instead, it stopped somewhere out of public notice, and there, in the car, they raped her. *They.* Multiple rapes, the newscaster said.

Gun had left at nine, with Carol's acceptance if not her blessing, and now he pictured her as he'd last seen her this morning in the rearview mirror of his pickup, bending to pick one of the last blooming chrysanthemums from the flower bed next to the garage. Then he thought of Diane's voice and its mock-daring edge as she asked him to meet her. My Red Supper. She'd laughed at the name.

Multiple rapes. And no known suspects. Gun's fingers were husk-dry on the wheel and his mind felt exposed to a hot wind. After the business in the car they'd killed her, cut off her air with a heavy rope or a twisted cloth. How long did that take? And dumped her body next to a natural spring in Theodore Wirth Park. Thinking of it now he wondered whether she'd died in the car or on the ground, the high trees rising above her and the fresh water running slow beside the struggle.

If he'd kept his word she would be living now.

You can't know that, Carol had told him. But he knew it. Gun gripped the wheel against a tide of self-disgust, as though he were related to the killers, would recognize their faces like distant cousins'. They'd done their part in Diane's killing, and he'd done his.

The unlucky driver from Metro Passage who had picked up the men was one Albert Iron Sky. He was missing. He was not, the report said, a suspect.

Harper LaMont's law office was on the sixth floor of the Steerman Building, a square hulk of old brick and new glass that looked post-*nouveau* cool: It had the high ceilings and unfinished walls, the polished wood floors showing authentic gouges from decades of loading dollies. It had a vegetarian restaurant and a cappuccino bar and officed a film company and a lesbian publisher. On the main level was a sports bar where, according to local papers, the hippest Twins relaxed after home games. Gun took the lift up with a group of three young men who looked like male models, guys with suits and stunning chins who stood shifting with the discomfort that rides perpetually in elevators.

LaMont's receptionist was a woman about Gun's age who wore a slim summer-white dress, wore it well, and didn't seem overly protective of her famous boss. "He's in his office but I'll warn you: He's moody today. What's it about?"

"Diane Apple. She was a friend of mine."

The receptionist said nothing but stood up and led him through a roomful of partitioned cubicles to an office with a heavy-looking oak door. The door stood half open and she said, "There you go," before turning snappily away.

LaMont was not at the desk but standing at a window, a short man with concave cheeks who sipped from a steaming cup. The window went all the way to the floor and he was looking east. The neighboring building topped out at five stories, and a dog, a lanky Weimaraner, was sitting motionless on the wide parapet. LaMont turned when he saw Gun in the doorway.

"Gun Pedersen," he said after a moment. "Not the fellow I would've expected. Maybe I should have." He had a deeper voice than his size suggested, full of practiced articulation, like Robert Seigel's on *All Things Considered*.

"Why's that?"

"Because you were supposed to see Diane the other night. She mentioned it to me." LaMont's eyes fastened to Gun's like a pair of blue hooks. "So did you?"

"Did I what?"

"See Diane." LaMont spoke quickly. "A couple friends ride along with you, perhaps? Wirth Park's beautiful at night."

Gun almost laughed but his anger squelched it. "Is there a judge in this room? All I see is a lawyer and an imitation writer. Maybe I'm in the wrong place."

"No, it's the right place." LaMont's eyes let go of him and wandered restlessly around the office. His hair was short but wild and almost frighteningly blond. "I'm sorry. I've been trying cases for twenty years, but this sort of random brutality—I need someone to blame. Tell me you don't."

Gun said, "Was it random?"

"Most likely. Do *you* know anyone who might've been after her?"

"No."

"So a group of hopeless cases rips off a taxicab and joyrides around the city. Diane Apple comes out of a restaurant and stands on the sidewalk. I don't know, maybe she was even *looking* for a cab, she might've waved them down."

The picture scrolled through Gun's imagination, Diane on the curb, maybe angry at his absence, seeing the cab approach, Diane leaning out with one hand extended and her hair swinging streetward. LaMont's voice was ironic saying, "Once again, the victim was asking for it."

Sure, honey, we'll give you a ride.

"So what happened, Pedersen? Why didn't you show up for dinner? The rib place, she told me."

"How do you know I didn't show?"

"Will you leave it be? I told you, I'm sorry for greeting you like Rumpole of the Bailey." LaMont pulled a blue ceramic mug off a shelf. "They told me at Homicide she was by herself at the restaurant. Had been for more than an hour. It was pretty clear she was waiting for someone. Besides—" LaMont handed Gun coffee, "a guy your size, I doubt she'd have much to worry about."

"I couldn't make it down. I tried to call."

LaMont seemed to think about what to say next. He sat at his desk, put his fingers over his eyes and rubbed while Gun pulled up a chair. A wooden chair, hand-built and straight-backed; it made a Mennonite of the sitter. When LaMont spoke again his eyes were pink, his voice subdued. "What are you doing here now?"

"I'm not sure."

"Is that right."

Gun didn't answer.

"You're not the guilty one, Pedersen. You probably ought to go home. There's nothing you can do."

A silver-framed photo was propped on the attorney's desk. A woman: red-haired and plain-featured, wearing a turquoise dress with a white lace collar. White spring lilacs bloomed behind her and she looked flushed, glad about something though possibly exasperated by the camera. "This is your wife?"

"Patrice."

LaMont's phone buzzed and he silenced it, punching a button, a viciousness in his movement that Gun understood. There was quiet in the office until Gun said, "Tell me about your meeting with Diane. Day before yesterday."

"I don't know that it would help you. I had only just met her."

"She mattered to me. I hadn't seen her in a while. I want to picture how she was."

The telephone buzzed again and a secretary's voice said, "Mr. LaMont, your one o'clock is here."

LaMont looked at his watch, double-checking. "I don't suppose you can come back later."

"I'd rather not."

The attorney held Gun's eye a moment longer, then pressed his intercom. "Radelia, I'm wrapped up at the moment. Give Carl my apologies and a pair of those Ordway tickets. Set him up for early next week." LaMont released the phone and rubbed his temples, slanting his eyes.

"Thank you," Gun said.

"I hadn't even met her before. The fact was, I'd hoped to write the screenplay for *Hung Jury* myself. But the producer was high on her work and sent me videos of that baseball thing she did for Tri-Star and a couple of *Cheers* episodes."

"She did *Cheers*?"

"Two episodes. I didn't think they were that funny, but I liked the baseball picture. Anyhow I'm busy enough, I'm finishing another novel and there's still law to practice here, damn it, so it was fine that they hired her."

"Were you supposed to help her with it, as a consultant or something? Is that why she came out here?"

LaMont shrugged. "It was never spelled out that way. She just called last week, said she was a little uneasy with some of the characters in the book. She had trouble with their motivations—I'm sorry, it all sounds like bogus artistic crap, especially now."

"Go ahead."

"Understand that my books mean something to me beyond the royalties. I'm not a mercenary."

"I haven't read them."

"At last, someone who'll admit it." LaMont smiled and seemed to relax, but his voice stayed serious. "They're 'thrillers,' I suppose, but they're also crusades. I've seen enough real cases to know what the back side of the species is up to. Child buyers, gang-bangers—it's kids that get hurt the most. You wouldn't believe the secrets an eight-year-old will keep."

Gun thought of Dotty, keeping God knew what secrets. "And your books help them?"

"I doubt it. I used to think I could be like Dickens, you see, reform the rotten system. But there are so many perverted step-dads out there . . . reviewers accuse me of sensationalism, but there isn't much I have to make up."

"So Diane was uncomfortable."

"We had a drink at Rosen's. It's so noisy there, we tried to talk but ESPN was all over us. So we went and got a booth at the Loon."

"This was—"

"Late morning. After eleven. She had a big wide briefcase—more like one of those canvas bags that holds two Thermos bottles with a lunch box in between. I never saw so many notebooks, and I'm a lawyer. Did you know she wrote in longhand?"

Diane came to Gun's mind as he had first seen her, her face blank with grief and striking by lantern light, sitting in the galley of her dead brother's boat. "No."

"She had all my books in there, not just *Hung Jury*. She was serious about getting those characters down. I guess we sat there two hours or more."

"Saying what?"

LaMont shook his head. "Nothing of significance. We hashed over characters and subplots, all that junk. Writers get incredibly self-indulgent over coffee and soup. Don't embarrass me."

"Did she say where she was going next?"

"She said she was meeting you later at Red Supper. After the old-timers game, is that right?"

"Yes."

The attorney's eyes became hooks again. "You two went way back?"

"I met her a couple of years ago. I didn't know her all that well, but we were close, somehow."

LaMont's phone buzzed again and he ignored it. "Not as close as you might have been?"

"Why do you want to know?"

"I'm not prying. But Diane mentioned you, more than once. She seemed regretful of using the past tense."

"You said you'd talked with the police. Did they tell you anything?"

"Not really. I know one of the detectives in Homicide fairly well. He questioned me yesterday. Apparently I was the last to see her. Well. Not *the* last."

Gun stood. The Weimaraner was gone from sight on the neighboring rooftop. "I appreciate your time, LaMont. Happy luck in the crusades."

The attorney held out a hand and Gun shook it. LaMont had a quick grip. "Drive safe," he said. The phone buzzed and this time he picked it up.

At the door Gun stopped. LaMont was talking to someone but Gun caught his eye. "The detective you mentioned. What's his name?"

LaMont hesitated a moment. Then he covered the phone and said, "Hanson. Bitter little bastard, but I think he's smart."

CHAPTER NINE

The Minneapolis police were located in City Hall. Standing on the street in front of LaMont's, Gun could see its gracious clock tower rising a few blocks away, a spire of gray stone looking like a solid citizen from a day when Minneapolis was just a big river town full of flour mills. Gun jacked quarters into the meter. The city was heating up hard and smelled like a plumber's sweaty hands after a particularly septic day. Gun longed for the cool strength of the north. He thought again of Carol and the girl and he knew his wife's conviction would be the same as LaMont's: *There's nothing you can do.* Maybe that was so. But the option was sitting still, hoping from a distance that the police would turn up something. And maybe they would. Maybe, Gun told himself, that was why he was walking through this spoiling city to talk with a cop named Hanson: to reassure himself that the job would get done.

City Hall could be a stunning place on a day with sun, and this was such a day, the building's stained-glass panels in the ceiling and upper walls pouring bright grace down upon a marble figure that looked like Poseidon in the middle of the floor. The statue was all classical musculature and bearded wisdom, but Gun lacked appreciation and asked at Information for Homicide. The old black man there was reading a rumpled copy of *Dianetics* as if it were the Bible. He gave Gun directions without looking up.

One floor up Gun approached a glass window with a

speaking hole and told a young woman he needed to speak
with Sergeant Hanson.

"He's off. Finished up an hour ago." The woman had on a
narrow black tie pulled tight at the throat.

Gun said, "What about someone else who's working on
the Diane Apple murder?" The words, so clear and factual,
made something drop in his chest.

"Do you have some information, sir?"

"No. I'm looking for some."

"I'm sorry. If you want to speak to Sergeant Hanson
you'll have to come back later." She broke eye contact as if
trained in the art. "Good day, sir."

"Listen. I was supposed to meet Diane the night she was
killed. At the restaurant."

Eye contact returned. "Are you Mr. Pedersen?"

Gun nodded.

The woman stood. "Please, wait right there."

He waited all of thirty seconds until a tall man with a
peppery beard opened a door next to the woman's window
and stuck out a hand. "Gun Pedersen," he said, "how about
that? I'm Lieutenant Conn. Come in."

The Homicide unit occupied surpisingly small quarters,
separated into cubicles by the same temporary-looking par-
titions you found in any office. The fluorescent lights
bleached faces to morgue complexion. There was a lot of
cop humor on the walls: bumper stickers saying ANOTHER
SHITTY DAY IN PARADISE.

"We've been looking for you," said Conn. He led Gun to
one of the cubicles and pulled out a chair. "We don't get
many ballplayers. Want a Coke? Coffee?"

"What do you mean, *get?*"

"Relax. Actually it's Hanson who wants you. He and McCaillen are looking after Diane Apple."

"And I was supposed to meet her. You must've learned that from LaMont."

"Hanson did. Also that you were at home and in bed with your wife by ten P.M. LaMont didn't tell us that, your wife did."

"You called Carol?"

"Hanson did. Not two hours ago."

"Stays busy, doesn't he? Am I in trouble?" First the lawyer, now the cops. Original or not, the bumper sticker was beginning to apply.

"No." Conn picked up his phone and asked somebody for McCaillen. He waited several minutes. Gun stood, restless. The next cubicle had a movie poster from *Lethal Weapon*, Mel Gibson and Danny Glover holding their big pistols. Someone had taken a Magic Marker and blessed Gibson with a drooping mustache. The young woman from the window marched back and told Conn, ignoring the phone, that an ambulance crew—accompanied by two of his detectives—was removing a body from a house across the street from the Washington Elementary playground. Kids were watching, teachers panicking. The principal was on line four.

"I told them to take it out the back," Conn said, his hand over the phone.

"They took it out the front, sir."

"Great. Get the principal's number, I'll call him." The woman retreated. Conn's phone spoke to him at last and he said, "Aw, man. Will you tell him—no, don't bother." He hung up. "McCaillen's not available. You'll have to come back when Hanson's on shift. Tomorrow morning."

"Tell me where he lives. I'd rather see him now," Gun said.

That perked Conn up. "No kidding. That's helpful." He wrote on a large yellow legal pad and tore off the page. In the voice of afterthought he said, "The city's full of bastards. I can recommend a trauma counselor if you need one."

"Save it for the school kids."

"That'll make the ten o'clock, you know. 'Hundreds of tiny children watched today as a murder victim was carried away.' They'll make me the guy responsible, like I told them to take the body out the front. I'm telling you, I'm screwed."

Detective Hanson lived in a neatly trimmed one-story on the edge of Dinkytown in Minneapolis. The sun was low when Gun arrived, the city's residual heat rising from the pavement to prevent any comforting chill. The house was white with lots of gingerbread around the windows and big empty flower beds flanking the front steps.

Hanson came to the door wearing Levis and black cowboy boots that brought him up to around five-eight. No shirt. Black hair, black mustache, skin that suggested Hispanic sires despite the Scandinavian surname. He was sweating hard but breathing easy and had a brown unlabeled bottle of beer in his right hand. He said, "Hey. C'mon back in the kitchen."

Gun followed him back through rooms that looked clean to the point of barrenness. The kitchen was another matter. It was full of weights: big round Weiders piled on the black-and-white Congoleum, dumbbells resting on old copies of *Esquire* on a hardwood table, and a padded bench with an impressively stacked bar sitting in the rests. Hanson said, "You interrupted my routine," laying back on the bench as he said it, gripping the bar.

"Don't mind me."

Hanson didn't. He lowered the bar to his chest and lifted, saying, "Beer in the fridge," the effort not showing in his voice.

Gun helped himself. This bottle too was without a label and he uncapped it, surprised at his sudden thirst. It was a dark smoky beer such as Diane had liked.

"Last of a vintage," Hanson said, finishing a set and resting his arms. "My wife made that batch before she left. Like a parting gift. She was an angel of a brewer."

"It's good."

"Don't repress. It's great." Hanson took the bar again, a little shiver in his voice this time. "So you were supposed to meet the lady friend at Red Supper. Bet you wish you had."

"Tactfulness suits you."

"You were pretty tactful yourself. I called your wife. She sounded gorgeous, man."

"She is. Man."

Hanson paused, the bar on his chest. There was a lot of weight on it. "Why don't you tell me the reason you didn't show for dinner? Your wife, she didn't know."

"Is this an interview? I don't see you taking notes."

"You wouldn't believe my memory. It's almost too perfect, it's like a Hasselblad. Why didn't you show?"

Gun took two long swallows from the bottle. Hanson was right: great beer. He said, "I'm not sure. Conscience, maybe. I drove around—tried to call Diane, actually, to tell her I wasn't coming. Then I went home."

"Head off a little domestic jealousy?"

Gun didn't answer. Hanson completed another set and stood from the bench. "We're all sinners, man. You were involved? Don't lie to me."

"No."

"Not at all?"

"We liked each other. At one time we could've been involved. It didn't happen. Why does it matter?"

Hanson said, "At this stage we don't know why anything matters. That why we ask the questions. Tell me why you came to PD."

"LaMont told me you were working on it. I wanted to see if you're getting anywhere."

That made Hanson grin. "You met LaMont. It's your day for short guys, huh?"

"He said it was a random killing. That you don't have suspects."

"If we did, we wouldn't have told LaMont about it. Ain't his case." Hanson picked a dish towel off the oven-door handle and wiped sweat from his face. "He tell you about his wife?"

"I saw her picture. Patrice."

"Killed herself, let's see, seven years ago. You ever read that guy, I forget his name, *The World According to Garp?* Patrice saw an open window and decided not to walk past it. I was a third-year cop at the time. She wasn't that high, six floors up. Just plenty."

Gun shut his eyes. He saw the woman's picture on LaMont's desk, her plain, uncomfortable expression endearing now and LaMont's quiet rage understandable.

"She was a lawyer. Specialized in children's defense. She'd been raped the previous year. It's not well known. You wonder why LaMont plays so hard against the shitballs?"

Gun hadn't wondered. Now he wouldn't. He wanted to get away from the sorrowful collection of facts and insights that was Hanson and flee homeward, but first he wanted what he'd come for.

"Is LaMont right? You don't have suspects?"

Hanson shook on a white T-shirt, stretching out the muscles in his arms. "No suspects yet," he said.

"No witnesses? I can't believe nobody saw the taxi grab her. She would've resisted."

"Is this your case?" Hanson was looking at him.

"I just want to know if there's hope. If there's a lead. I just want to make sure something happens."

Hanson repeated quietly, "Is this your case?" and Gun understood suddenly that the question was not rhetorical.

"It's my case," he said.

"All right. There is one possible witness, a woman. She was out walking Hennepin Avenue at eleven night before last, which tells you what her calling is. She said there was a taxi in the alleyway between Fourth and Fifth. The cab had its fog lights on and motor running. She said she could hear a woman screaming inside."

Gun took a breath. It felt like swallowing a balloon. "What else."

"There were two guys in the front seat. No descriptions."

"Where was Diane?"

"We don't know it was her. She would've probably been in the back."

"With a third man."

Hanson nodded. He opened the refrigerator and took out a heavy cardboard box. It rattled with bottles of homemade beer. Hanson shoved it at Gun. "Here, Pedersen. Consolation prize. Bet you never played in such a shitty league before."

• • •

He drove the dark streets preoccupied, turning an old man's slow corners and noticing nothing until the skies broke open and his windshield blurred with rain. He let up on the gas, coasting, and it was like floating down through a storm-swept lake, calm once you reached the middle depths and promising a soft place at the bottom. He could see his hands on the wheel but not feel them, and then his eyes were drawn by a piece of red neon that showed through the rain and led him in: ROYAL-T, the neon said. VACANCY.

A balding clerk accepted his cash and gave him a key to 118, where he sat on the bed facing the window and uncapped a bottle of Hanson's. It was past midnight and he had no idea which part of the city this was. There were three locks on the metal door, two dead bolts and a chain, none of them latched. He thought distantly of locking them but didn't move from the bed. Overhead the rain made a boiling noise on the cheap skin of the Royal T, and he thought: three men. Three men, a taxi, a short piece of rope. He thought, *I can't go home.*

Sleep arrived minutes later, with Gun still in his clothes and the bottle unemptied, the anthem of the sinners' league rising in sirens outside. He dreamed he walked in uniform. His spikes clicked on cement in an echoing tunnel, and he walked toward the light of a clamorous park, and the violent swell of a crowd.

CHAPTER TEN

Outside his wide motel-room window in the soft light of morning, two women stood nose to nose, screaming. One wore leopard-spotted tights and a high pile of red teased hair. The other appeared dressed for church, all starch and buttons. Both looked very well-fed, and apparently they wanted to kill each other.

Yawning but vaguely curious, Gun propped himself up on an elbow in bed. At issue, he gathered, listening, was something about a birthday.

"Get him what? Then I guess being the favorite gives you the privilege of being the bitch!" This from the woman in the leopard tights. The window glass trembled. "You want to know the truth, Dad's not gonna give a shit one way or the other."

These two are sisters? Gun thought. He was lying in bed not more than a yard from the confrontation, and he considered tapping at the glass to get their attention, save them from hurting each other. He didn't need to. Abruptly the women fell silent. Their bodies, tilting dangerously close together, now separated, and their faces swiveled toward Gun, who threw aside the covers, stepped fully clothed from the cheap bed, and swept the heavy shades closed.

Without his customary joy or satisfaction, Gun did his morning push-ups, rolled a cigarette, and smoked it quickly, just to be done with it. Then he took off his clothes and got into the shower—a dark narrow place that smelled of decay, like an upright coffin. The water thankfully was hot and Gun let it pound his back, then his chest, wishing for a kind of cleansing he knew he wouldn't get here or anywhere. Inside his head was a picture he couldn't shake. It was Diane Apple after they'd finished with her: naked, purplish bruises on her belly, a bloodied mouth, one long arm twisted crookedly beneath her.

When he finally stepped dripping onto the wrinkled linoleum floor, he knew what he wanted from the morning. First, though, he needed to find out where he was.

The woman at the desk in the motel office had on leopard-spotted tights and big red hair. Gun smiled at her.

"Oh, my God." She ducked her head and raised chubby fingers to cover up her face. She moaned and peeked at Gun through her hands. "It *is* you. I'm so embarrassed."

"No need."

"I saw your name in the night book when I came on this morning, but didn't figure on the real thing. And then when I saw you"—she pointed sheepishly toward Gun's room across the parking lot—"I thought, yeah, might be. Oh, God. Gun Pedersen."

Gun nodded. "Well . . . I'd just as soon settle up."

"My husband Bob, he was on last night when you checked in, he doesn't know baseball from summer gourds. Didn't say a word to me." She shook her head, and when she lifted her light green eyes to meet Gun's she put a good part of herself into them. "Gun Pedersen," she said once more. "I used to love watching you. I grew up in Detroit, see."

Gun turned and looked out the window at his truck. He

hated what she was showing him, the frankness and vulner-ability. "Thank you," he said.

"I saw one of the Series games in sixty-eight. Those two home runs?"

Gun said, "I made a local phone call this morning. You'll want to add it to my bill."

"Of course." She seemed to get it now, and turned away to riffle through credit-card receipts. The color of her face was still impressive. "It was certainly a surprise to see you," she persisted, "in the flesh. Oh, okay—here it is." She plucked a receipt from the file and scratched on it with a pen. Sliding it foward on the counter for his signature, she said, "I couldn't help wondering what you—I mean, a man like you—what you're doing here at my place. This place. You know?"

"Not really," Gun said. He signed the receipt. "By the way, where *is* this place? Suburb, right? North? West?"

"Crystal," said the woman, cocking her head. She looked at him sideways and pointed a pink-nailed index finger. "Minneapolis is thataway."

"Thanks."

"One more thing," she called out, stopping Gun at the door. "You always sleep in your clothes?"

"Don't you?"

She laughed, a touch of something cruel in the sound. Gun turned and walked into a morning sun-soaked yet still cool, and entirely too benign.

The alley was paved with squashed cans and empty ciga-rette packs. It was narrow enough to prohibit most sun. Given the businesses the alley served—a porn shop, a pawn shop, a low-life bar—Gun imagined it contained more than its share of ignoble stories. Only one of them mattered. It was here that a prostitute had stood, rooted, listening to screams from an idling taxi. Gun walked the alley up and down, imagining the parked cab, looking at doorways, placing the whore in this spot or that. He found nothing of interest nor did he expect to. A fluffy brown sparrow hopped behind him as he walked, wanting bread.

Following directions he'd gotten from Hanson on the phone, Gun took Highway 100 to Glenwood Avenue to Wirth Parkway, then south a hundred yards into a small parking lot overhung with elms and oaks. He shut off the motor and sat in silence for a minute, relieved at what he could sense taking place inside himself: the soft heat of guilt turning to anger, a swelling hatred which he now promised himself he'd direct with all the strength he possessed.

He stepped out of his truck and walked down the small dirt hiking path Hanson had described. The forest floor was heavy and fragrant with dying wildflowers. The trees were past their greenest weeks, yet still full enough to keep out all but the daintiest lacework of sun. The dirt path angled downhill to a simple log shelter, three walls and a roof set upon a cement slab, crude picnic table and benches within. It was on this table that Diane's leather purse had been found, emptied. Gun sat down. He rested his elbows on the scarred, knife-initialed, cigarette-burned tabletop.

For a place surrounded by city, it was surprisingly quiet here. An even hum of cars on the interstate half a mile to the south. The occasional diesel blast on Highway 55 to the north. An invisible squirrel above, pissed off. If you listened harder you could hear the small breeze disturbing the oak leaves, the distant rhythmic tap of a woodpecker, and then finally, if you let yourself—and Gun did—a coarse panting and the *shhhh* sound of a body being dragged.

"Sons of bitches," Gun said.

He opened his eyes, stood, and moved quickly down the rest of the trail to the spring. It looked the way Hanson had said it would look. A round clear pool in a small bowl of dark stones, its issue slow. The trickling runoff left a trail of rust. Her hair, said Hanson, had been soaked with springwater. Her cheek resting just beneath the pool, her face tilted toward it. "Eyes open," Hanson said.

At the time, Gun had resented this detail. Now, looking up at the oak trees and the patches of bleached sky beyond them, he reconsidered. Maybe for the soul-numbed cop as for Gun now, it helped to think of Diane, in death, remaining open somehow to this small piece of country still breathing here in the midst of so much failed civilization.

Gun knelt and touched the water. Cupped his hand and was leaning down for a drink when he saw a stone lying at the bottom of the shallow pool. It was quartz, the size of a penny and smooth-faceted by nature. Reaching for it, Gun thought of Diane's old nickname from her brother Billy.

Diamond.

CHAPTER ELEVEN

Gun's daughter Mazy lived in a town house two blocks from Lake Harriet. A very nice part of the city. Hilly, the streets overspread with mature elms and maples, the houses old and solid. In the early seventies, Gun and his first wife had spent an afternoon touring the neighborhood with a realtor. It was fall, about this same time of year, and rumor said Gun would be traded to the Minnesota Twins before season's end. Amanda fell in love with a Spanish stucco hidden from street view by a hedge gone mad, and they made a preliminary offer on it. The trade, of course, never happened.

Now, twenty years later, Gun was visiting his grown-up girl just three blocks away.

Mazy worked for a Minneapolis newspaper. At twenty-seven, she'd already been there for nearly four years. She was a good writer, she was smart, and she'd moved up fast. Two months ago, in fact, they'd made her editor of the Entertainment section—though according to Carol, who was much better than Gun at getting the scoop on Mazy, the new job wasn't what Mazy wanted. Like Carol, Mazy was a hard-news woman, this being only one of many ways in which the two were similar. Both considered themselves absolutely right in what they thought, a trait Gun admired regardless of the trouble it sometimes caused. Both liked Japanese cars. Both ate way too much without noticeably suffering for it. Both loved him, and he imagined how they commiserated with each other about the obligations entailed in that.

At exactly ten o'clock he walked up to Mazy's door. He told himself he was foolish for coming; what he needed now was objectivity.

Mazy answered the door immediately, and her smile—natural, surprised—told him Carol hadn't called. It was, of course, Amanda's smile, the same full lips and summer-blue eyes. Her hair was Amanda's too—down past her shoulders, heavy and straight, more blonde than red after months of sun.

"I thought now that you're an editor, you'd have to go to the office in the morning like everybody else." Even as a little girl, Mazy had been a night owl. A late sleeper.

"I go in when I'm good and ready," said Mazy. Her smile caught the sun and flashed her confidence. Then, seriously: "Of course, I'm there till nine, ten at night, Dad." She led him inside and they stood awkwardly together in the all-white kitchen—white floor tile, white cabinets, white ceiling, white table and chairs. Red roses in a vase on the table. A lot of them. He wondered who sent them.

"Well, sit down. We'll have some breakfast."

She sat him at the table, placed bowls for both of them, poured out some kind of flake cereal and added milk. Honey for sweetener. Then put a teapot on the stove and sat down to eat.

Gun waited until they were finished, until they were drinking the sharp orange tea Mazy served, before telling her why he'd come. He had to provide background; aside from the stories she'd read about the murder, Mazy hadn't known about Diane.

Her face was solemn when he was done. She said, "So you're down here to do what, exactly?"

"To learn what I can about Diane's death." He lifted his hands as if to say, *It's that simple.*

"And what does Carol think of this?"

"That's why I'm here to see you, honey."

"Dad—" she drew out the word—"if she's upset, you can hardly blame her. If I were Carol, I'd be furious."

"You'd feel betrayed?"

"Think about it. It *is* a betrayal, of sorts. You're down here because of this—Diane. I'm sorry it happened, Dad, really, but it's cop business now. Not yours. And here you are anyway, poking around. This isn't the sort of thing you do for just anybody."

"She wasn't just anybody."

"Listen, Dad, please. I know you love Carol. But when it comes to love, a guy's allowed only two categories of women. First category is the woman he loves. Second is everybody else. Now Carol's wondering which group she belongs to. You're screwing up, Dad."

"Lord, no wonder they made you an editor. You could always boil it down," Gun said. He sipped tea. "So you think I should go home? Forget Diane?"

"Speaking as a woman? Yes. Speaking as Carol's friend? Yes."

"Speak as my daughter."

She said nothing, and Gun closed his eyes, tried to force his ideas into a straight line. "I see it this way, Mazy. Here I am, and Carol's unhappy about what I'm doing. She's going to stay unhappy. Maybe she'll think less of me. Maybe she'll think how I feel about her has changed. Maybe our marriage will be diminished in some way. But if I give up and go home, then I'm guilty. I'm at fault for Diane's death, and I'll hate myself."

"Don't, Dad."

He continued, "And if I hate myself, what will *that* do to Carol? What'll it do to us?"

He opened his eyes and saw his daughter's looking back, weighing, considering.

"Be careful," was all she said.

He used Mazy's phone to call Carol, who picked up after one ring. In the deadness of her voice he heard that she had something against him.

"What is it?" he asked.

"Are you coming home soon?"

"It might be a few days. I've talked to some people and learned some things." Gun watched his daughter moving around her living room, swinging into a jacket, pretending not to listen. "There's more for me to do here," he said.

Carol was quiet for moment. "What is it you're after?"

Gun covered the mouthpiece of the phone and laughed without humor.

"Gun, it's not your fault. Or your problem, for that matter. It just isn't."

"Right," he said.

"So just come home."

"Soon," he said.

"Look, it's an awful, awful thing that's happened. But Gun, the world can be an awful place. There's nothing even you can do about that."

"Not even me?"

"I'm sorry, Gun."

He checked his impulse to hang up and instead took a long deep breath.

Carol said, "I've got to tell you something."

"Go ahead."

"Something happened last night. I would've called then if I'd known where you were. If you hadn't just disappeared."

"I'm here now. Tell me what happened."

"This is nuts. It's sick. A woman gets killed and you go running off you don't even tell me where, and then think you can give me a call whenever you damn well please and say you'll be home in a week."

"She was murdered, Carol. She was a friend of mine, not a *woman*, and I didn't say a week. I said a few days. Now what happened last night?"

"Oh my God." Carol was suddenly out of breath. Or maybe she was crying.

"Carol—"

"They scared the crap out of me, Gun. They really did. They called me in the middle of the night—"

"The guys from Hawk Lake?"

"I don't know who it was. Two-thirty in the morning and the phone rang. I picked up and some guy was whistling into the phone. A Christmas song, Gun. 'What Child is This.' I asked who it was and he just kept whistling. And then in the middle of it there was a gunshot, loud, right in my ear, and the whistling stopped."

Gun felt his lungs empty of air and his pulse become swift and urgent.

"Gun, are you there?"

"I'm here."

She blew out a long shaky breath. "He—they, whoever—called again, half an hour later. Three A.M. I answered the phone and there he was, whistling that song. I didn't stick around for the shot."

"Carol, I'm leaving now. I'll be home this afternoon."

"I'm all right. It's daylight now. You know something, Gun? I saw the sun come up this morning."

Before leaving, with Mazy grim at his shoulder, Gun tried calling Hanson both at home and at Homicide. Both got him only the detective's taped voice. He left Hanson a message: "I'll be up north for a day or two—call me if anything happens."

It was a five-hour drive from the Cities to Stony. The morning had the ripening smell and taste of autumn and Gun thought of his boyhood in Upper Michigan, hunting geese or ducks with his father—though today would have been more suited for upland game. A grouse day. The sky was high, cloudless, and without color, the sun a mere baseball that you had to look hard for.

Many times, after a morning's shooting, he and his father had come upon a field of cut grain and lay down in the stubble to soak up what was left of summer, chewing on shafts of yellow straw, breathing in the dirt and the vegetable dust, the sharp blood scent of their birds, then dropping off to sleep and waking stiffly into another season, a pair of Rip van Winkles the two of them, the recent sun gone quietly into the sudden clouds of afternoon, the morning hunt almost out of mind.

At a familiar spot along Highway 71, Gun pulled off onto the gravel shoulder, shut off the truck, and got out. Immediately to the west a treeless, breast-shaped hill rose up out of the pines. The half-mile walk took Gun's breath and made him appreciate his heart, which he'd inherited from his father—still strong in his late seventies—and grandfather, who'd died angry at ninety-nine. On the nipple

of the hill was a large, well-placed rock and Gun sat down
on it. The sky was as clear as he'd ever seen it from here,
and he sensed that today's count would set a new record.

Which it did, by three. Turning slowly on his rock until
he'd completed a full 360 degrees, he found seventy-four
lakes. From this height, most of them looked small and
round, a generous scattering of Scandinavian blue eyes staring up out of pine forest. But there were also larger lakes,
one in particular, glittering and narrow, which extended
south as far as Gun could see, out of the pines and down
into the beginning of farm country.

Most he couldn't name. Very few. Yet it seemed to him,
sitting here, as though in a small way they were his. Almost
thirty years ago the view from up here had convinced him
he belonged in this part of the world, and now he couldn't
imagine belonging any place else.

Gun stood up and began his walk down the hill to his
truck. The afternoon was getting long. The air was clean,
the wind cool out of Canada, and he felt ready now for the
next stretch of his life, however hard and complicated it
might get. He felt ready for Carol, hurt and bedeviled, and
for the demands his own conscience was making on behalf
of Diane. He felt ready to do whatever was necessary to go
on living with himself in this place where life was sometimes beautiful.

CHAPTER TWELVE

They began as low purple hills Gun knew weren't there, and they grew to thunderheads by the time he drove through Stony. He turned onto the lake road, slowed the truck as he neared the stand of birch surrounding Jack Be Nimble's, but continued on by. He was an hour past due already. And anyway, Jack the Confessor would be sweating at the grill now. No time to sit and talk. Supper hour.

Out over Stony Lake, Gun saw long black fingers of rain trailing from the dark gray bottoms of clouds which moved with a speed you could almost hear. Freight cars, water-haulers. He rolled down the window of the Ford and took in the wind and the smell it brought. Rain advanced in a line across the water, dark-texturing its already rough surface. The rain was heading southwest, Gun was driving due north, and their intersection happened at the end of his long dirt driveway. He had to put his wipers on high to negotiate down among the birches and pines, though the ruts of his driveway were old enough and deep enough now to lead a blind man home.

He was sitting in the cab, had just shut off the engine and was waiting for a lull in the rain to run inside, when a quiet blue Toyota Camry pulled up next to him. He recognized the car as Donna Wright's. Probably out to check on Dotty. She looked up and he saw her nod. Her face was blank and featureless through rainwater that ran like clear honey on the window glass. Gun lifted his hands and shrugged at the sky.

• • •

Inside, there was coffee on and cookies in the oven. Chocolate chip again. Having a child in the house—if you could call Dotty that—had its advantages. But Gun wasn't about to point this out to Carol. If she was feeling more than usually domestic, best to just stay quiet about it.

The news—and the reason for Donna's visit—had to do with Dotty's parents. They'd been found. At least her father had, and now Donna and Carol were huddled at a corner of the kitchen table, talking strategy. Gun sat at his usual spot on the end and watched the cookies blooming through the oven-door window.

"So, don't worry," Donna said, "he can't just show up and take her home. We *will* know what he's like, at least on paper. We're running every check on him there is." Donna was a large woman with large expressive hands which she used as a forceful accompaniment to her voice, which in turn always surprised Gun with its low pitch. Most everything about her was masculine, except her decidedly feminine habit of dress. Whenever Gun saw her, he thought of a farmer in drag.

"But you're dead right," Donna said, aiming a huge index finger at Carol. "There's good reason to wonder about him. I mean, how does a kid thirteen, or however old she is, end up where Dotty ended up? You've got to wonder about the parents. That's why I'm saying we can't let her know he's on his way."

"You think she might run?" Carol asked.

"That's part of it. Of course, she might run if he's the best father in the country. More than that, though, in these sorts of cases we like to meet the parent first, get a sense of how they're going to react to their child. Then set things up accordingly. Make it as easy as possible for everybody." She put out her hands as if slowing someone down. "I'll tell Dotty when it's time. After I've met the guy."

Gun stood up and went to the oven and with the hot pads lifted out the pan of cookies. They were perfectly domed and just beginning to brown at the edges. With a spatula he started to remove them quickly from the pan and set them on a wire rack to cool. If you set them instead on a solid surface, the moisture as they cooled would seep down into the cookies and cause them to lose their crispness. "How do you know she's not listening right now?" Gun asked.

"She's off in the guest room, moping." Carol's green eyes were exasperated. She shook her head. "I've run out of things to do with her."

"It's okay, she won't be here after tonight," said Donna. "I've made arrangements to get her into the detention center in the morning, early. The father's driving up tonight or early tomorrow and I'm meeting him at ten, and if that goes all right, I'll bring them together."

"What do you know about the guy already?" Gun asked. He brought a small plate of cookies to the table and refilled coffee mugs all around.

"Mmm." Donna took two cookies from the plate and set them on her napkin. Then she took a bite and chewed slowly, all the time holding on hard with her eyes to Gun's question. "Mmmm, very good. Well, we know his name. Fordrick. Edward, I think. He lives in Minneapolis and was divorced from Dotty's mother, who has since died. He's in some kind of retail business, I'm not sure what. This is what we got from him over the phone. Like I said, we're running checks on him."

"How'd you find him?"

"Pretty much textbook. A missing-persons report was filed almost two years ago, and the photo from that report lined up with the one we sent down. Interesting thing is, it was Dotty's mother who filed the missing persons. Her father and she had split already. So when they matched up the photographs this week, of course it was the mother they tried calling. Who it turned out died a few months ago. From there it wasn't hard to find the dad."

"Aren't there times when the photos are actually two different people?" Carol asked.

"It happens. But the father, Fordrick, he said he's absolutely certain." Donna bounced one large fist on the table. "We've got a match here, I'd say."

Gun swallowed the last of a second cookie and stood up from the table. Looking out the window above the sink, he saw that the wind had blown the storm completely out of the territory and then been sucked away itself, leaving calm the evening that remained. The sun, half an hour from setting, was throwing long rich light on the soaked world. The lake glittered as lakes do in movies, and Gun had a sudden intuition. If he were a fish, he would be powerfully hungry right about now.

"Excuse me," he said to Carol and Donna, "but I'm going fishing."

Both women looked up at him and frowned—not unhappy with him, just confused. Gun tiptoed out of the kitchen, walked down the short hallway to the bathroom, pushed open the door and saw Dotty standing one-legged in the puddle of her clothing. His entrance had performed a stop-motion on the girl. She was about to thread one bare foot into a lavender bikini and was bent slightly forward, looking straight at him. He couldn't help but take note of her tan, the way it turned her small breasts by contrast into beacons. He muttered an apology and backed out of the room. Blinking hard, trying to get his mind to shutter this picture down. As he closed the door, he heard her say, "Nice swimming night."

A few minutes later Gun was sitting in his sixteen-foot aluminum boat, rigging his line for walleyes, when Dotty came strolling down from the house and stepped onto the dock. She walked with a self-conscious ease of motion most women didn't find until college age and every few steps she threw her hair from her face with languid movements of her head. Gun hadn't noticed before how long she was, coltish all down through her high hips and narrow legs.

"Isn't the water a little cold?" he asked. She'd stopped on the dock next to him. She wore Carol's lavender swimsuit and had the heels of her hands set on the small rise of her hips, her fingers angled down toward her crotch. The middle finger of one hand was tucked inside the waistband. Posing, but posing well.

"*You* still go in, don't you?"

"But I'm used to it." He looked back down at the knot he was trying to tie in his line. The girl didn't move off, and he could feel her eyes on him. He looked back up. "Don't stay in long," he said.

"Why not?"

"You'll catch a cold, or something worse."

Abruptly, she laughed, her head tilting back. Then she sobered and looked down at Gun, her eyes focusing, the pupils black and deep. "Like it matters if I get a cold," she said. "Like if that means anything."

"Just a suggestion."

"So you're not telling me I can't go in, then."

"What if I did?"

"I'd say you're full of shit."

"And go in anyway."

"Probably," said Dotty. "Probably."

"Then be my guest."

The girl lifted her hands from her waist, looked at them, then adjusted her bikini top, fingers lingering there, affectionate. Finally she said, "Thanks a lot," bitterly, Gun would think later, and dove—perfectly, without splashing, her toes aligned and pointed as they disappeared.

CHAPTER THIRTEEN

She swam well, he could see that, a very fine crawl, each stroke long yet quick and he watched her for a moment before walking up to the house for the leeches he kept in a styrofoam cup in the refrigerator. Carol didn't like having the walleye bait alongside the salad dressing, but there were still a few principles Gun held beyond compromise.

When he got back to the dock, Dotty was out of sight.

He scanned the calm surface of the water. The lake was free of boats this evening, completely quiet. Where had she gone? A wooded island lay a quarter-mile out, due west—in the direction Dotty had been swimming, but there was no way she could have reached it already. And if she'd turned around to swim back, where was she?

Helplessness seized Gun's chest and he felt like sitting down; instead he dropped into the boat, threw off the line and yanked on the starter rope. The engine spat, caught, roared, and died. He yanked three more times. The motor wouldn't fire. "Son of a bitch!" he shouted, and bent to the fuel tank to pump the primer bubble. When he pulled the rope again, the engine caught and held.

He twisted the throttle all the way open and set the bow on a straight line toward the island, cutting the same path as Dotty had only minutes before. *You damned kid.* He couldn't believe this—and Carol and Donna were inside right now, chatting it up at the kitchen table, sipping coffee without guilt. *Damned father that'd let this happen to you.*

At the spot where he'd last seen Dotty, he throttled down and the boat died in the water. The wake rocked into the stern, shoving him forward. He stood and looked around, feeling dumb and desperate. There was nothing to look for, not up here. The kid was gone. *Goddamned, pitiful men that'd pay for a girl your age.* Gun started a circle in the water, running the engine at a fast troll, expecting to find nothing, knowing he'd find nothing but doing what he had to do before he could let himself go inside and make the phone call.

He'd made several circles and was about to give up when he saw something white flash beneath the surface, starboard. He cut the throttle and shoveled the anchor over the gunwhale. Yes, there *was* something down there, close against a bed of crappie weeds at a depth of five, six feet. He stepped up onto the bench seat and dove in, remembering in the half-instant of air between boat and water that he still had his wallet in his pocket and thinking, *So what.* Then the plunge, and thinking how the water didn't seem so cold this way, when you had all your clothes on.

Five, six, seven feet down, his lungs getting warm but holding out fine. At least eight feet now, deeper than he thought. He blinked and tightened his focus against the haze of water, tightened his stomach against discovery. Hesitated before the final few strokes. Please, no. Then thrust himself ahead.

No. He felt relief and a trickle of forgiveness, and he almost swallowed water. He'd seen bodies in the lake before, and this was not a body, though it looked like one from a few feet off. Reaching out, he touched the smooth surface of a large, white, beautiful branch of driftwood.

Probably birch, probably blown here from the island. He kicked for the top.

Inside, he made the call, then sat for a few minutes with Carol and Donna, neither of whom seemed capable of speaking. The dread they were generating, all of them here together in the kitchen, was too much to stand, and Gun got up and left.

There was time to put on dry clothes and walk down to the dock, time to roll and smoke a single cigarette. Time to wish a lot of things there was no use wishing. Then the trucks and boats started pulling in. Three outfits, all county equipment, Sheriff Jason Durkins presiding in his tired way.

Night was nearly full but a big moon was on the way up, promising the small, necessary light.

"You're sure she didn't just swim out to the island? Maybe wander off down the shore?" Sheriff Durkins had his hands jammed in his pockets, and his shaking head answered his own questions. His eyes were sad and tired and pouchy. As usual, the effort of keeping them open seemed not only conscious but difficult. Although not yet out of his thirties, Durkins seemed to have survived his particular allotment of years, and then some.

"Can I ride with you?" Gun asked.

Durkins nodded. His deputy and the water-crisis volunteers had the trailers backed into the water along the most gradual slope of Gun's shoreline. They worked quickly and without talk. The boats were aluminum eighteen-footers, their big Mercury outboards geared and cabled for steering wheels.

"Wish you hadn't called. It's my girl's birthday," said Durkins.

"Marla, right? How old is she?"

Durkins frowned and looked up at the moon. "God, she's eight," he said. He shook his head, an epiphany.

It occurred to Gun that Durkins's daughter had still been in diapers when her mother decided it would be more fun to live in California with her old boyfriend than stay up here and raise her kids.

"Maybe you need a new job," Gun suggested.

"There's an idea." Durkins actually seemed to be thinking about it. He reached for a cigarette from the slash pocket of his windbreaker, brought it to his lips, and snapped a sleek silver lighter. In the nearest boat a man lifted a large treble hook, working free a tangle in its line. It looked to Gun like the size hook you'd use for sharks. "Hope you like to fish," Durkins said, and walked down toward the lake.

As it happened, they didn't have to fish long. Ten minutes were required to catch the large piece of driftwood Gun had found, another ten to get Dotty. She was thirty yards past the place where Gun anchored and gone in, her body adrift in the shallows above a sandbar. She'd drowned in five feet of water.

His first view was of her face, for she was caught by the hair and as she surfaced the moon hit her directly. Her skeptical mouth was partly open, turned up slightly at the corners, as if about to deliver an insult. Her eyes were closed. Gun stood in the stern of the boat as the others brought her gently aboard. Her body seemed younger and smaller than it should be, and of less consequence. A long stripe of lake weed ran diagonally across her chest and Gun thought of the ribbons that beauty queens wear, announcing their place of origin. He wondered whose job it would be to tell the girl's father.

Then came the fast trip to shore and a half-hearted attempt to revive her, though Gun couldn't imagine that anyone here tonight, seeing how she looked, being lifted so palely from the silver-black water, could be so foolish as to think that Dotty's body held anything still sparkable. There was no urgency in the paramedics who crouched above her. They moved with careful efficiency and without faith. They worked like men not accustomed to feeling useless.

Carol didn't speak until the body had been zipped into its cavern of blue vinyl and transported away. They were standing with Donna on the long slope of grass, watching the red lights of the Stony ambulance pull out of the drive.

What was as hopeless as a slow-moving ambulance?

Carol stood next to Gun yet remote from him, slumped and crooked, her head bent oddly to one side. She looked as Gun had never seen her: older than her age, and confused. He put his hands on her shoulders from behind, kneaded them like chilly clay until she leaned back against his chest and gripped his fingers with her own. She said, "My God, Gun, forgive me," and he held her while the dam gave way, feeling something like heat lightning inside himself as Carol wept.

At last Donna Wright said it was late and Gun and Carol walked her to her car. Gun said, "I saw you talking to Durkins. Who tells Dotty's father?"

"I tell him." Her voice was even deeper than usual. "But I can't say how."

Carol breathed in heavily, breathed out, seemed to be anchoring herself. She said, "I'll tell you how. You'll say she was staying out here and shouldn't have been. That she went for a swim and drowned. You'll say she ought to be alive right now. She *would* be alive if I hadn't brought her

out here." Carol's voice trembled and Gun touched her arm
but she pulled away.

"I'm not sure it matters if Dotty was staying out here, or
someplace else," Gun said. He said it gently, not wanting to
follow it up.

"What does *that* mean?"

Gun said, "I don't think she was going to let her dad have
another crack at her."

"You're saying she drowned herself," Donna said.

"I'm saying I think so. Yes."

"Just because you found her in five feet of water?" Carol
asked. "You know how fast the bottom drops off on either
side of that bar. The currents could have pushed her up
there."

There was sudden anger in Carol's words and Gun let
them dissipate for a few moments in the cool air. Then he
said, "She knew her dad was coming. She knew he'd been
located. She heard us talking tonight in the kitchen."

"How do you know?"

"She was right next door. In the bathroom. I walked in
on her by mistake when I got up to go fishing."

Carol turned and walked up toward the house.

CHAPTER FOURTEEN

By midnight the wind had gone to the east, coming persistently into Stony smelling of rain and dying algae and entering the window of the tavern where Gun sat with Jack LaSalle. It was Jack's tavern, called Jack Be Nimble's. It was nearly empty. The walleyes hadn't been hitting of late and the two seemed to parallel, catching a good stringer and then finding an audience gone tolerant with beer.

"Who told the father?" Jack said.

"Donna Wright over at Social Services. They tried to call him but he was on the road. She had to tell him when he drove in."

"What a job. Poor Donna. You meet the guy?"

"He called the house afterward." Gun shook his head. They had a back booth where Jack had thrown open the square-paned window and the white muslin curtain moved against the bottle of brandy sitting between them on the table. "He's going to sue my ass into little pieces. Those aren't his exact words, but that was the essence of the call."

Jack poured brandy. His right index finger was missing and it suited his humor to point instead with the concave depression that was left. He set down the bottle and pointed at Gun. "Not to question the bereaved, but what good's a lawsuit do him?"

"I don't know. He was just talking, letting his reflexes kick. Maybe he just needs some time." Though Fordrick had sounded like a man who needed a lot more than time.

Jack said, "Did he ask anything about the girl? How she acted, how you found her, I don't know."

"It was a short conversation."

"Lawsuits." Jack rubbed his crew-cut temple with the missing finger. "He mention his daughter by name even?"

"He didn't mention her at all."

They stayed quiet in the booth while the gently rising wind pushed the curtain into slow waves and delivered scents of pine and cooling water.

"Carol," Gun said finally, "is not doing well."

Jack didn't answer.

"First she gets the scary phone call. Of course I'm out of town for that—"

"As if you'd have been any help," Jack said.

"It would've helped her not to be alone. And now the girl drowns—"

"If you're worried about Carol," Jack said, "what're you doing here?"

"I don't know. Once they took Dotty away, we needed different things. Carol went into the bedroom and shut the door. I looked in after five minutes. She's hard asleep." Gun shrugged. "I needed to move around. Here I am."

"Carol can handle this," Jack said.

"Yeah, that's what I told myself. That's always how I've played things with her—doesn't matter what happens, Carol can handle it. But this whole mess with the casino and the girls—it's got so much weight, and somehow it's all landed on her."

Jack took a swallow of brandy. When he spoke, his voice seemed almost muted. "Gun, it wasn't you who arranged for the girl to stay out at your place. That's the county's job."

"She was trying to do some good, Jack. Think how long

you've lived up here, and when did anyone try running whores in your backyard? Now some bastard comes in, he's got girls not even full grown living that life. Thirteen-year-olds. Carol figures if she can get Dotty talking, she's maybe rescuing some other kid. Or a bunch of kids. You think she should've followed protocol?"

"Ease up, Gun. I wasn't judging Carol." Jack spoke calmly, taking his time. "You know, I can understand you taking off after Diane got killed. But you said something, and it was true. It would've helped Carol not to be alone."

Gun said he had to leave, and stood. In his mind he saw his wife, the white sheets rumpled against her skin, a bottomless sleep her slight defense from the incalculable evil of the day.

There were no lights in the windows when he arrived home, and he closed the truck door softly and made his way through the grass that blew against his ankles in the intensifying wind. The house looked so dark it was impossible to imagine a living person inside, and the warmth that touched his face and hands when he entered was a small marvel. He turned on the light over the kitchen sink and moved down the hall to the bedroom. Carol had barely moved. The star-patterned quilt had slipped from her shoulders and he reached for it, letting his fingers brush her skin as he pulled the quilt snug. She didn't wake, and he didn't wish her to; her sleep was a harbor reached at high cost. But Gun remained restless. He slipped from the house and sought the lake, walking as if by daylight between the black trunks of pines and down the easy well-worn slope to the dock. Wrapped in dark, cold mist Gun thought of Diane Apple and of her unapprehended killers. He shut his eyes, imagined the men asleep tonight beneath dirty blankets, breathing slowly, on one closing in. He felt his balance tip and jerked his eyes open. The moon was gone behind clouds. Still the waves were visible by their somehow phosphorescent crests, and he watched them soar past below him as if they knew where they were going and were neither anxious nor afraid of getting there.

It was some time later when he went inside. The quilt had slipped from Carol's shoulders again and she had shifted to her back, arms forming a white diamond above her head. She wore the summer-weight cotton nightgown Gun had ordered away for in the spring, her favorite, with embroidered daisies circling the neck. A good omen and heaven knew they needed one. When he sat down on the bed she woke, or nearly woke, and reached for him with a peculiar strength in her arms saying words only another sleeper might have understood.

•••

It was black outside. Hours later. Her whisper was edgy. "Gun. Listen."

He was still all tangled up with her, arms and legs not wanting to wake. "I don't hear it."

"There's a car in the driveway. Out by the road—by the mailbox. It's been idling out there for five minutes now."

Gun swung out of bed. Now he could hear it—a faint squeal in its fan belt—and he could see a soft halogen glow through the pines.

"I'll call Durkins," Carol said.

"Not yet. Wait."

"You weren't here for those phone calls. God, they're driving in—"

Gun pulled on long johns and went to the closet. The Winchester Model 12 leaned in a back corner. The car's high beams were bouncing through the window and the shotgun's long blued barrel flickered when he brought it out.

"Please," Carol said.

Gun was aware of the hair rising along his shoulders and the back of his neck. He yanked open the top drawer of his dresser and dug among the socks. Found one shell, a number-eight birdshot from the previous grouse season.

"For God's sake," Carol said, but now the car was idling outside, twenty feet away, its headlights locked on the window and the bedposts white as bones in the glare.

Gun went down the hall barefoot, moving fast. He went through the kitchen to the front door, slipped to the porch and eased the screen open. The grass was stiff with dew beneath his feet and his arteries jolted as if filled with mercury as he ducked past the corner of the house to the woodpile and from there to the broad stand of chokecherry bushes. He knelt and got his first good look at the car. A disconsolate Chrysler from the K-Car era. One man was silhouetted in the dash. The fan belt whirred. Exhaust showed in the red glow of taillights, climbing from a pipe too close to the ground.

Gun moved without thinking. He knew the ground and trusted it. He came in low on the driver's side. The grass bent quietly under him and he smelled besides exhaust the new cold beginning of an autumn day. It was hunting weather, the Winchester a smooth effortless weight in his palm. The last few yards felt noiseless, windless, a glide in the dark; he was invisible right to the moment he slid the muzzle inside the window, notching the man's temple with it, the man freezing solid in the car without saying a word.

CHAPTER FIFTEEN

The man slumped back against the seat and slowly rolled his eyes to Gun. The dash lights showed on his face the dirty trenches and excavated planes of the habitual drunk. Also a reach of bald scalp and a circle of salt-stiff hair that stuck out over the ears. His breath floated to Gun like a ghost from the sewer.

"You wanted to shoot me then?"

He was pathetic enough that Gun was embarrassed by the Winchester and lowered it. He knew the man now—that voice thin and rough as a rat-tail file—but said, "You lose your way, fella?"

"Now there's a question. Damn good one. Let's see," the drunk said, inhaling heavily through his nostrils, "I suppose the answer would have to be Yes. You know Mama wanted me to go to seminary—"

"I'm not waiting for you to sober up," Gun said. "Turn around and get. If you can't drive, I'll give you a ride. Make up your mind."

"How about this, ballplayer? How about if I just puke?" The door of the Chrysler squealed open and two old wing tips sought solid earth. "I stocked up on Scotch whiskey, there in the motel. I sat on the bed and drank it. Way too much. Way."

"You'd better go, Fordrick. You'll screw up my sunrise."

"Tha's good, you know who I am. In about one minute I'm going to lean forward and puke on your feet. I stocked up just to unload. Did it on purpose and came out here. Whad you think of that?"

"I think it's a pretty cheap memorial for your little girl. It fits you all right, but it's not good enough for Dotty."

Fordrick straightened. He was short with sloping shoulders and long blue wrists. His rough voice was an indignant slur. "Dotty wasn't her name! Laurie was! And you," Fordrick tried putting a fist near Gun's face but the motion was too much for him and he clutched the car door, "you'll go to hell for what happened to her."

Behind him Gun heard the bedroom window slide open. Carol called, "Gun? Who is it?"

"It's Mr. Fordrick."

Something crossed Fordrick's face. "That's a pretty wife," he murmured.

Carol's voice was relieved. "Well, Mr. Fordrick, your brights are hurting my eyes. Please turn them off."

Fordrick touched Gun's elbow. "I hadda wife."

"Turn them off," Gun said.

Fordrick leaned into the Chrysler to comply but his balance went and he thumped face-first across the bench seat, his wing tips coming off the ground and hanging pigeon-toed out the door. Gun heard his plaintive caw: "Awwww, God—"

"Carol—"

"What are we going to do with him, Gun?"

Gun shrugged. Light was lifting in the eastern sky and overhead the siskins chipped and skittered in the still-black pines. He squinted into the car where Fordrick was softly vomiting onto a pile of empty cigarette packs. Gun looked at Carol standing at the bedroom window. "He mentioned a motel. Checkout won't be for a few hours yet. I expect I'll drop him there."

She stood there wearing what had come first to hand, an enormous burgundy hooded sweatshirt of Gun's. It made a waif of her. A gently smiling waif. "Samaritan," she said.

"Yeah." Gun reached down and got hold of Fordrick's ankles which felt loose enough to come off in his two hands. He said, "Probably I should've just shot him."

He pulled the drunk man out of the Chrysler and steered him mumbling and mouth-wiping to the garage. Fordrick opened the door of Gun's new sea-green pickup and tried gamely enough to climb in, but in the end Gun had to lift him as he would've a child: one arm under Fordrick's legs, the other supporting his back, bony as a chicken's. Fordrick leaned bodily against him breathing hell in his face.

"Which motel?" Gun asked when they reached the highway.

Fordrick was sleeping, sagging forward into his shoulder belt. Gun turned on the radio and knobbed around until he found the public station. They were playing something New Age, music with no rhythm and no melody filling up the hours when no one listened. Gun jacked it up until Fordrick moaned and wrapped an arm over his head.

"Which motel?"

"Ah, don't remember. It's pink. Stucco."

That would be the Lakeside. Nineteen bucks bought you a serviceable mattress, a window full of Stony Lake, and all the free TV you could watch. In the summer they put lawn chairs down by the water.

Gun said, "Tell me something. What happened with your girl? How old was she?"

"Why should I talk to you? I'm gonna sue your ass."

"I wouldn't be surprised."

"Half my friends are lawyers, you righteous prick. My girl shouldn't of been at your place at all."

"No." That took Gun back to it again: standing on the dock, the last bit of daylight coming yellow off the double birch, not much wind, the lake sipping easy at the shore. The noise of the screen slapping shut up at the house; then the girl stepping down the path in Carol's lavender swimsuit.

"We were trying to help her, Fordrick. I'm sorry." *She knew you were coming,* he almost said, but looking at the man he couldn't.

"Righteous prick," Fordrick repeated. The phrase seemed to please him.

"How'd you lose her?"

Fordrick turned and fixed Gun with a glare that looked almost sober. "She ran off from me, damn it. Two years back. Whoever she found to take her in, they made her what she was."

"You had nothing to do with it."

"That's right, by God, so shut up now. I got a lawsuit to protect."

The town of Stony was graveyard quiet at five A.M. and Gun drove through it slowly, his window rolled down. The sun was still some distance off but blue-gray was rising in the clouded sky and the mercury street lamps on Main blinked uncertainly. With Labor Day over, Stony was bracing for the end of tourist season. The brick facades of the dime store, the hardware, the Lucky Day Cafe looked stricken and colorless, old faces set for winter.

At the motel Fordrick managed to get out of the truck and walk by himself to Number Five. Gun stayed behind the wheel. Fordrick dropped the key at the door, went to his knees getting it. "Hey. What about my car?"

"I'll park it out by the highway. Here to there's a little more than five miles; the walk'll be good for you. Keys will be under the seat."

Gun watched Fordrick work the key around until the lock submitted and then the drunk man went in without fanfare and the door shut, opening again one second later to show Fordrick's creased face. "I'm still gonna sue," he shouted.

"I know. Sue me into little pieces." Then on impulse, "Did you love her, Fordrick?"

Different things moved over the man's face. Gun read some of them, fairly or unfairly, and the first was a vacant question that Fordrick didn't voice. *Love who?*

A sick ache hit Gun's belly, sadness and intolerance and fury. He pointed at Fordrick. "When you pick up your car, don't come to the house. Do you understand? Don't let me see you again."

"That's a threat, that's verbal assault, you righteous—" Fordrick began, but Gun was backing out of the lot and missed the rest. Leaning across the cab he rolled down the passenger window until a hard cold wind scissored through.

CHAPTER SIXTEEN

Carol was up already, dressed in sharp tan khakis, chambray work shirt, and burgundy vest that buttoned in front and cinched in back with a light brass buckle. All this though it was not yet seven and Carol no early riser. She wore dark lipstick, her only makeup, and her black hair fell straight and full to her shoulders, the bangs swept to one side. She said, "Here's coffee."

"Mm, keep it. I want some of that lipstick."

She gave him some, warm and too quick.

"I couldn't sleep after you left with Fordrick." Carol's eyes crinkled with dismay. "So that's Dotty's father. What he must've been like to live with."

"He said her name was Laurie. He intends a lawsuit."

"Of course."

"You think he has a case?"

"I suppose he does. It's hard to care, isn't it?" They sat at the maple table Gun had built, a long time ago now, twenty-five years. The sun was up and shoving at the cloud cover, poking holes. Steam lay over the lake, growing up from the skin of the water and raising itself in peaks to drift westward. The lake was a range of gray cumulus with angels riding here and there where the sun touched peaks. Carol said, "I should have let the county take her. It wouldn't have happened then. I'm sorry, Gun."

He pulled her close to him, feeling the muscles tremble along her shoulders.

• • •

The Hawk Lake Casino was called all sorts of things. The people who worked there, including several hundred Ojibway Indians who'd never drawn steady paychecks before, called it a blessing and bought new cars. Most of the whites who lived within ten miles called it a blight on the landscape: Just look at the place with its blazing facade, its shining swooping marquee entrance, miles of denture-white limousines queuing up to unload. An editorial in a nearby weekly paper carried the headline, IT'S NORTHERN MINNESOTA, HOW MUCH NEON DO YOU NEED? Some of this sentiment Gun attributed to jealousy, to louts who could only tolerate Indians as long as they were poor. The land seemed suddenly brimming with fearful bigots, guys at the Standard station or in resort taverns saying "Sure those poor bastards need *something* to help them outta the hole, but why this? White people can't open a casino! They're raking it in over there!" A rich Indian, Gun gathered, was worse to have around than a poor one. What would they want next? Their land back?

On the other hand, Gun was personally acquainted with two men who were good men otherwise but lacked some necessary piece of will or spirit and so lost, before the casino was a year old, not only their businesses and homes but their families as well. Gun's own favorite name for the casino was what the tribal leaders called it, watching the bus loads of old people come in from Minneapolis and stand in tottering lines at the video slots, struggling to break open rolls of quarters. They called it the New Buffalo, and they were right. There hadn't been such a slaughter in 140 years.

"I'm worried about this," Carol said. They'd parked her

Mazda Miata in the casino lot and Gun stood on the asphalt trying to get his knees to unfold.

"Look at this parking lot. Big as a prairie. It's like North Dakota," said Gun.

"There are more people here than in North Dakota."

They walked in silence. The lot was close to full though it was only nine A.M. They passed a purple Jaguar with Oregon plates. A Plymouth Horizon with a stick-on Garfield in the window and a bumper sticker saying WHY WORRY? THERE'S ALWAYS WELFARE.

"I know what you think of these men. Just remember we don't know they're responsible for those phone calls."

From the casino's neon entrance, walls stretched back in plain gray windowless cement. Who-cares architecture.

They reached the door. An Ojibway in a white suit nodded soberly and opened it for them. They gave their names to a girl of twenty or so behind a U-shaped console next to the door.

"Security will take you down in a minute," she told them.

It was actually less than a minute, so they had little time to stand adoring the spectacle. Half circus, half Dante: rank upon rank of nickle and quarter video slots, dogged attention being paid nearly all of them, the color and metal and shine of the machines a fit for the constant noises they made, the blinking and bopping and the sometimes chatter of payoff, of spitting quarters. Blackjack tables, change machines, brass and green felt. Indian dealers in white shirts and black ties. There was a stunning preponderance of gray-haired heads among the gamblers and Gun asked half rhetorically why these people weren't at church suppers.

"Because blackjack's more exciting than bingo," Carol

told him, and then a suited Ojibway wearing a two-way radio on a wide black belt approached and led them away from it all. He drew his radio and spoke softly into it as they walked, then opened a door into a narrow hall where the carpet lay frayed against the sideboards and damaged slot machines stood awaiting repair.

"It's a ways down," said the security man. He wore a long shining ponytail and a nameplate: ARNOLD. "How do you like the place?"

"It's big," Carol said. "Do you like it?"

"I like the work." Arnold led them past wood-veneer doors, a set of metal lockers built into the wall, the hall twisting and continuing before them like something you ran through to reach the cheese. "There was nothing here before. Just a field. I liked that too."

They went through an open area full of smoke and old styrofoam cups, stopped finally at a door that looked made of real wood and Arnold opened it, leaned in. "Two for you, Mr. Stanky."

"Thanks, Arnie," said Stanky from inside. His voice was big and beefy. Gun wished he were at home.

"Carol, I'm glad to see you. It's about time." Ronald Stanky was at the door, every ounce of him, relating to them heavily, shaking Carol's hand. "I wasn't expecting you, Gun."

"Along for pleasure." Stanky's handshake was zealous and Gun suppressed a childish urge to crush it.

"Well, excellent. Have you been here before? Seen our little enterprise?"

"Once, with a friend." Jack. "He lost twenty bucks."

"Cheapskate," Stanky grinned. He nodded at a pair of tan office chairs and took a seat himself behind a slate-topped desk. "I've asked Rich to come by and sit in on this, I'm sure you don't mind. He should be here in a few minutes. You remember Rich Morton?"

"FBI. Lot on his mind," Gun said, and Stanky grinned again, *We're all in league here.*

"Ron," Carol said, "I'm not here for an interview. I'm here because someone's harassing me, and I think it's someone connected with the casino."

"What? Geez." Stanky's eyes seemed to get closer together. "Sit down, folks. You're serious about this?"

"We're just here pulling your leg, Ron," Gun said.

"What happened? Carol?"

"A couple of nights ago somebody called our house. They whistled a tune, into the phone. Then there was a gunshot, and quiet. Middle of the night. They phoned twice, as if once weren't enough."

Stanky stared at them a moment, then reached for a pack of Camel Wides on his desk and shook one out. "You mind? No?" He lit, inhaled, appeared to relax. "This is what I think, folks. I think somebody's got a sick funny bone. Maybe it's somebody you stepped on doing a story, Carol, or maybe not. Look, when I was a junior high kid my friends and I would phone up Kentucky Fried Chicken on a Saturday night, say, 'Hello, how large are your breasts?' You don't want to get too grim about a crank call."

Carol said, "I can't believe you're in PR, Ron. You don't even patronize well."

"Oh, I see. So I'm the stupid bastard trying to scare you now, giving your number to some phone sicko." Stanky took an irritated pull on the Camel and let the smoke out with his words. "That sort of shit is for the movies, Carol. Don't overestimate your importance here. If we were that

worried about your little paper—and it's a dandy, honest—
we'd come after you in ways that made more sense."

"Ah. You'd appeal to the sensibilities of my advertisers."

"We do a lot of good on this reservation," Stanky said. He
tilted back in his chair and the words came without effort.
"Nine hundred jobs, three hundred and twelve of them to
Native Americans. You know what the biggest industry on
the Rez was previous to this? Wild rice. Rice! A few hundred Indians kneeling in canoes, hoping to harvest enough
rice for their families plus a few pounds more to sell to
tourists. You ever walked inside the average home here on
the Rez? Lucky if they have plumbing. I moved here in the
winter, I saw houses, people living in them, snow sifted
down through the roof every night. Drifts piled up they had
to shovel a path to watch TV."

Carol said, "I told you, this isn't an interview. Besides, I
haven't noticed a lot of Indians building new homes yet."

"That's weak, Carol, and you know it. We've only been
open ten months. Also you know what we've got on the
drawing board. A new school, new hospital, city sewer and
water, day care. You've seen the blueprints. The tribe's looking down the road. These people aren't stupid, Carol. They
know a gift horse when they're riding it."

Gun said, "You're riding it too, aren't you? What's the
percentage? Fifty percent to the Rez, fifty to the company
that manages Hawk Lake?"

"The tribe gets sixty, Pedersen. We've been open about
that and if you'd asked your wife she could've told you. It's
a sliding scale. After two years it goes to seventy–thirty."
Stanky's eyes held a magnanimous shine. "It's only right.
You walk a mile in their moccasins, you want the money to
go where it should." He stubbed out his cigarette. His fin-

gers were white and chubby. There were three taps at the door and Rich Morton stepped inside, nodding greetings while not looking at any of them.

"Rich," said Stanky. "You remember Carol and Gun."

"Sure." Morton's eyes were the dry transparent blue Gun remembered but there was something else in them this time, something besides annoyance. Fatigue. Morton couldn't have been fifty but when he reached behind the door and drew out a folding chair and opened it to sit, the movements of his arms and wrists and the way he held his head made Gun think of old men in barbershops in his hometown in Michigan. Morton said quietly, "Heard about the trouble at your place last night. Young girl drowned. That's damn tragic."

Carol's face hardened. "That information hasn't been released. I'd like to know how it reached you."

Morton didn't answer right away. He met Carol's eyes evenly. "I happened to hear Search-and-Rescue on the scanner. They were slim on details. The girl was staying with you?"

"She was," Gun said. He was aware that Carol wished him to be quiet. He said, "Her name was Dotty Fordrick. Or Laurie. Does it ring any bells?"

"No."

Carol shot him a look that wished he wasn't there and said, "We think she was a prostitute. That she was working out of the casino." She hesitated. "She was young. A kid."

Morton said, "Aw God," sitting back in the folding chair. He didn't look at Stanky and his manner was as if Stanky wasn't in the room at all. With eyes closed he said, "She tell you anything worthwhile?"

Gun had a sudden picture in his mind of Morton the day he'd driven out in the Range Rover with Stanky, Morton

moving the muscles in his jaw around, his eyes quick
behind the sunglasses. Morton saying, *You mind if I walk a
little?* "You knew she was with us. The day you came out."

"We suspected."

"Rich—" Stanky's voice was startled and Morton pointed
at him as if pushing a button and Stanky was silent.

"What I'm saying, we suspected you had somebody out
there. Couple nights ago a guy came in here, guy from
Minneapolis, one of these assholes you can tell from the
look on his face, and he loses a ton. For him, anyhow. Say a
couple thousand. One of my security, a woman, recognized
him when he came back in. Said she'd seen him leaning all
over some junior-high-looking little girl. That he left with
her. Kid like that should've never gotten in here, but they're
damned creative. You see what kind of customer I mean."

Stanky said, "I think you're misrepresenting our clientele.
An evening of entertainment here costs the average person
less than twenty-five—"

"Stanky," Morton said, "tonight I'll take you out and buy
you six beers and let you talk my ear off about an evening
of entertainment and any other shit that doesn't matter.
Until then, will you shut up?"

Stanky went white and short of breath, reached for a
sheaf of memos, turned his chair sideways to the desk and
began reading.

"This guy leaves here, I'm told, around one in the morning. With the girl. Before three, he's back again. By himself,
and it's like he's crazy. He's all dirty and got his face cut,
he's beat to hell. Yelling in our entryway, hollering about
suing us for this and that. We had new security on the door
that night, a big kid, Charlie Lapoint. The guy called Charlie
some names Indians don't like to hear. Charlie forgot all

about our policy, which is firm courtesy. Tossed the guy and I mean ass-over-teakettle tossed him, put a big dent in the hood of a limo under the marquee. I had to suspend Charlie. Against my wishes." Morton had been talking to unoccupied space but now leaned forward to address Gun. "The name James Swanson familiar to you?"

"Should it be?"

"That's up to you. Were it me who hit the bastard I'd not waste time remembering the name."

Morton straightened in his chair, stretched his arms out hard as if waking them to the day, and relaxed. The man had an attitude of tired forthrightness that made Gun want to accept his intentions as clear and right. But there was tension in Carol, a reporter's doubt, and for now Gun stayed with it and didn't commit.

"All right. It doesn't matter anyhow. This guy Swanson came back alleging crooked dealers, rigged machines, anything. Wanted his money back. He was pathetic. One of the things he said was that he'd been assaulted on our property. He named you, Pedersen. Story was, he bumped into you in the west parking lot. You started shoving him around."

"Wow."

"Mary—she's the security who saw him before, with the girl—Mary asked him where she was. He said, Pedersen took her."

Carol said, "So you came to our house looking for little wayward footprints."

"Partly that. But we couldn't say it that way. Admit it, Carol, the slant you've taken on this casino hasn't been very positive. I read your paper. You think we're going to come to you saying, 'Hi Carol, we're looking for a prostitute who ran away last night and thought we'd stop by?' Hell, we knew you'd been looking around for contacts and that's why Swanson mentioning Gun Pedersen was about the only thing he said that made sense. Naturally we thought you'd make hay if the girl was with you. For all we know you've got your story written already. Maybe you've sold a special to the *Star Tribune*."

"Maybe I have. What else did Swanson tell you?"

"Squat. I wasn't surprised. He won't file any lawsuits, but he wouldn't tell me the truth either. Not even the girl's name, not that it matters anymore. He told me her age, though. Kept saying she was eighteen. Repeated it so often it was plain he didn't believe it."

"Thirteen," Carol said.

Morton sat silent with his ghost-blue eyes full of some experience or dread damning him from inside. "It's true what we've told you before. We know they're out there, these girls. But thirteen—we can't have it."

Carol straightened in her chair and Gun could see her wishing for notebook and pen. "You can't have it because it's wrong and deadly, or because it's bad for business?"

Morton's pale eyes came into focus. "I have a girl, eleven. Don't preach to me, Carol. I'm saying if that kid told you anything that would help us find out who's doing what out there, that I'd be grateful."

"And more grateful still if I didn't break the story."

Stanky looked up with some silly hope in his soft face. Morton saw this and squashed it. "No, there'll be a story all right. Just wait until you can get the whole thing. Does that sound fair?"

"I want the exclusive. Your word on it now, or everything I have comes out in my next edition and the AP wire takes it national."

Morton said, "Give me one week. Then it belongs to you."

Stanky returned to his memos. Gun could hear his breath, shallow, coming and going in the stale office. For a man who'd just been sitting all morning, it didn't sound good.

CHAPTER SEVENTEEN

"He thinks you know more than you do," Gun said. He felt reborn emerging from the casino's stale close hallways into a day that had matured wonderfully without them. The noise of the place faded as they reached the car and the air was bracing and the aspens at the edge of the lot were well into gold. Among the aspens and the birch and occasional red maple, sharp pines swayed under a yellow sun.

"I'd be more flattered if it were true."

"You think Morton is genuine?"

"I don't know. I think he's being truthful about the corporate attitude, that they've simply accepted that prostitution happens and that the casino's presence helps it along."

Gun cradled his legs into the Miata, working them into place while Carol got fluidly in and started the car and checked herself in the rearview. Gun said, "You don't buy him, though. Morton. That he wants to stop it."

Away from the casino Carol wore a look of satisfaction that belied the edgy belligerence she'd shown inside. "Morton's the casino cop. If this place sponsors hookers, if it even *looks* like it's sponsoring hookers, it's Mort that gets sacrificed. If he didn't want to stop it before, he does now."

"You're assigning old Mort a pretty self-serving motive."

Carol looked at him. Her green eyes on sunlit days threw light like emerald water and he enjoyed the light and reached to touch her hair. She smiled. "If good things happen, who cares about motives?"

"What's next?"

"The oldest profession is about to take a hit. Not everything from Vegas transfers to the sticks. You can play some games but others you have to leave behind." She was so pleased she seemed to flicker in the sunlight and Gun watched her readjust the mirror and move the stick into reverse. There weren't many things that put Carol into a gladdened state of mind as quickly as this, a story going her way. Carol enjoyed a good crusade and would allow herself to gloat when victorious. But this seemed too easy and Gun kept silent and was grateful she did not notice.

They pulled out of the lot onto the highway and hadn't gone half a mile before Carol's eyebrows rose and she slowed and took a sudden left onto a gravel lane that led through pines.

"How come?" Gun said. It was the road to Loreen's place.

"I think," Carol answered, "we ought to stop and see Loreen. If there's going to be some sort of roundup, this might be a good time for her to change careers."

Daylight failed to defend Loreen's trailer house. Icicles of brown rust were mapped across the white metal walls. The left end of the trailer had sunk half a foot into boggy earth. The night's rain had gathered in dark pools that made molasses of the yard. A man was kneeling on the sand-packed tire in front of the door. He wore a stone-washed jean jacket and murky Adidas. His back was to them, his head tilted back in some relief or agony. Gun heard the flat sound of driven water striking mud.

"Oh to be male and unabashed," Carol said. The man's shoulders shifted a little as he heard this but he finished up anyway, making them wait. Finally he stood and stowed it away and turned to face them, a blond smooth-faced man with forty pounds of Crisco hanging over his belt and an open proud smile on his face.

"When you really have to go," the man said, "there's no stopping. Know what I mean?"

"Loreen inside?" Carol asked.

"Ah." The man poked hands into pockets and yanked his pants higher, the motion jerking him from youth to middle age. He smiled at Carol. "You a friend of hers?" Eyed her. "Colleague?"

Gun smiled also. He'd been twice to this trailer now and twice encountered men so mortally witless it was a wonder they'd survived in the world. He said, gently, "Time to leave," and to his surprise his softness of voice sunk in and the man blinked and stepped off the tire. He stepped without caution and mud swallowed his shoes and lifted the cuffs of his Dockers. Struggling toward a blue Honda Accord parked on higher ground the man gasped, "Who you with?"

"Vice," Gun said. "And you?"

A woman's voice spoke from the trailer. "Damn. Damn it. You can't be serious."

Carol let the man reach the Accord, shoeless now, wake it abruptly and rev it bouncing backward through the pines. "Loreen. It's me, Carol."

A narrow window slid open near them and a woman craned through it. Not Loreen. Brown-skinned and wide-faced with penciled brows and frosted hair. She said, "You're no Vice. I've seen Vice, and you ain't him."

"We're looking for Loreen." Carol glanced at Gun and went on. "I'm a reporter. Loreen's been helping me on a

story. If she'll be back soon, we can wait. Otherwise I'd like
to leave a message."

The woman laughed and shook her hair, the motion
releasing an odor of perfume and hard use. "Carol, honey, I
don't know your Loreen nor anyone else's Loreen. Now I'm
new here, moved in day before last, but this is my place and
I live here all by myself. You sure you know where you are?"

"Of course I'm sure! This is Loreen's trailer—" Carol's
color was coming up and she pointed in sharp jabs around
the yard—"that's the sandbox she put up for her kids.
That's their swing set."

The woman in the window was quiet through this, her
face showing no discomfort. She wore some purple-based
makeup that was incongruous with her penny-toned skin.
Her pores where the makeup had rubbed away were large
and oval. "All right, all right. You're saying your friend
Loreen had this place and I'm sure you're right. But she ain't
here now. This is just a rental, see? She wasn't here to stay.
I ain't either I hope to God. She must've just moved sudden.
Forgot to tell you."

"It's a rental? Who's the landlord?"

"Who are you asking me that?"

"What about the car?" said Carol. "That's Loreen's."

"Hey, that's my Geo, I'm making payments. And what
the hell are you doing here anyway? I don't think I gotta
talk to you anymore." The woman's head disappeared and
the window came down hard.

Back in Stony Carol got out at the *Journal* office and asked
Gun to pick her up later. Her confident mood had turned.
She was confounded by Loreen's disappearance, and deter-

mined to find Loreen herself. Gun suggested calling Sheriff
Durkins about it, but Carol told him it was needless, that
she'd simply look at the county plat book and learn the
name of the landlord and call him directly. She said Durkins
would only bumble into Morton's own investigation. She
did not mention her own hold on the story nor her wish to
keep that hold exclusive, though both were plainly visible in
her impatience with herself.

Gun went about preparing lunch with a strange pleasure he
could not name. He was hungry and his tongue tingled at
the back corners when he opened the refrigerator and saw
the brick of bright cheddar. He unwrapped a loaf of cracked-
wheat bread, baked by his daughter Mazy on her last visit,
sawed off two thick slices with a long serrated knife. He
spread both slices with brown Dijon mustard, then let the
bread sit while he ground coffee and started the pot. He cut
heavy curls of the sharp flaking cheese, enjoying how the
pieces tilted away from the mother brick and thumped onto
the board in the quiet kitchen. A ripe tomato lay on the win-
dowsill over the sink and he sliced it down into steaks and
laid them atop the cheese on the bread. He took the pepper
grinder, loosened the top screw for the coarsest grind, and
cranked it over the open-face sandwiches until the tomatoes
grew dark and textured. The coffeepot blew steam as the
carafe filled. Gun sought and found his favorite mug, a hand-
thrown one of Norwegian design with blue-brown glaze. A
friend, Dick Chandler, had made it years ago.

He sat at the table alone and, eyes open, asked a blessing
on the food. The phone rang at his first sip of coffee. Carol
said, "Two things."

"All right."

"First, Loreen's trailer is sitting on Reservation land. It's not privately owned. I called the tribal secretary and he says there shouldn't be housing on that land at all."

"What else?"

"I was reading the AP wire from last night. The police found an empty taxicab in an abandoned garage on the west side of St. Paul."

"Albert Iron Sky."

"His," Carol said. "Still no sign of him, though."

Gun could feel his mind disengaging from the telephone. He said, "I'll have to go back down."

Carol drew an audible breath and released it slowly and he saw in the sound her fingers opening and a clutch of grass drifting free. "Go ahead. I'll get a ride home."

"I'll call you tonight," he said.

He ate the sandwiches deliberately, trying to draw from them the pleasure he'd noticed earlier, but it wasn't in them. Nor in the cooling coffee in the Chandler mug. It wasn't until he'd packed to leave, throwing spare clothes and his shaving materials and a bag of McIntosh apples into a canvas duffle, that he came near to understanding the root of the feeling. He suspected it stemmed from quiet. From the small stillness of an unrattled kitchen and the zip of a knife through bread. It occurred to him that the peace of the lonely was possibly the most unbroken, and he wondered how long a man could embrace that peace before it claimed him and he chose not to leave it any more.

CHAPTER EIGHTEEN

He reached the northern suburbs at supper time and stopped off at a place called Hunters Inn to phone Hanson. He tried Homicide first, waited ten rings, and was about to hang up.

"You've got Minneapolis PD. Homicide."

"Hanson, Gun Pedersen."

"So you get the papers up there."

"My wife saw it on the AP wire. She *is* the paper up there."

"So where are *you*?"

"In your town, or almost."

"And you're wondering what the wire story didn't say."

"I guess so. How about if I come over?" Gun asked.

"There's not a lot I can tell you, man. But if you're hungry and like Chinese . . . I was just wrapping up here. Wanna meet?"

Gun said sure and took down directions for a restaurant in Robbinsdale, about twenty minutes from where he was now.

"You finish up that stuff my wife made?" Hanson asked.

"You just gave it to me."

It was a place Gun remembered from years before, just across Highway 81 from Crystal Lake. An old steak house he'd been to in his playing days, when the Tigers came to Minnesota. Now it was called the Yellow Garden, and the people who ran it, Gun thought as he pushed through the door into the entryway, had to be authentic. He inhaled deeply and could feel the garlic burning clean the thousands of little air sacs in his lungs.

The inside was darkly paneled, gold and red Chinese carpets on the walls, furnishings in red and orange. Gun took a booth next to a window and asked for coffee.

Up the aisle, a couple with two small children struggled through their meal, the father getting up every few minutes to chase the youngest, a boy two or three years old who decided now that he wanted to sit with Gun. It wasn't easy, trying to ignore the little guy, his round face and round green eyes deadly serious about the business of making a new friend. Three times the father had to come and remove the child from Gun's booth.

Hanson arrived as the young family left, and the detective caught Gun waving at the boy, who waved back over his dad's shoulder.

"Grandpa Pedersen," said Hanson.

"Not yet."

"Me neither." Hanson sat down and signaled the waiter who in turn smiled and pointed at Hanson, familiar.

"Any kids?" Gun asked.

"Two, and they tend to side with Mom. Both girls. I think they've sworn off men." He had on a worn denim shirt with pearl snaps, rolled-up sleeves.

When the waiter came Hanson ordered for the two of them, something with shrimp and chicken. Also a Chinese beer for himself. "Tinny and weak, that stuff," he said as the waiter left. "But it's the spirit of the thing."

Hanson closed his eyes and rubbed them hard with his index fingers. "Love my work," he said. "Love my goddamn work." He blinked and folded his hands on the tabletop. His eyes were exhausted, red spider legs in the corners. He said, "Forensics finished up yesterday and we sent Diane back home to her family."

"Who'd she have left?"

"Nobody to speak of, Gun. Parents are gone. No siblings. A cousin in Baltimore. That's where she's going."

Gun tried to remember where Diane's brother had been buried. Couldn't. He imagined Diane lying next to Billy in a green lawn beneath yellowing maples. It didn't help.

"Nothing new, Gun. She may have died of suffocation but they're not positive. The bruising says she fought pretty hard." Hanson looked out the window and softened his voice. "Raped twice, at least. But all this you got on the news."

"What do you know about Iron Sky?" Gun asked.

Hanson lifted his glass of ice water and kept it lifted until it was gone. "God, I'm thirsty—" he tipped his head at two plates of food half eaten across the aisle—"just smelling it." He slid the empty water glass to the center of the table. "Like I said, there's not much to report. We found the cab. And yeah, I'd say some pretty bad shit happened inside it. The lab's working now."

Gun waited.

"Blood, semen," said Hanson. "About what you'd expect. Some hair. The lab gets done and what we're gonna know is—the blood belonged to Diane, and some of the hair. So what? I mean, who do we match the semen samples to?"

"You find Albert Iron Sky, for starters."

Hanson's beer arrived, and he took a long swallow and twisted up his face. "Worse than I remembered. Always is. Just gets worse and worse. But the food—you wait."

"Where's Iron Sky from, up north? One of the reservations?"

"He's from the sewer, via the shithouse, Gun. That's my guess. The people we've talked to either don't know or don't want to say. We think he hasn't been in the city very long. There don't seem to be a lot of people that know him."

"Where'd he live?" said Gun.

Hanson shook his head. "Doesn't work that way, Pedersen. I asked you before if this was your case, and you said yeah. Okay, I'm respectful of that. But it doesn't mean I'm required to give you anything. All it means is, I'm not gonna have your substantial ass thrown out of town if I bump into it once in a while." He smiled quickly, finished the bottle of beer and reached for Gun's water glass. "Mind?"

Gun shook his head and watched Hanson drink. Then the waiter came with the food, and Hanson tucked his napkin into the collar of his shirt. His body seemed to tense for eating and he lifted his fork. Instead of spearing a chunk of the well-spiced meat, though, he aimed the fork like a teacher's pointer at Gun. "Quid pro quo, buddy. Pay as you go. And the way I see it, that's generous on my part: putting you on equal footing with me."

Gun ate a few shrimp, which tasted fresh, though he knew in this part of the country there was no such thing as fresh when it came to seafood. He said, "Then I don't guess you'll be telling me the name of the prostitute, the one that heard the screaming that night and put you onto Iron Sky."

Hanson smiled with a full set of capable-looking teeth, yellow and straight. The bottom jaw was missing an incisor. "It'd be different if I thought I was finished with these folks. If I thought they'd given me what I needed. But no, I'm not there yet so I can't just hand them off. Of course if you go out of here tonight and stumble over something interesting, and you want to tell me about it, then my attitude changes. It's simple, isn't it?"

"What about the taxi? Where was it?"

Hanson was chewing slowly and with obvious satisfaction, his eyes starting to drift. "Wouldn't do any harm, I guess. You could've gotten it from Channel Four, if you'd bothered to watch."

The time was eight-thirty when they left the Yellow Garden. Night was fully arrived. To the south, rising out of the highway and reaching into the lower stars, were the several towers of Minneapolis, clustered pillars of light dots.

It was almost beautiful, Gun thought, the city at night, from this distance. Though it had no right to be. He wondered if Diane had flown in after dark. And if so, had the sky been clear, as it was now? Had she admired the view?

He drove Highway 81 to I–94, entered downtown on Fourth Street and parked a few blocks short of the address Hanson had given him. Across the street was a surplus store, still open, a blue neon sign in the window saying, WE'VE GOT IT. He walked past a strip joint of historic reputation called The Service Center and past another bar, in front of which a tall rugged-faced man dressed up like Cupid asked Gun for a light. Gun looked away and kept walking.

At the end of the block he took a left, walked to the end of the first building, and took another left down a concrete alley-drive. Sixty yards in, behind The Service Center, was a flat-roofed brick garage, a dim light bulb burning away above its door. Painted on the front was an old sign, faded almost beyond readability: LOUIES FIXIT. Gun stood well back from the building, out of range of the light bulb.

Only two blocks away was the alley behind the bookstore where Diane had been raped, if the whore's word was any good. Gun felt the sudden need for a cigarette and reached for his makings. The sweet-dirt smell of the tobacco calmed him, the habit of his fingers on the paper. He shook out his match, a shiver at the back of his neck.

Rising close on both sides of the alley were brick walls. Above was a single lit window—second floor, the back side of the strip joint. A yellow shade pulled down tight. Gun dropped his cigarette, stepped on it, and walked up to the garage. He bent to take hold of the door handle. He twisted it and lifted and the door slid open easily. For several minutes Gun stood looking into the small, dark, close-smelling interior, at first waiting for his eyes to adjust, then waiting for the history of the place to reenact itself. For bloody men to step out of a materialized taxi. For their coarse words to fill up this small damp room. This did not happen. Light from outside slowly seeped in, showing nothing here but an oil-stained floor and dirty brick walls. The muteness, the absence of ghosts, seemed a harsh miracle.

CHAPTER NINETEEN

He took a room at the Sheraton Downtown and spent a dizzy hour channel-jumping, putting off the phone call he knew he must make. Finally he clicked off the TV and reached to the nightstand for the phone. He lay back against the maddeningly slippery, synthetic pillows and set the cheap plastic telephone on his chest.

His resolve dwindled and he let it go. Turned his mind instead to his stomach, which had never been satisfied with Oriental fare and hadn't been tonight either. He dialed room service and ordered a filet mignon and a bottle of beer. Turned the television back on. Found a ball game.

The steak was done right, bloody at the center, a little charred on the outside, and the beer tasted so good—Moosehead from Canada—that he ordered another. When the second bottle was gone, he dialed his Stony number and waited, stomach clenched, for his wife's voice.

"Hello, this is Carol."

"Hi."

"Gun, thank God you called." And she sounded as though she meant it.

"Yeah?"

"Yeah. How's it going?"

"Fine." He told her he'd seen Hanson, seen the place where the taxi had been found, learned nothing.

"Busy night," she said.

He could feel Carol's tension over the wires, knew she had something to say. He could see her sitting at the kitchen table in her red cotton one-piece from L. L. Bean, her lips zippered shut on that bit of news she had for him, her slender fingers tapping an arrhythmic pattern on the varnished maple.

"What is it?" Gun asked.

"Want to know what I just learned?"

"I just said, What is it?"

"Morton's gone. Canned."

"Ah," said Gun.

"Ah?"

"It doesn't surprise me a lot, Carol. Who'd you talk to?"

"I called Hawk Lake to see if he was around and got hold of Arnold. Remember Arnold? I just had this feeling tonight I should get Morton alone someplace, away from Stanky. Get him talking. Last we saw him, he seemed fed up. Ready to talk. And now I'd bet anything I was right. Arnold told me he left this morning. Resigned, Arnold said, but the *way* he said it, Gun, he meant fired. Stanky got rid of him, I bet anything. It's getting weird, these people disappearing. Loreen, and now Morton."

And Dotty, Gun thought, but didn't say it. "Did you get hold of Stanky?" he asked.

"Sort of. I caught him at home an hour ago, but of course he said he couldn't talk, he was on his way out. Said how bad he felt about Morton leaving. He sounded like he always sounds."

"Any idea where Morton's at?"

"Arnold didn't know. I've been trying Morton's home number, which is listed, but no one answers."

"You could try Durkins. I've seen him and Morton at Jack's place a couple times, drinking coffee."

Carol said she'd do that, then was quiet for a moment. Gun could feel her mind working a different angle, finding a way in.

"Gun," she said, "as long as you're down there, I was hoping you could talk to someone for me."

He let her wait, listen again to her own words. "Sure," he said.

"You ever heard of Lou Gorman?" Carol asked.

"Nope."

"You should've. He heads up Club King Incorporated, the outfit that runs Hawk Lake and a bunch of the other casinos. The newspapers've got more of Gorman's quotes than the governor's these days."

"Then maybe he should run for office."

"He just might. The guy's ambitious and he *loves* attention."

"Okay."

"Use some of that old baseball charm. Ask him what happened to Morton. Gorman likes to hang out with the local jocks. He's always showing up in photographs with people like Christian Laettner, Andy MacPhail."

Gun closed his eyes and listened to the faint shadow of another conversation on the line. He said, "Maybe we can have our portrait done together, Gorman and I."

"Gun, seriously, I could use a little help here."

"Have you thought about this, Carol? If Gorman's clean, he won't know a thing about Morton. If he's not, he won't be talking to me or anybody else."

"I've thought about it. All I'm asking is that you go see him, Gun. Don't be aggressive, just . . . interested. Tell him your wife's a nosy journalist. Appeal to his civic-mindedness. Don't push the guy, just get a read on his reaction, then tell me what you noticed. That's all."

"I'll do my best."

"Thanks. I appreciate it, Gun."

"Carol—"

"Yes."

"I'm sorry about all of this. About being down here at all."

She didn't answer. The silence deepened until he had to do something, hang up or wade in. He said, "I can't explain myself very well, but I'll try. First, maybe I shouldn't have agreed to see Diane. But I did, and then I didn't follow through on it, and look what happened. That makes me feel responsible. If you think I've abandoned you to chase phantoms, I'm sorry. I mean that, Carol. Right now it's not easy to know where my place is."

He wasn't sure what response he'd expected, but at least not the resentful laugh Carol gave him. "I guess your place is this whole roomy world, Gun. I hope you can find your way home." She was quiet for a moment, then: "We all have our goddamned tragic flaws, don't we?"

"I'll call you tomorrow," he said, and hung up.

He got out of his clothes and into bed and lay there without finding sleep. For most of an hour he kept hearing his conversation with Carol, the relief in her voice when he'd first called, her polite request, and at last the bitter laugh that marked his failures. At last he rose and dressed again. He pulled a chair up next to the window which looked out toward the western suburbs, lights as far as he could see, smoked four cigarettes—more than his usual daily quota—ordered coffee from room service, drank it while rolling and smoking one more cigarette, then decided to go out for a walk.

CHAPTER TWENTY

One A.M. Hennepin Avenue. Clear and chilly. Gun walked in
the direction from which he'd come two hours earlier, noticing how the streets were more heavily peopled now. A block
from the hotel he stepped carefully across the legs of a young
woman lying on her back on a steam grate. She looked sixteen, had a lovely full face, a nose ring and scalped hair, and
wore the uniform of tough city girls: big black lace-up boots
and secondhand clothes—in this case baggy green coveralls
with the name "Fred" stenciled above the breast pocket.

At the next corner a dark-skinned man with one frosted
eyeball lifted an open palm and said, "Donation." More out
of guilt than sympathy, Gun took a five from his wallet and
gave it over, turning aside the man's thank you, disgusted
by it. For it occurred to Gun now that he was wanting to
blame these people out here for Diane's death; that he saw
them as rodents and predators. As if it was *their* fault. As if
the culmination of their weaknesses and their filthy unions
had killed Diane. And wasn't this partly true?

Beneath a streetlight, a neon-lipped prostitute with six-
inch heels and fat-dimpled thighs cleared her throat and
stroked herself, Madonna fashion. Gun stopped and looked
at her, squeezing into his eyes all the corruption and stink
that was growing inside of him. The ugly whore looked
quickly away and he walked past her, increasing his pace
and refusing to see any person or thing for the next five
blocks, until he'd arrived at The Service Center.

He pushed open the windowless door and walked in. A rush of rotten heat swept over him and he wavered off balance for a moment. The air was humid and musky ripe, the music hard-driving Canadian rock and roll from the early seventies, The Guess Who doing American Woman.

Gun recalled his first time in a strip joint, eighteen years old, and what he remembered now about that night was how hard he'd tried to have fun and how miserably he'd failed, standing around with a couple dozen men drunk on beer and their imagined potency. The only excitement coming when a couple of young guys started in over who-knew-what, ripping each other's clothes and pounding each other's faces bloody with their fists. The stripper had even stopped to watch, and when the fight was over she'd been so desperate to win back her audience that she ignored city ordinance and removed her G-string, revealing a shaved and remarkably innocent-looking crotch. At the time, Gun had been amazed that all present weren't paralyzed by a sense of their own depravity.

Not much had changed in thirty years, though it did all seem more understandable to Gun now. The men did not appear happy, excited, or particulary horny. They seemed merely angry and wanting someone to receive the consequences of their little power, someone to punish. Most sat, leaning forward in their chairs, cutting away at the girl with their eyes, fists balled up on the tabletops or white-knuckled around their brown bottles.

The dancer was a redhead. At least her wig was red—and it was pushed far forward on her skull, giving her an oddly masculine look. Her limbs, too, were manly, muscled as if from hard lifting, the quadriceps standing out like narrow cables on the fronts of her thighs, her arms and neck sinewy. Her breasts were large and loose, and they shook, careened, wagged, flapped. Her face was set in a grin as hard and expressionless as the clench of her buttocks. Gun could not imagine how the men watching could possibly want her. Yet a few hooted and called out, their rolled-up bills held aloft in their fingers or teeth.

"Over here, Sweetie. Got a big one for ya." A high-pitched, barnyard squeal of a voice.

Without a hitch in her moves, the redhead angled herself in the direction of the caller. "How big is big?" she asked.

"Come and have a look."

She strutted backwards to the edge of the small stage— her high heels sounding like gunshots against the hard-wood—and squinted down over a freckled shoulder at the green bill in the young man's fingers. Apparently it wasn't worth the pride it would cost her to get it. She laughed at the guy, and he reached up and grabbed for her leg but missed as she swung away.

"Bitch," squeaked the man.

"But not your bitch."

Gun took a stool at the bar, wondering what good it was being here, wanting to be gone. He'd thought, simply, that he ought to get a good look at this place at night, a look at the men who liked being here. He'd imagined in some undeveloped part of his brain that he would be able to look around and pin guilt to a pair of eyes. In fact, every pair of eyes, every profile, every hunched or straight set of shoulders looked the same.

The bartender walked over and knocked on the bar. "Big fella, what can I do¿" he said. He was big himself, as tall as Gun and wider by far and he wore his long gray hair pulled back in a tail. Three earrings in his right lobe, all diamonds. Diamonds on his thick hairy fingers, too. His T-shirt said, DON'T LIKE MY SERVICE¿ DIAL 1-800-FUCK YOURSELF.

"What's wrong¿ My shirt¿" the bartender asked.

"Yeah," said Gun.

"You could talk to the manager, but I pay his salary."

"Well, I hope it's substantial," Gun said, and he ordered a Coke.

"Just a pop¿"

"That's right."

Gun heard a collective hoot and swiveled on his stool. A thin bald man in a blue suit held a rolled-up bill in his teeth and was in the process of inserting it between the two halves of the dancer's muscled buttocks, which she ably presented for the reception. Gun felt his soul go in for a crash landing. He swung around toward the bar, thought once more of leaving, then gave in to curiosity and turned in time to see the rolled up bill slip safely home and the man pull away—except the girl lost her grip now and the money dropped to the wooden stage.

The stripper swooped down to snatch it up, but another hand got there first.

A dumb "Ooh" rose from the crowd but a high sharp scream slashed through it and released a flood of silence. The girl was not dancing anymore. Instead she was grinding a wicked heel into the top of a man's hand. Beside the hand lay the rolled-up bill, and the hand's owner gaped up at the dancer above him, his face contorted in pain and disbelief, the bald top of his head glistening.

"Let him go!" somebody yelled.

"Fuck you," the woman shouted back.

"Let up!" This from the bartender, standing to Gun's right. "Prudy, let up now and get your butt over here!"

The girl lifted her foot then, and the man whose hand had been speared bellowed and curled himself around his wound. Meanwhile the girl was off the stage and marching toward the bartender, the men at their tables scrambling to clear a path for her. Gun watched her come, saw what she had in her eyes, and was glad he was not her target. She swept on past and planted herself in front of the bartender.

She wasn't saying anything or even trying to. But the muscles beneath her skin rippled and convulsed with a trapped energy that made Gun think of horses. The bartender's right fist shot out and gripped her upper arm and yanked her to her toes.

"Kind of thing's uncalled for. I'm trying to run a business here." His large face was stretched in anger. "You're gonna go get your clothes on and then get out of here, and I don't wanna see you tomorrow night, hear me?"

The girl was still nude, and this fact seemed finally to reach her. "Just let me go," she said, and glanced down at herself. She pried at the fingers that held her arm, but the bartender, her boss, whatever he was, did not let go. Instead he raised his left hand to her chin and squeezed it between his thumb and forefinger. His light gray eyes narrowed and ran down her body.

Gun said, "Let her go now."

The man blinked once and took his hand away from the girl's face. "Huh?"

"I think you heard me."

The bartender did not look at Gun but kept his eyes on

the girl, who in turn had lost her nerve and was staring miserably at the floor. "This is my place," said the man. The fist that held the girl was descending, though, and now the fingers that gripped her opened, leaving red prints on her pale arm. She ran with compromised dignity around the end of the bar, a forearm in front of her breasts, and disappeared into a back room.

"Thank you," Gun said. He looked around and saw everyone staring, their eyes impatient for the next diversion.

"I want you outta here," said the man.

"I was about to order another Coke."

"We've got a McDonald's down the street."

"I don't like McDonald's."

"Get out of here." The man motioned toward the door with his head while pointing a finger toward the far end of the bar. "Hey, Lanny," he said.

From the last of the leather-covered stools a bearded man stood up. The top of his head was like a pumpkin, bald, with pumpkin-like creases, and he wore a sweatsuit the same color gray as his beard, the sleeves cut off high to show his beefy arms. He carried in his hand a short length of pipe, duct-taped at the handle.

"Yeah, Steve?" He came forward. His eyes seemed passive, his face bored.

"Our friend has it in his mind to stay," Steve said.

Lanny nodded, then looked at Gun and shrugged. "I guess you gotta go." He aimed his pipe at the door.

"I was telling your boss here, I'm not ready to go yet." Gun was splendidly aware of just how much he wanted to piss these guys off. In fact, he couldn't help smiling, and when Steve's blow came, Gun wasn't ready for it—a surprisingly fast right hand landing precisely at the center of

Gun's stomach beneath the sternum. The punch doubled him up and ruined his defense against the hard left that now caught him on his right ear and dropped him cow-like to his knees, where he stayed, sucking without success at the air and trying to focus his eyes on the boots which he knew must be Steve the bartender's. He felt a hand grasp the back of his collar and pull up.

Lanny had not moved. Steve, however, was panting, excited, his head bobbing, his tongue tasting his lips. "Okay, are we done?"

Someone in the crowd said, "Attaboy, Steve."

Gun turned and looked for the one who had spoken, but all were quiet and stiff at their tables. The only movement Gun noticed in the whole place was along the far back wall, where a man in an old-fashioned fedora was gliding along the booths, probably headed for the rest room. Gun turned back to Steve the bartender, whose light eyes had grown suddenly darker.

"Now I'm going to hit you, Steve," Gun said, wishing it didn't have to be this way. With an eye on Lanny's pipe, Gun brought up his fist and caught Steve on the chin, snapping back the man's head. The pipe rose in a blur and Gun blocked Lanny's swing, forearm on forearm, then smashed a knee into the shorter man's big stomach. But the fat there was hard fat, and Lanny kept his feet, and then Gun heard sliced air behind him and fell away but not quickly enough and a bottle broke on his shoulder, glass rained on the floor, and he turned in time to catch Steve's fist with his cheekbone.

Gun did not fall but sat down hard on a leather-topped stool, his lower back slamming against the bar. He looked beyond the two men and into the crowd that watched, saw no help there, considered a sprint for the door, which seemed both prudent and possible, then heard at his right shoulder the sound of a revolver's hammer being cocked. He turned and saw behind the bar a man in a misshapen brown fedora. The face Gun recognized but could not yet name.

The man said, "Let's go," and bumped Gun's shoulder with the flat of his hand.

CHAPTER TWENTY-ONE

Harper LaMont sat down across from Gun at a cherry-wood table in the lounge of the Sheraton. LaMont still wore the ridiculous hat and his clothes were old and woolly, Salvation Army issue. Gun hadn't been able to match the face to a name until they'd driven a couple of blocks in LaMont's Wagoneer, and then only because of the lawyer's voice: the courtroom articulation, the deep bass tone that had surprised Gun when he'd first heard LaMont speak.

And now, Gun realized, the eyes, too, would have done it. They were Paul Newman blue, almost unapproachably calm.

Gun ordered coffee. LaMont asked for tea, then offered Gun a prefab from his pack of Marlboros, but Gun was already reaching for his papers and tobacco.

LaMont said, "I don't need to ask what you were doing in there tonight, but I will say that's a hell of a way to dig for clues."

"So I take it you heard about the taxi. Where they found it."

"Ah, Channel Four." LaMont took off his hat and raked a hand through his stand-up platinum hair. He looked around the room, nearly empty now—it was after two o'clock— and put on his worn-out hat again. He smiled into Gun's eyes and touched the floppy brim. Laughed apologetically. "I don't often go to this length to avoid being recognized."

"Why the getup?"

"You might've noticed where I was."

Gun leaned ahead to accept an offered light.

LaMont said, "I wasn't there for the same reason you were. That's not to say I'm uninterested."

"You and that place," Gun said. "It's not a fit."

LaMont's smile showed teeth absurdly white and straight. Money teeth. "Lately I'm going around town, checking out dancers, watching the guys who check out dancers. Research for a novel I'm planning. Getting the atmosphere." The lawyer leaned back in his chair and took a drag on his cigarette. He kept the smoke in his lungs for so long there wasn't anything left when he blew out. "There've been a couple of writers in the last year who did novels on strippers. They made some money on them, too. One's headed for the screen next year. All of which is fine by me. I don't begrudge any writer his luck or money which are one and the same in this business. What I don't like, do not like, is when people glorify subjects that don't deserve it. I don't like it one bit."

"You don't like it."

"I don't."

"And you aim to set the record straight."

"I do," said Harper LaMont.

Gun nodded, remembering what Lieutenant Hanson had said about LaMont's wife. "How'd you get started with all this?" he asked. "Exploited children. Beat-up women. There's got to be a better way for a lawyer to make money. You weren't always writing novels. And you sure don't strike me as a bleeding heart."

LaMont shrugged. "In fact, I'm a Republican. A damn good one since I started making all this book money. But what I've done, Pedersen—what I do, it's all inherited. I had a wife, she's dead now, and that woman *was* a bleeding heart. A lawyer, too, and a good one. Specialized in children's defense. She was smart, she was low-profile, and she worked her ass off. And when she had the floor, believe me, there wasn't a person in the room who didn't know she was telling the last truth about the most important issue of our time."

"And she died," Gun said.

LaMont ground his cigarette into the ashtray between them and looked off toward an empty corner of the lounge. "I always used to wonder what she saw in me." His voice was soft, unsure of itself.

Gun waited a moment. LaMont was silent. Gun said, "I'd guess by now you've found out."

"Sure as hell've tried." The lawyer took off the floppy hat and scratched at his scalp like an old man.

Gun nodded his agreement, understanding too well that if once you came up short for a woman, and then she died, you were bound to come up short in everything.

They both smoked, their eyes deflecting each other's all around the darkened room. Finally Gun said he had to think about getting some sleep. LaMont coughed once and drained his tea.

"I wish I could help you, Pedersen."

"Tell me something. Say these animals get caught—what happens then?"

"State prosecutes," LaMont said shortly.

"I know that. But what happens to them? Do they go away and stay away?"

"Oh, man." LaMont shook his head and offered a dry laugh, took off his hat yet again and scratched at his scalp. "This is Minnesota we're in, right? If there's ever a trial in this case, and it ends in a guilty verdict, we *still* won't see justice. We can forget it. No matter what, the animals win. I know."

Gun laid his hands flat upon the table; his knuckles felt stiff and hard and old. LaMont leaned forward and there were pinpricks of light pulsing in his eyes.

"The question is, Pedersen: If you catch them, will you hand them over? To anyone?" He smiled and shook his head. "I don't think so."

Gun slept until nine o'clock and by ten was squeezing his pickup truck into the lone vacancy in the small parking lot out front of the address Carol had given him by phone yesterday. Small brown letters on the tan-brick building spelled out the name CLUB KING INCORPORATED. Inside, a white hallway with mauve carpeting. Manufactured prints on the walls, pastel. And Muzac, of course: Clapton's ballad about his son, a piece Gun had liked, eviscerated.

Club King occupied a suite on the main floor. Nobody here but a secretary behind a radiantly golden oak counter. She was not smiling and appeared unable to. Gun said good morning and she sighed, asked whether he'd been here before.

"No, I haven't. I'd like to see Mr. Gorman."

"Appointment?" She spoke with unhidden sarcasm. Her blue eyes utterly cold.

"I don't have an appointment," Gun said.

"No appointment," said the receptionist.

Tact, Gun told himself. "I'm afraid not."

"Then *I'm* afraid there's nothing I can do for you, sir."

"Gorman's not here?"

"He's in a meeting."

"I could wait."

"He'll be in a meeting all day, sir." She began to peck at the computer's keyboard.

"Maybe I could catch him at lunch."

The woman continued typing. Gun cleared his throat. The receptionist's eyes flashed up at him. "Mr. Gorman always has lunch plans."

"Important ones, too, no doubt. Could I make an appointment?"

"Of course." She began tracing her finger across the mostly empty squares of a large calendar blotter. "How would October fifteenth be?" she said, without looking up. "In the afternoon. Two o'clock."

"That's almost a month away," Gun said.

"Yes." The receptionist smiled for the first time. Her teeth were not filed to points.

Gun spent the rest of the morning and most of the afternoon pounding the blocks between Blue Books, behind which the whore had supposedly seen the taxi, and The Service Center, where he'd nearly gotten his head knocked in last night. It was a kinder place in daylight: the prostitutes someplace sleeping, the pimps off snorting their dough, the bums out of sight. Still, it was dismal—the sort of neighborhood where you stepped with care, watching for vomit, or dog shit, or worse.

He spoke with a dozen bartenders, twice that many early drinkers, and a handful of retirees and hard cases who rented second- and third-floor apartments. Everyone knew about the murder. No one had a thing to say about it. No one remembered anything unusual, and no one would admit to hearing any street talk. Many said they'd already been approached by a detective from Minneapolis PD. Hanson was doing his job.

Most seemed nervous at being questioned and anxious to see Gun leave. A few asked to see his badge. One old woman with only a scattering of hair on her skull and a missing arm tried selling him a handgun.

By two-thirty, tired and fighting a headache, he drove six or so blocks to a yuppie café across the street from Harper LaMont's office, sat down in the smoking section, and ordered a bowl of wild rice soup and a turkey and Swiss on wheat. He sat in a window booth and watched men in dark suits moving with hurried importance down the sidewalk and women in dark suits trying to look like men. He smoked like he hadn't smoked in years, one cigarette after another, and he finished two beers before his food came. He had to admit that he didn't know what to do next, or where to go, or who the hell to talk to.

CHAPTER TWENTY-TWO

By four-fifteen Gun was back at Club King Incorporated. He pulled into the front lot and found a space, hesitated with his hand on the key, and backed out again. Gorman hadn't returned Carol's phone calls and Gun reckoned against his own chances of landing an audience with the man. In low gear he followed the row of cars to the end of the building. There was a high woven-wire gate, the door standing open with a sign saying EMPLOYEES ONLY. Gun turned in. This back lot was smaller than the front, and dirtier. Blue signs mounted near the rear entrance showed where the money parked: VP FINANCE. VP OPERATIONS. EXEC SECRETARY. And, closest to the door: CEO.

The CEO spot was filled by a yellow Suburban, its back windows conspicuous with fly-fishing gear. Gun parked next to it, appointing himself vice-president. The Suburban had hip waders in the back and three Orvis cylinders Gun assumed were full of good fly rod. A basket creel. A brim hat in a tasteful olive-brown.

Gun tuned the radio to WCCO. Steve Cannon was holding forth there like Raymond Chandler as he had for a lifetime, talking booze and broads and the disappointing Twins. Gun opened the waxy white bag on the seat beside him and withdrew a long john. Glazed and nut-sprinkled. He ate it in four mouthfuls.

At five o'clock Cannon gave way to news and the latest from a neutered weatherman and at long last a red-complected man swung through the door and headed for the Suburban. Gun stepped from the truck. Gorman wore a gray unbelted duster that went past his knees and flapped in the wind as befitted a craggy adventurer. He'd clearly chosen the duster to complement his hair, which was as white as Gun's own. His eyebrows were dark and arched like Sean Connery's and he carried himself as if to exploit the resemblance.

Gun met him at the Suburban. "Mr. Gorman, Gun Pedersen. If you have a minute to spare, I'd sure like to talk to you."

"Gun Pedersen. I'll be damned. Roberta told me Gun Pedersen had dropped by and I thought she was making it up. Having some fun with the boss man." Gorman had a deep soft old-boy voice and he held out a wide hard hand and Gun shook it. Gun had never heard anyone use the term "boss man" in real life before. Gorman said, "Say now. Weren't you at that CCO sports banquet last spring? No? My table, me and old Sid Hartman and Joe Montana are sitting around a few platefuls of king crab. Montana's a gentleman, signs some napkins for folks coming over, it's only right, and then this girl sashays over to say 'Hi.' I'd say she was pretty but all I remember is lipstick. And Joe, he starts saying 'Hello' and what comes out? A belch! No polite little airy one either but a hard-edge monster like to burn your throat out. He had no idea it was coming! So this makes the gossip column in the *Star Tribune* and I'm mentioned too and now the goddamn office help won't let it go. 'Mr. Gorman, Jim McMahon is on the phone.' 'Mr. Gorman sir, there's a Mr. Puckett wanting to know if you're available for lunch.' Gun Pedersen! I'll be damned." Gorman laughed. "I'm sorry sir, that's one hell of a long way to say hello. You can take the boy out of Wyoming . . . now what can I do for you?"

On the whole Gun would've preferred hostility. He said, "Guess I'll pass on the crab."

"Heh. How about steak then? I've got a dinner meeting, nothing formal. Just pull up an extra chair."

"Thanks. I don't think so. But I need to ask you about Rich Morton."

Gorman squinted. "I know the name."

"Your head of security at Hawk Lake."

"Sure, I got him now. Used to be FBI. What about him?"

"Maybe you could tell me why he got canned."

Gorman's eyes tightened in their sockets. "What is this? You a friend of his?"

"Not exactly." Gun stopped here but realized Gorman was going to wait him out. He said, "Morton's been in touch with my wife. Now she can't get hold of him. She was told he'd been fired."

Gorman began to speak and stopped. When he continued his voice was still the old-boy but not soft anymore. He was the boss man all right and accustomed to getting answers he desired. "Let me ask you this, ballplayer. Why in the hell is your wife needing Morton so bad?"

"She runs a newspaper up north. Her name's Carol Long. She's been trying to reach you, but real important guys always seem to be in meetings."

Gorman stood staring at Gun through a whisk of wind that snapped the duster around his knees. "And she sent you to find this out? Damn, Gun, this disappoints me. I thought you were here on your own business, not for some gutter journalist who lives to screw careers. Wife or no wife, Pedersen. A man who swings the bat like you shouldn't have his balls snipped."

Gun took a breath. Steady. He opened his mouth hoping

for Carol's sake it would opt for diplomacy. Instead it said, "If you had any balls, Gorman, you'd return my wife's phone calls. I can see that's unlikely. If you suddenly grow a pair—" and then Gun stopped. This was going nowhere and he turned from Gorman and moved toward the truck.

"Listen, you almighty shit—" Gorman was saying, but Gun, walking, heard it as one hears hailstones on a distant roof. He slid behind the wheel and turned the key.

"Piss-ant self-important—"

Gun's hand on the shift knob felt dry and nerveless.

"Has-been—" Gorman was fading, in the rearview now, his face enraged but satisfaction evident in his own locution, his clean even teeth moving efficiently around the words. As Gun turned the corner of the building a gold-trimmed Seville coming in blared its panicky horn, and he realized he was driving in the left lane. He eased to the right, reaching to brace the half-cup of coffee balanced on the dash and splashing it across the cab. He smelled its cold smell on the seat and on his clothes and felt its cold wetness on his knees. He wondered how it was that everything he touched he spilled.

Chapter Twenty-Three

There was a bantamweight match on HBO when Gun got back to the hotel. The standard cable fight, black kid–Hispanic kid, pick the one in blue shorts and hope the other guy goes down. The Hispanic had a flyswatter jab that looked like it would wear on you. Gun left the fight on while he took a shower. The hotel kept its water hot enough to take Gun's breath a moment but it wouldn't take away the picture of Gorman he kept seeing, of Gorman's teeth snapping up and down, nor the almost physical discomfort of having gone to Gorman as some sort of emissary for Carol. He'd felt strangely hobbled. He dreaded talking to her, telling her he'd just screwed every contact she ever made at Hawk Lake.

He stepped from the shower and dried, standing at the mirror with his flesh cooling to prickles and aware that he'd done too much sitting lately. Too much driving and thinking. He dressed. On HBO the fight was over and a movie had started, a bargain thriller with rotten dialogue and Alan Alda as the psycho. Alan looked old and ungrateful for the work. Gun turned it off and picked up the phone.

Carol didn't answer and he hung up after eight rings. He lay back on the bed but it seemed wooden and mean. Heat was coming from somewhere, blowing from a vent in the wall near his head, and like all hotel rooms this one warmed too quickly and became stuffy. He searched fruitlessly for a thermostat and finally went to the sliding glass door and

opened it wide, stepping out onto the balcony and allowing
the sharp wet wind inside. Down twenty stories he saw
cars on the one-way going east with their headlights pushing before them through the gloom. The balcony was of
black gap-welded iron shafts so you could looked down
between your feet and saw the vulnerable scalp of whomev-
er stood on the balcony a floor below, but the wind was
coming down from the north bitter and laden with a mist
chilled at ten thousand feet and Gun stood alone tonight.
The cold renewed his urge to move, swing, press. He went
deliberately to his knees, straightened out on his gut with
his chest against iron. He stiffened his legs, finding the safe-
ty rail against the tips of his toes. The push-ups came hard
at first, as they usually did, stayed hard through the first
twenty and the second and then the third. He'd done no
push-ups this morning nor the previous night. Nor the
morning before that. Gasping toward eighty Gun felt his
shoulders shake and his legs begin to cramp. Eighty reached.
Eighty-one. There was blood between the fingers of his
right hand. Eighty-two. Long ago doing this work on the
grass beside Stony Lake he had started slow and gone faster
all the way to finish, easy doings, muscles and boneblades
incapable of failure, and age a demon yet incomprehensible.
At eighty-six Gun's chest touched iron and did not rise
though his arms braced and shuddered and he at last
allowed defeat. He lay like a struck dog, soaking, the curtained light from inside showing real drops now as the mist
became a rain.

Sometime in the narrow hours beyond midnight a tiny
bright *snick* brought Gun alert. He lay among the stiff

sheets, tensed to the silence and waiting. The next *snick* was louder and came clearly from the door. The faint glow of city entering the window was devoid of natural dawn. Gun heard the slow agony of a withdrawing dead bolt and with numb extremities he rose in his shorts and crossed the carpet. A heavy ceramic ashtray lay beside the television and he picked it up just as a vertical blade of light appeared at the door. The blade widened. Gun's heart went leaden— and then exultant, as the light became a rectangle full of promise.

Diane Apple walked through the door.

Her eyes laughed at him standing in his Jockeys gripping a stupid ashtray in his own defense. She said, "Gun, I've brought you something."

"Diane." He was too smitten and aghast to say anything else. Her hair was as she had worn it in Florida, in an untamed auburn braid. She was barefoot. She wore black jeans and pearl earrings shaped like conch shells and a man's button-down shirt, ripped at the cuffs. He wanted her to speak again but she smiled quietly and came forward. She smelled of a wild perfume and mahogany and of oil soap such as she'd used on the deck of her small cruiser. He held out one hand. She reached for him and as she did her knee bumped a corner of the low TV cabinet and the noise opened Gun's eyes where he lay in the strange bed and he shut them now and strove to breathe slowly and not like a man startled from dreams of redemption. He breathed heavily and looked through slits at a dim form frozen near the television. He knew nothing except that it was not Diane Apple.

He watched the dim figure resume movement, going to the luggage rack which Gun had placed beside the sliding glass. A pencil-thin shaft of directed light appeared and the man fastidiously emptied Gun's suitcase, removing handfuls of clothing, Gun's shaving kit, a pair of good Avias. Gun thought of his billfold. It was in the pocket of the trousers he'd shucked off before showering. The tiny beam left the suitcase and explored the room like a restless wasp, lighting upon the balding upholstery of an armchair and dancing over the silver change spread across the nightstand. Gun shut his eyes and drew a deep unflattering breath that whistled in his nose and he felt the light pass cautiously across his lids. The man advanced. Gun lay having to think about every breath, in, out, sensing the shape of the man nearing him and knowing a sudden sweaty fear of knives. He opened one eye, saw the flashlight beam slide to the floor directly at the foot of the bed. The heaped trousers were there and the burglar knelt without hesitation and began rifling the pockets. Then decision took Gun and he was motion unthinking, ripping the sheet away and the burglar popping upright even as Gun flung the sheet with a high stroke. Coming off the bed Gun saw the white sheet ballooning and the man's arms fighting it off and sure enough a weapon there, dark and heavy and whistling as Gun ducked beneath it, his head slamming the man in the V at the bottom of his rib cage. Air was expelled, sick-smelling air, and Gun was on the floor atop the man whose face was still covered by the sheet. Gun wrapped him tighter, the makeshift straitjacket twisting as something thumped the floor and a blind knee came up trying for Gun's groin. He grabbed a hank of sheet behind the man's head and with the other hand found the first hard thing offered in the dark, his own black-soled boot, raised it high, and gave the downthrust every drop of juice he had. He heard and felt breakage and the man went loose without even groaning and Gun rolled away. The man's breath was a sucking wound in the muted room. The odor of urine rose swiftly and Gun, not caring whose it was, got to his knees and found a light switch.

The burglar lay besheeted from head to middle thigh, the white cloth wicking scarlet at the head and light gold at the crotch. On the floor lay a black penlight, still shining, Gun's open billfold where the man had dropped it, and a leather-covered sap the color of teak. Gun knelt. Shallow breathing came from under the sheet and Gun unwrapped him, afraid for the damage he'd see.

He was a young white man, no more than thirty. Light brown hair medium-long and prematurely receding. His eyes were blue and flat and while open gave him a deathly look and Gun closed them with his fingers. Three teeth were broken that Gun could see and blood was pooling at the back of the mouth. He was breathing through his nose, a fine-lined nose that appeared untouched. Gun turned the man on his side and blood ran from his open mouth and he took a larger tattered breath and moaned.

Gun went into the bathroom and brought out towels and a wet washcloth. Cradling the man's head in one palm he wiped blood from the young, slight, clean-shaven chin and concave cheeks. The burglar moaned again through lips somehow not ruined though Gun now saw another broken tooth, four in all. As if he'd been open-mouthed, about to screech when the boot landed.

"Hey," Gun said. He said it softly, sounding ridiculous to himself and thinking for some reason now of Hanson, the homicide detective. "Hey," he said, and the man came awake with a convulsive dry heave, his thin white hands reaching before him like a child's. Another heave and Gun helped the burglar sit upright, the man's shoulders shaking as if fevered.

"Easy. All right, that's over. Lay back now, use your hands—here, keep the towel over your mouth. Keep the pressure on and you won't lose so much blood." Gun lowered the burglar back to the floor. He picked up the phone.

"Uh-uh," the burglar said. He'd lifted his head and was shaking it.

"Room service," Gun said, and the burglar shut his eyes and let his head thump back to the floor.

Gun ordered hot tea with lemon and a bowl of crushed ice and was told by the surly night cook that a minimum order of ten dollars was necessary for delivery past one A.M.

"I'll leave a big tip," Gun said.

When the tea arrived Gun brought it in and set it on the floor while the burglar propped himself against the bed. The towel came away full of ocher clot and the man's eyes watered but he was quiet and took the cup and held it close to his mouth and let the steam come up into the raw places. He stirred ice into the tea with his finger until it cooled. Gun waited to speak until the man had sipped.

"I'm sorry about the teeth. Maybe you have a dentist in the family. Meantime you'll have to enunciate carefully. Start with your name."

The burglar's mouth labored. "Annie Moon." He shook his head, frustrated.

"Annie?"

"Uh-uh."

"Ronnie."

With effort the burglar said, "Danny. Moon."

"Danny Moon."

"Mood."

"Your name is Danny Mood."

"Uh-huh."

"Better be truthful here, Danny."

The burglar crossed himself.

"You didn't come in here to take my money, did you?"

Danny Mood shook No.

"Why then?"

Mood considered a word, tried it out. "Conhidenshal."

Gun leaned over Mood. He smelled cold tea and the lemon in it didn't mix well with the other odors in the room. He said, "Danny, nothing is confidential here. If you wanted confidential, you shouldn't have woke me up. Next time I pick up that phone, you think it's going to be for room service?"

Mood lowered his gaze, worked his mouth quietly. When he spoke again his voice was soft, as if to cushion pain, but he'd found his consonants. "I'm a private investigator."

"A detective."

Mood nodded. "Looking for Iron Sky. His family hired me."

"The taxi driver?"

"Yuh." Mood sipped tea, looked down and shut his eyes. "Aw, I wet my pants. Goddamn."

Gun went to the sliding glass door and opened it an inch. "You think I know where Iron Sky is? Why?"

"I saw you earlier. At the garage where the cab was. You were poking around in there." Mood was feeling enough better to have some resentment in his eyes. "Thought maybe you found something. You get it now? I don't find Albert I don't get paid."

Gun thought it over. "Let me see your ID."

"Don't have one. I'm part-time."

"Iron Sky's family, where are they from?"

"Reservation up north," Mood said.

"There are lots of reservations up north."

"Fon Du Lac."

"And you live here. In the city."

"No. Up near the Rez."

"Finish your tea," Gun said.

Danny Mood finished it. Gun took the cup, then scooped the blankets off the man and helped him up. Mood's balance wasn't good and in standing he vomited a little tea and Gun's innards momentarily jerked. He went into the bathroom and found a clean washcloth.

"Take it with you. You should get to a hospital. I'll call a cab if you want."

"I can drive."

"Drive then." Gun opened the door. Mood went out holding the washcloth to his mouth with his left hand and extending the fingers of his right before him as if to locate a line of equilibrium.

"Mood," Gun said. Mood had reached the elevators and now looked back. "I shouldn't need to say this. Find other work."

The elevator bell rang and as the door slid open Mood's eyes took on a shade of sudden malice. It hadn't been there earlier and it changed his face entirely. Stepping aboard Mood dropped the cloth from his mouth and laughed once, hoarsely, giving Gun a grin as bloody and lewd as a Halloween dream.

Alone in the room Gun took his time. He turned on every bulb he could find, bathroom too, evicting shadows. His muscles ached with used adrenaline. He re-packed his

clothes. Balled up the sullied sheet and blankets and opened
the sliding door and dropped them onto the balcony in the
rain.

He had the feeling he had misplayed Danny Mood. That
grin, when Mood got on the elevator. There was something
more wrong with that grin than any number of ruined
teeth, and it put into Gun's blood an unreasoned anxiety he
hadn't known since childhood. He could contain it now,
but the sensation was there. He sat on the bed with every
bulb burning, thinking as he had not done in years of being
small and in his parents' home, tucked in bed upstairs and
sweating, eyes shut hard, listening for the sound of breathing not his own and fearing the closet that stood open as a
grave across the darkened room.

CHAPTER TWENTY-FOUR

At sunrise Gun was sitting in a freeway Perkins drinking coffee with cream and watching the sluggish early commute. He hadn't slept and he wasn't sleepy. He was thinking about the dream he'd had of Diane Apple. He'd believed it completely, even down to the smell of deck soap when she reached toward him. Your mind was capable of such betrayals, Gun thought; it was like getting clubbed, a kind of peace followed by a hell of a hurt when you woke up. She'd even spoken to him, "I've brought you something," her voice low and confident, Diane's own voice.

He thought: brought me what?

Breakfast came in the hands of a pretty waitress, forty or so, brown hair pulled into a bun and rimless glasses on her nose. Pancakes, syrup, poached eggs, bacon, and hash browns. Wheat toast. Gun ate watching the rain, cars down there on I–94 moving toward the city like fish getting reeled in, no choice in it for most of them. Halfway through the meal he was sick of food and looked at the clock. Eight-fifteen. He went to the pay phone by the entryway.

"Homicide," Hanson said.

"That's a crummy greeting, first thing in the morning."

"Pedersen, you're still in town. Hit any homers this trip?" Hanson sounded edgy, uncomfortable.

"Gosh no, Hanson. What about you, have you shot anyone yet today?"

Hanson chuckled. "All right. Tell me what you've got, but be quick. The lieutenant thinks you're getting old."

"Some days I feel my knees."

"You know what I mean."

Gun said, "There's a private investigator looking around for the cabdriver, Iron Sky. He looked me up last night."

"Why you?"

"Apparently he saw me looking around the garage where they found his cab. Has he been in touch with you?"

"Local guys usually don't. The lieutenant discourages PIs. What's his name?"

"He's not local. Danny Mood. Lives up by the Fon Du Lac Reservation, where Iron Sky's from. The family hired him."

Hanson was quiet a minute and Gun could hear the click of computer keys. "Pedersen? There's a little more on Iron Sky. I'm checking here . . . he doesn't come from Fon Du Lac. All we've been able to find out, Iron Sky's a Red Lake Chippewa. And I'd be surprised if his family could afford a private eye."

A man was waiting for the phone. He had a briefcase and a dripping trench coat and a mouth that looked made to complain.

"What'd this guy look like?" Hanson asked, not sounding worried now about the lieutenant.

"Ah, normal. Five-ten, brown hair, medium build."

More clicking. "Private investigators' register shows no Daniel Mood."

"I'm not surprised. He seemed mighty unofficial. Said he was part-time."

The man with the briefcase coughed and started poking through the big pockets of his trench, as if he might find some billable hours in there. Gun put his hand over the phone. "I'm sorry. Are you extremely important?"

"'Brown hair, medium build.' Can you do any better than that?" Hanson asked.

Briefcase decided to use the bathroom.

"He didn't stay long," Gun said.

"Come on, Pedersen. How many amateurs do I have to deal with here?"

"Listen, Hanson, he didn't talk much. I'm sorry. Now I've got to make another call. If I see him again, I'll get his number."

"Oh, thanks."

He wasn't sure why he hadn't told Hanson what happened with Danny Mood. He'd been conscious of pulling back and he knew the detective knew it too, Gun calling up and then turning soft-focus on details. Well, he'd given Hanson something, anyhow, and he'd gotten something back: Mood was no investigator, and he was no friend of Iron Sky's. Didn't even know what rez Iron Sky was from.

Gun didn't know what any of it meant.

Rain was still falling when Gun pulled into the Holiday Inn lot, downtown Minneapolis. He'd checked out of the other place because he didn't feel like explaining the bedding. Holiday Inn ran ads on the radio saying "No surprises," and that was better than he'd done lately.

They allowed him to check in early because he would accept a smoking room. Everyone else in Minnesota had quit. It was ten in the morning and he shut the thick orange drapes and undressed and locked the door twice, bolt and chain. He went into the bathroom and saw for the first time a smear of dried blood up next to his ear. He remembered turning to the briefcase guy at Perkins and the guy's quick departure thereafter. He smiled and his own smile looked strange in the mirror—like a language reversed.

After the shower he lay on his belly on the bed, his feet hanging off the end, the long sag hitting hard at last. As his eyes closed, he had the sensation of seeing ahead through hours of empty dark. No Diane in there, no Danny Mood. He'd make it last, stay in that dark as long as he could and then get up and see what was on the other side.

CHAPTER TWENTY-FIVE

He woke gasping as if he'd held his breath for hours. His mind felt thick, oxygen-deprived. The red numerals of the clock read 5:58, and Jack LaSalle was pounding on the door.

Jack was two hours earlier than Gun had expected him.

"What were you doing in here?" Jack said when Gun let him in. "Yoga? I knocked for ten minutes."

"Anybody else would've had the desk ring the room, see if I was in."

"Well, I didn't think of it. I'm just the help."

Gun pulled the drapes and late sun poured in. There were clouds but they were thin, and the sun was warm through the glass. Gun had to blink to focus. "I slept all day."

Jack was carrying an Army duffel which he slung onto the bed. He opened it and took out a pair of brown vinyl wing tips, khaki janitor pants, and a suit coat. The coat was a shiny brown polyester blend with wide lapels and white stitching on the pockets. The clothes smelled like a basement.

"Camouflage," Jack said. "Look, I haven't even shaved."

"I don't know what to say. Should I shake your hand or buy you a hot meal?"

"The meal. Potatoes, red meat if you can still get it down here." Jack slung on the suit coat and held up the wing tips. "Some good proletarian beer."

•••

They found steak at a storefront place downtown, two blocks from where the whore had reported the taxi. The table had the standard red-and-white checked cloth and Gun sat across it watching Jack eat, Jack all business going after his New York Strip. In that getup he looked like a hard-timer who'd been begging all day and finally hit up the right guy. That morning, when Gun had called asking his help, Jack had sounded like a kid being invited to Disneyland. That hadn't bothered Gun; in fact it had helped somehow, taken a little of the poison from his blood. Even back in the hotel, the way he pulled those clothes out of the duffel: happy, calling them camouflage, Jack clearly on a hunting trip. But out here he was different. He sliced meat and ate it without meeting Gun's eyes.

"Jack. You don't owe me this."

Jack looked back surprised. "Of course not. You're the one with the debt. I'm just reaching down, help you pay it."

"You don't have to."

Jack went back to his steak. He said, "Where's Carol in all this?"

Gun decided on the short version. "She's at home. I think she understands it."

"Yeah? That's some woman, understanding you going off to rescue some girl who's already killed." Jack looked up. "Sorry, Gun. It's not my business."

"It's all right. She's entitled to be angry. I didn't ask her not to be."

"She's trying to reconcile you with her own conscience."

"I respect her conscience."

"And what does yours say? You think it'll tell you when to stop?"

"That," Gun said, "is a dandy question. Anything else you'd like to know?"

Jack pushed his plate away. He said, "If we get what we're after, how many Hail Marys am I gonna have to say?"

They started at nine P.M. at a place called Spanky's: charcoal stucco, no windows, and a big blue neon kitten above the door. The kitten had what was supposed to be an oversexed expression and it had a neon bikini top that blinked on and off every two seconds, the kitten's eyes getting wide when the bikini disappeared. The door was painted black on the outside and a livid pink inside when Jack swung it open to a mix of smells, cigarette smoke foremost and others less pleasant the farther inside Spanky's you got. A bar ran along the left wall, all the usual Miller and Pabst and Bud signs strung above it with visible extension cords. Jack moved to a stool and Gun heard him call for whiskey neat, looking the part and wasting no time. The place was half empty, half full for an optimist but Gun didn't see any of those here, certainly not the two women dancing naked through pink smoke on a plywood stage nor any of the men who'd swiveled on their bar stools to watch. Some sort of thudding music was in the air, no real tune but an electric bass counting out rhythm. Gun found an empty booth where he could see Jack at the bar. The air was sticky, full of body sweat and fruit-flavored liquor and the gamy smell of the chronically horny. Men who'd somehow grown used to such atmosphere were talking loud here and there, fat guys laughing up their shitty bosses and shitty neighbors and their ex-wives. Others just stared stageward as though their lives had gone out and left them immobile. Onstage the women swayed, a redhead and a counterfeit blonde waving their chests around without ambition, their eyes saying, *Wow, showbiz.*

A waitress arrived and Gun looking past her saw Jack toss back the whiskey and hold up his hand for another.

"Coffee," Gun said. The waitress had dark hair, almost black, tan skin a little slack around the eyes, probably from the lousy hours. She had a bright red bow at her neck and a slim gold wedding band on her left hand.

"Nothing else?" she said.

"No, thanks." He wanted to ask her how she could stand the job. How her husband could stand it. Or maybe there was no husband: She just wore the ring, kept these losers at a distance.

She said, "You have to have something. There's a two-drink minimum. We've got the nonalcoholic stuff, if that's a problem for you."

At the bar Jack was tilting back his second whiskey. The guy to his left was laughing, watching him. The guy to his right was one of the staring zombies, looking through the dancers.

"Is the coffee good?" Gun said.

"It's fine. But that's not—"

"Bring me two coffees." Gun laid a twenty on the table. "Charge me for the minimum. Keep what's left."

The waitress said, "Oh, my Lord."

"What's the matter?"

"You're that baseball player. Gun—Larson."

"I'm sorry. I'm really not."

She stood tapping her pen on her receipt pad, smiling. "You're embarrassed to be here. I understand." She lowered her voice. "Believe me."

"OK, I'm embarrassed to be here. And I swear, I'm not Gun Larson."

Jack was doing away with number three up there and

now he was laughing too. And holding his hand up. The waitress was blushing—in this place!—saying, "Oh boy. I apologize. You really do look a lot like him, though—" running off at last to get the coffee.

By the time it arrived, two cups of lukewarm water the color of tobacco spit, Jack had finished four whiskeys and his voice was rising. Gun rose too and started for him, wanting to slow this down somehow.

Then Jack said, addressing the bartender, "This is one odd shitty part of town, you know that?"

The bartender was a slight dark-haired man with sideburns and a limp. He ignored Jack.

"I'm down the street last week and outta luck, I'm walking along got a beef sandwich in my pocket. Late at night, now. And I go past the alleyway and out comes four big coloreds: 'Whatcha got, man, whatcha got?' Four tall guys telling me to give 'em money."

Gun thought: *coloreds?*

Jack went on, "So I ask 'em, 'What are you, the Dream Team? This is what you're doing now, rolling little white guys?' Shit. So I hand 'em the wallet and of course it's dry as a monkey's red heinie. So they hand it back! I'm home free, right? And then the tallest one, looks like Charles Barkley, leans down into my face: 'You got nothin else for us?' 'Well, hell. A beef sandwich if you want it. Here.' Barkley takes the sandwich and sniffs it like a goddamn retriever. 'White bread,' he says; like that's a bad thing. Then he says, 'You Marley, you got a cold. Here's a hanky for you.' Taking the bread off my sandwich. Marley steps up and he's got the sniffles, no doubt about it. He folds that bread around his big nose and gives a honk and you can see the bread fill up. Barkley sticks it back on top of the beef and hands it back. Barkley says: 'Snack time.'"

"Aw, God," said the bartender. Jack had drawn a small crowd and he motioned for another whiskey. Gun sat a few stools away watching their faces, grins all over them: This poor schmuck ate a booger sandwich!

"Didja eat it?" asked the guy to Jack's left. He couldn't wait.

Jack said, "What would you do?"

"Man, I'd run away!"

"Remember those commercials?" Jack said. "Builds strong bodies twelve ways. Damn right I ate it."

There were gigantic laughs. Gun thought: I don't even know this man.

"That was Tuesday. Next night was worse."

They were expecting something even funnier than boogers on bread and seemed surprised when Jack sobered up on them. Gun wondered what happened to the whiskey. Jack said he'd seen a taxi in the alley in the middle of the night. Two or three men in it, one woman. The woman screaming.

"Never forget it," Jack said. "One of the guys looked out and saw me."

"You see the action?" asked the man to Jack's left.

Gun saw Jack brace up at this. Jack said, "You sorry jerkoff. You think I was lucky to be there, don't you?" his voice without a shade of drink.

Gun left Spanky's and went to his truck where it was parked opposite the bar. The wind struck his face from the east, then switched abruptly to the north. You couldn't gauge the wind in cities and that was something he'd always disliked; the streets and structures messed up his barometer. He started the truck and sat, feeling befouled and cold and the heater taking its time. In ten minutes Jack came out, stood in apparent indecision, and walked west down the block. Gun watched him, Jack walking at a slow roll, the bad suit coat flapping open. Just another street troll.

No one followed him out of Spanky's. Gun waited until Jack was three blocks distant and pulled out to pick him up.

"Well, that's one," Jack said. He rubbed his hands under the heat.

"You plan to drink that much at every stop?"

"Actually, I plan to slow down some," Jack admitted. "You have to admit, it loosens the tongue."

"Uh-huh. You seemed right at home. Where'd you get that story?"

"Heard a guy tell it up at my place. Fellow who came up for the ice fishing. He was a whiskey drinker and that brought it back somehow. He was lying too but it's a funny story. Was I as good as I think I was?"

"I could hardly stand to watch. Now let's try again."

They tried a bar called Cap's and an adult bookstore next to it, Gun staying in the truck now to watch the door, and a strip place across the street called the Woodpecker where Jack said there wasn't a spot on the floor your shoes didn't stick and where he'd gone into the men's room to find cocaine spilled all over the toilet seat and a man on his knees licking it off. They tried a nameless place where the drinks were served in Dixie cups and a fat girl bobbled around behind a back-lit screen for an audience of three, two sleeping. They drove a short distance and tried a spot relatively upscale, where the dancers had spotlights and pretty faces as well as silicone and where a lot of the men wore ties and some had women with them, and where Jack in his K mart wing tips looked displaced. The Shore, it was called; and when Jack left the Shore a little before one A.M. a slim white kid with white albino hair left also and took Jack's path around the corner.

There was traffic on the street and it was a full minute before Gun could get across. By the time he'd done so Jack already had the kid and was kneeling on his chest behind a dumpster, the kid's hair spread on the ground white as a lab rat's and squeaking noises coming from his mouth.

"Look who's here," Jack told the kid when Gun walked up. "You think I'm fast? Try him."

The kid told them his name was Joe Sampler. He was maybe twenty-two, chest hollow as a rock star's under a thin gray-patterned shirt, no jacket. His eyes were watery like two popped blisters. Jack kept him supine while patrons leaving the Shore walked past in small suddenly quiet groups. Sampler told them he'd followed Jack out of the club because he wanted to talk.

"Talk about what?" Jack demanded.

"What you were sayin. The woman in the taxi, back the alleyway."

Jack rose in one motion, hoisting Joe Sampler up like a Tom Petty rag doll and setting him afoot.

Gun said, "Tell us what you saw. Don't skip anything."

"You guys detectives?"

"Does it matter to you?"

Sampler grinned now, grabbing his elbows. "Cold, isn't it? I think we can work something out."

Jack hooked one hand in Sampler's shirtfront and put him back on the ground.

"Joe," Gun said, "we've already worked it out. If you've got anything to say, we're going to hear it. That should be plain to you."

"Listen, I didn't actually *see*—" Jack rolled Sampler to his belly and turned his wrist up behind him—"ow, didn't see it happen. I heard about it. Some guy talking it up. Hadda be the same thing, taxi, alley, three of 'em. Oh man, the arm there, could you please?"

"Who was talking?"

"I can find out," Sampler gasped.

Gun told Jack to let him up and Sampler stood, ill-postured and bits of dirt clinging to his chin. "I need a couple days."

"You have one day."

"A day! I don't even know what this guy looks like."

Gun said, "A thousand dollars for one day's work."

Sampler stopped. "That a real offer?"

"Come back tomorrow night. Midnight, right here. You tell us who he is, we'll pay the thousand."

"What if I can't find out?"

"I think you will."

Sampler wiped dirt off his chin. He said, "Yeah, you know, I think so too. I gotta hunch." He looked cocky now and he walked away from them with his hands in his pockets, swishing some change around in there, his thin shirt rippling across his back in the rising street-confounded wind.

CHAPTER TWENTY-SIX

So they had a day to kill.

They spent the first twelve hours of it sleeping and woke at noon to a bright September sun barreling in through the south window of the big double room. Downstairs in the hotel restaurant they ordered the largest breakfast they could find on the menu and then over coffee debated what to do with the afternoon.

"Tell me," said Jack, "if I haven't worked my middle-aged butt off for you." He was sitting up straight in his chair, his beard past the sandpaper stage and heading toward fur, dark muskrat salted with gray that started just beneath his eyes and disappeared into the unbuttoned collar of his woolen long-underwear shirt.

Gun smiled, noncommittal.

"We've earned a little fun, I'd say. Now, I know you don't care for the Metrodome but I'm sort of fond of the place, and remember, it's not often I get down here. Haven't been to a game since, geez, the Twins won the Series in ninety-one."

"Go, then."

"Hell, Gun, can't you just call them all up on the phone? We get back from the game at four, spend an hour on the horn and snap, we're done. What's wrong with that?"

Gun hailed a waitress, told her he'd like cream for his coffee, and she sailed off leaving a wake of sweet perfume. A pungent gardenia.

"You don't take cream," Jack said. "Tell me you don't take cream."

"The city'll do that to a man."

"I'm disappointed. Cream in your coffee and you want to skip the ball game."

"The Twins are what, in last place now?" Gun shrugged, and his hand rose to the left side of his face, where his fingers surveyed the bruise on his cheekbone. It was swollen and felt like a small hard disc beneath the skin but at least it didn't hurt much. "Jack, look. I'm going to find this guy somehow. And the phone doesn't work for the sort of thing we're talking about. Fact is, I don't think I'll have much luck face-to-face either."

"You're sure you don't need me?"

"Hey, if you're not along I might actually get some cooperation. Go to the game. I've got a friend that'll put you in close, right next to the player's wives. Chat 'em up some, do a little name-dropping."

"What, drop your name?"

"Of course my name."

"Most of those girls were in training bras when you retired, Gun. Watching their boyfriends play kickball at recess."

The waitress showed up with the cream and Gun nodded thanks and picked up the small glass pitcher and moved it toward Jack's cup. "Want some?"

"Aw, why not."

There was enough grease in their breakfasts to slide to hell on—bacon, eggs, corned-beef hash, potato pancakes—and getting down to the business of eating it, Gun realized just how hungry he was.

Halfway through a stack of cakes, Jack put down his

fork, straightened, and looked out the window. The recent morning dazzle had given way to gray mountainous clouds that had come riding in from the west, their dark underbellies swelled up with something—rain or hail or sleet if the temperature dropped. A puzzled look darkened Jack's face, and since Jack LaSalle was a man who rarely seemed puzzled, Gun stopped eating too.

"Tell me," Jack said. "What are we gonna do if that kid doesn't have a name for us tonight?"

"What *can* we do?"

"We can throw him in the river."

Gun smiled.

Jack did not. "Tell me something else, Pedersen. How come you let that guy walk that snuck into your room? Danny Mood. Just because you felt bad about hurting him?"

"Partly, yeah." Actually, Gun had been asking himself the same question all morning. "And partly, I believed him," he said, hearing in his own voice an odd tightness. "It makes sense, doesn't it? Iron Sky's family wanting to know what happened?"

Gun shifted on his chair as Jack's cool dark eyes regarded him skeptically from across the table. Sitting there waiting for more.

"And besides, I wanted him out of my room. I wanted him away from me." Gun blew out the air he'd been holding in his lungs. "I just wanted to see him leave, okay? At a certain point I didn't care about anything but getting rid of him. He's a spook if I ever saw one."

Gun remembered Mood's grinning face in the elevator, the bloody gap where his mouth should be, the small, low-wattage eyeballs. All at once the smell of the bacon cooling here on his breakfast plate was a sour offense to his stomach. He pushed the plate away to the center of the table and reached for his tobacco and papers, needing them now like he'd always believed he didn't. "You were scared," said Jack.

Gun said nothing, unable to disagree.

Jack smoothed the palms of his hands down over the stubble of his cheeks, then rested his thick fingers on his face in an attitude of thought, like a priest weighing out the exact price of a sin. Jack said, "I have a very bad feeling about this Danny Mood. I wish you hadn't let him go."

But Jack's bad feeling wasn't cause enough to make him skip the Twins game, so Gun went off on his hospital rounds alone. He went to North Memorial, Fairview St. Mary's, Hennepin County Medical Center, and several hospitals in the surrounding suburbs before finally giving up. He talked to emergency room receptionists, to nurses, hospital spokespersons, and doctors, and from each one he received the same answer. They were not legally able, they said, to hand out the information he requested. It would violate a patient's right to privacy.

Gun didn't bother to mention that in this case the broken-mouthed patient in question had flagrantly abused Gun's own right of privacy.

Finally, not surprised by his lack of success but disappointed nonetheless, Gun gave up on the hospitals and stopped at a bagel café in a New Hope strip mall for coffee. He sat by a window and watched the afternoon darken. It was only four-thirty, but the overcast was heavy and bringing early dusk. With a wind out of the east, rain was inevitable. And appropriate, Gun decided. It was hard to imagine talking to Joe Sampler beneath a clear sky.

Before leaving the café, Gun skimmed the Minneapolis paper, looking for Mazy's byline. Didn't find it. He did notice, however, in the celebrity nitwit column that Donald Trump—between impregnating Marla and then tantalizing the media with wedding hints—had managed to uncover an ugly conspiracy. Indian gaming, he charged, had become tainted by organized crime.

What? Gangsters involved in gambling? Poor Donald.

The phone's red message light was blinking when Gun got back to the hotel. He called the desk and learned that his daughter had been trying to reach him all afternoon. He dialed her work number at the *Star Tribune*.

"Mazy Pedersen."

"Hi. It's Dad."

"God, at last. Will you please tell me what's going on?" She sounded breathless, angry.

"Something I don't know about, obviously."

"I can't *believe* you sometimes. You've been down here for how long this trip—three, four days? And you haven't even bothered to call Carol. Remember her? New wife? Married her just last summer! What, are you trying to win dead-beat-of-the-year?"

Gun said, "Have I ever told you, you sound exactly like Bill Rigney?"

But Mazy was just getting warm. "She called me this morning, wondering if I'd seen you. If I knew where you were. She hadn't heard a peep from you since your first night down here. She's on the Richter scale, Dad, way up there. And I don't blame her."

Gun said, "I did try calling," which was true. He'd tried once, to tell her about his Gorman failure.

"Well, try again. Then drive home. Get down on your knees with the biggest bunch of flowers you can find and tell her the truth. Which is: You're unforgivably lucky to have her. You love her wildly. And you're a jerk to treat her this way."

"I'll tell her I'm sorry," Gun said.

He heard Mazy, slowing down, on the other end. He expected her summation now, and got it. "Dad. I got Carol's call this morning, I spent fifteen minutes defending you. Telling her about the talk we had at my place last week, how hard you're trying to do what's right. Then I get my assistant calling round to every hotel in town to find you. Then I try your room every half hour since eleven this morning. And now here you are, and I'm telling you, just plain sorry isn't going to do."

Gun's instinct was to defend himself. Tell her how twisted his life had become, how he hadn't had time to think of Carol. But it was an unflattering truth, and he lowered his guard. "Mazy, if you'll let me go, I'll call her now. She'll be getting home from the paper."

A short pause. Gun could sense his daughter deliberating, and wondered if she was about to deliver another piece of her mind. Apparently she decided against it.

"Okay, Dad. Make the call. Is it okay if I call her myself, then, in a little while?"

"I hope you will. Thanks," Gun said.

"Don't blow this, Dad. Please," said Mazy.

Gun knew by this she meant *Don't let her go, don't lose her,* and he saw with a sudden and distinct clarity that such a possibility existed.

Carol was home. She expressed no surprise at hearing Gun's voice, no relief, no anger. She asked how he was doing, what he was learning. He told her about his talk with Gorman, asked her about the casino story.

He apologized.

Angels did not break into glorious strains.

But she forgave him, with more graciousness than he knew he deserved, though he could hear in her voice a withholding of herself that he both regretted and accepted.

CHAPTER TWENTY-SEVEN

At midnight Gun and Jack drove past the front of the bar where Jack had hooked and reeled in Sampler, then parked half a block down. The instant they stepped from Jack's old Toyota Corona a hard up-and-down rain started to fall. It was a rain released from the clogged sky with mechanical precision, as if somewhere above them a Hollywood rainmaker had been activated. They were drenched in five seconds.

Next to the dumpster in the alley crouched Sampler, his body unbelievably thin, his long hair flattened to his narrow skull and shoulders by the bulletdrops of rain. He squeegied water from his face with a white blade of a hand. As Gun and Jack came up to him, he coughed, loud and rattly, something vile in his lungs. He took a step backward. "Freezing out here," he said.

"You're supposed to have a name for us," said Jack. "We're buying." He slapped the chest pocket of his ancient black letter-jacket.

"Uh-huh, yeah, the name." Sampler nodded fast. "Let's go someplace where we can talk."

Jack grabbed the lapels of Sampler's dirty white sport coat and looked at the young man's Adam's apple which was at a level with Jack's eyes. "We'll talk here." Jack spoke slowly, enunciating each syllable. It was the way he might have spoken to a child or to someone whose understanding of English was limited.

Sampler said, "Hey, man, take it easy. There's just, it's not so simple." He wrapped his fingers around Jack's fists, then apparently thought better of this and dropped his hands to his sides. He tried to smile, but succeeded only in showing the brown rot of his teeth.

Jack lifted him off the ground and walked him up to the side of the building. "So if you've got a name, let's hear it."

With impressive ambiguity, Sampler managed to shake his head while nodding at the same time. Jack's arms straightened as if by hydraulic command and Sampler's flimsy body hit the brick wall and slid down onto the paper- and glass-littered dirt.

"Let's go," Jack said, and he started off down the sidewalk.

Gun trotted after him. "You sure about this?" Playing along.

"I'm sure."

Behind them, Sampler shouted whining from the alley: "Just a minute, you guys."

Jack only sped up.

Gun turned and saw Sampler running toward them on the sidewalk, moving with surprising speed, his clothes flapping in the hard rain. "Hold it," said Gun, and he caught Jack by a shoulder. "The kid's got something, just hold on."

"Yeah?" Command performance now, Jack's square face twisting and his voice pitched high with disgust. "*You* get what the guy's got. I don't want to have to look at the little ferret." He broke Gun's hold and crossed the street, moving quickly toward his car. He got in behind the steering wheel and started the engine.

Meanwhile Sampler had caught up to Gun and snatched hold of the back of his canvas jacket. "Listen to me, please. Just listen, I've got something, really. You owe me that money; give me a chance."

From inside of his car Jack motioned impatiently, then rolled down his window to say, "Forget it, Gun. Let's get out of here."

Sampler was still latched firmly to the back of Gun's jacket, though, and Gun dragged him like an oversized albino rat across the street toward the old Toyota. In the driver's window Jack's face grinned and winked. He was perfectly merry with excitement.

"I need five minutes, give me five minutes. You'll be sorry if you don't, I swear to God you will, you've gotta give me a chance . . ." Sampler's irritating squeal of a voice going on and on.

Gun went around to the passenger door and popped it open and Jack looked over, his face transforming suddenly to pure disgust. "I won't have that piece of trash in my car. Get rid of him."

"He wants to talk," said Gun.

"Oh? Okay, then." And Jack swung out of the driver's bucket to the street, rounded the front of the car at practically a dead run, took hold of Sampler by the hair, and walked him to the back of the car. He opened the trunk and told Sampler to climb the hell inside.

Sampler said, "Shit."

"You do that and I'll kick your ass into your throat and pull the rest of you through it. I said, Get in."

From Sampler came an "Uh-uh" and a shake of the head, for which he received from Jack a fist in the gut. Sampler bent over double and was grabbed by the seat of the pants and the collar of the coat and shucked into the car's trunk. His body landing made a pathetically small thud, which was followed immediately by a small rusty squeak of the shocks.

Jack slammed shut the trunk lid, wiped the palms of his hands on the front of his jacket, a self-congratulatory well-done, then he got back in behind the wheel. As soon as Gun had joined him in the Toyota, Jack asked, "Where to?"

"You're doing fine."

"I think he's wasting our time, Gun."

"I have a feeling you'll find out fast."

"Am I that good?"

Jack shifted into first and pulled into the street. From the trunk came muffled shouts and the weak thumping of fists on Japanese sheet metal. With a sad shake of the head, Jack reached out and turned on the radio.

Two blocks down, he took a left on Washington Avenue and headed north. They drove through the eastern edge of the old warehouse district, and soon the old brick monsters gave way to a zoning commissioner's hell, blocks that didn't seem to know what they wanted to be: a crumbling little bar next to a brand new gas station next to a tar-papered house next to a low-riding commercial building. Then a scrap-iron yard, then another.

There was no one about in this part of town at this time of night, and the streets were poorly lit. At a Salvation Army store Jack took a right. "River's over here someplace," he said, muttering to himself now.

They moved forward slowly, one block, two, and straight on past a dead-end sign. In front of the locked gate of a chain-link fence, Jack stopped the car. To the right was a high billboard-size sign reading RIVERBOY SALVAGE. It was lighted by two uptilted flood lamps, their hot wide lenses steaming heavy white coils in the cool rain. Jack reached over into the glove box at Gun's knees and removed a .45 revolver. He got out of the car.

Standing in the glare of the Toyota's headlights, he fired one shot into the padlock at very close range, then he pushed open the gate and came back to the car.

Gun said, "Invite the neighborhood."

"Sound doesn't travel in this kind of rain." Jack affected a lopsided smile, Dr. Science, and he pulled through into the salvage yard and Gun hopped out and closed the gate behind them. They drove in a winding, looping pattern among scrap heaps of steel and iron—car bodies, bedsprings, stacks of wheels and barrels, old farm implements, all of it curtained by the rain. They came finally to the far eastern edge of the yard where a steep brush-covered bank fell to the Mississippi River, wide here and black, fearfully unknowable and emanating cold air as it slipped on by, soundless but for the low dark drumming of the hard rain that battered its moving surface.

CHAPTER TWENTY-EIGHT

Jack had parked the car out of sight from the street behind a large pile of rusty, heavy-gauge springs, had taken Sampler out of the trunk, had told him to shut up when the young man started begging, and had cuffed him into silence once already, the heel of his hand on Sampler's ear. Now the three of them formed the points of a triangle, Sampler sitting on the wet ground, Jack on his haunches, Gun alight on a large rusty overturned file cabinet.

"I'm willing to listen for two minutes," said Jack. "Talk fast, please. Give us the name you said you'd have, or names. No bullshit."

Long hair was pasted all over Sampler's face and now he pushed it clear of his colorless eyes. He blinked through the rain and straightened his shoulders. He said, "I'm the sort I hear a lot of things." His eyes rose timidly, yet shrewdly, Gun thought, toward Jack. "Last night, you talking about that girl and shit, and I'm thinking that's a loud piece of news. I can go out and hear it if I listen hard enough. You know?"

"No," said Jack. "Are you some kind of a moron? You ever go to school? I told you, Give us a name."

"I can tell you the perfect spots to hang out and listen. Places where folks talk, that shit. You'll hear names."

Abruptly Jack stood and walked to his car and opened the door and started rummaging in the backseat. When he returned he had a length of rope, the plastic marine kind, yellow, and a look on his face, *What'll I think of next.*

"Ah, man, shit," said Sampler.

Jack pointed to a big tireless tractor wheel that lay several yards away, weeds growing up through its center. "Stand that thing up and roll it over here," Jack said.

By now Sampler knew better than to argue. He got up.

Gun watched him work the wheel loose, lift one side of it with effort, and roll it toward Jack. The thing looked like it weighed a hundred and fifty pounds, or more than Sampler, in any case.

"Thank you," Jack said, and Sampler let the wheel fall. "Now, sit down on it."

Sampler sat down on it, slowly, and Jack knelt beside him, rope in hand. "What the hell?" Sampler said.

"Shut up and hold still." Quickly Jack tied one end of the rope to Sampler's waist. He made several knots and he pulled them tight, grunting.

"Hey, man, I was bullshitting you. You go around flashing that kind of money, what do you expect? I was bullshitting you. I'm not the guy for it, all right? I don't got what you want."

Lifting the wheel easily to bring the rope through, Jack said, "First you do and now you don't. What are we supposed to believe?"

"I'm telling you, I don't know a thing. I don't know nothing. I wanted the grand, okay? I figured I could go out, you know, and *hear* something. So I went out—God did I— I haven't slept in a day and a half. I went out and I talked to everybody in town. And I didn't get it, I'm tellin' you. I didn't. I don't know who it was in that car, and I don't know anybody that knows. I don't have a goddamn name."

With clean, efficient movements Jack tied the knot securing the other end of the rope to the tractor wheel. "There," he said. "Gun, I'm gonna put you to work now. The bank's pretty steep here"—nodding toward the river—"but still, we've got to be sure we get him far enough out."

Sampler sneezed and dug in his nose. "Keep your money, I don't want it. Just keep it. Just let me go and you'll never hear about me again. Or no, maybe you need some help, yeah, anything, and I'm your man. I'll do anything." Sampler was shaking his head in steady rhythm. His whole body trembled as if diseased.

Jack said, "Maybe you're more afraid of them than you are of us."

Sampler looked for a moment as if he might laugh, then he started to cry. "I'm afraid of dying, man, that's all. I don't wanna die, I'm scared to die."

"Who'd you talk to?"

"Everybody, everywhere, I talked to 'em."

"Who?"

"People that'll kill you and forget about it the next day. I talked to people that dig up graves, no shit, all right? People that sell their kids and then have some more and sell them."

"Give us some names," said Gun.

"They don't have *names*, that's not how it works."

"Sure it is."

"Oh, shit. This guy Lizard that lives in a basement, I talked to him, and he had some good shit that night and a girl, which is all he remembered. And this guy called Peterkin, he knows everything, and there's always about five big black guys with him all the time, and he had them kick my ass out of his place. And I went and talked to a guy named Fordrick who runs a mail order business, and nothing there either—"

"Fordrick?" Gun cut in. "Tell me about him."

"He lives above that bookstore, you know, where the whore heard the screaming. That's why I tried him."

"He didn't know anything?"

"No."

"What do you mean, mail-order business?"

"Whores long distance, is all. People call him, and he sends 'em out. Outside of the city sometimes, different parts of the state. I don't know, I guess he does pretty good." Sampler rubbed the rain from his face, cleared the hair away. "Please, I'm not shittin' you. Nobody knows a thing, at least nobody's saying anything. Just forget the money, I don't want it."

Gun said, "Fordrick lives above that bookstore?"

"Yeah. But he's small-town, he's nothing. Anyway, he was up north when it happened. He comes and goes."

Jack crossed his arms on his chest, looked over at Gun and tilted his head, as if to say, *What else can we do?*

"Maybe he'll catch pneumonia," Gun said.

They left Sampler in the rain, tied to his wheel in the scrap-iron yard, and drove back to the hotel. It was past two o'clock. They flipped a quarter for who got the first hot shower, and Jack won.

Gun sat down wet on a straight-backed hotel chair and twisted the dial on the wall heater to low. He could feel himself starting to get used to being here, and he felt smaller for it. Smaller and everlastingly dirtier.

Tonight had been useless for Diane, unless Fordrick knew more than what he'd let on to Sampler. And that seemed doubtful. Most likely Dotty's father was simply part of the ugly background. Spend enough time in a dump, and sooner or later you were going to run into the rats. Minneapolis, after all, was not a large city and the stinking heart of it was limited to a rather small area; it made sense the dwellers therein were more or less acquainted.

"You're thinking about Fordrick," said Jack. He was wrapped like a fighter in a white bath towel so large it hid his feet. Steam drifted from the open bathroom door behind him.

Gun nodded.

"Did it surprise you to hear his name tonight?"

"At first. Not after I thought about it. How about you?"

"About the same."

"We'll look him up in the morning," Gun said.

"Doesn't sound like he's gonna be much help, though. You think?"

"Not to us, I'd guess. Not to Diane."

"No," Jack agreed. He sat down heavily on a chair, said, "I'm asleep," and a few seconds later: "Are you going to get Carol out of bed?"

"I suppose she'd want me to," Gun said.

"I think she'd want you to."

"Yeah." Gun got up to take his shower.

CHAPTER TWENTY-NINE

Twenty minutes later, despite the hour, Carol's hello was hard and quick, prepared for middle-of-the-night news. Gun said, "Everything's fine, Carol."

She let out a breath. "Okay."

"Jack and I got something on Fordrick tonight. I thought you'd want to hear."

"Let me get a pencil."

It didn't take more than a couple minutes to tell her what he knew. She listened without interruption, then said, "Gun, this is incredible. Do you see what it means? It's gonna be the break I had to have. Now, you've got to get to him right away, all right? You've got to bring him to me. You can do that for me, can't you?"

"I'll try," Gun said. "Jack and I. Right away in the morning."

"Thanks." She was quiet for a moment, before saying, quietly, "Gun?"

"Yeah."

"What else are you coming up with down there?"

"Not much, Carol."

"No luck, huh?"

"Not much."

"Gun, I miss you," she said.

The words put a bitter pang in his rib cage. "I love you, Carol. Do you know that?"

She said, "Mazy called today. We talked a while."

"Get me all figured out, did you?"

"Will you tell me something? How did that girl grow up so well adjusted?"

"I'm as mystified as you are."

Carol said, "I need to see you, Gun. I feel—" she hesitated—"I feel like you're moving away from me. Like a storm's come in and picked you up, and you're getting farther and farther off. I need to see you soon."

"It'll be a day or two." A throbbing rose in Gun's throat. "Maybe more."

"That long."

"I'll call when I know something. Good-bye, Carol." He eased the receiver down into its cradle.

By eight A.M. he and Jack were climbing the steps that led from the street-front entrance to the second-floor apartment above the bookstore. The mailbox at the foot of the stairs was marked, sure enough, with the name Fordrick, and inside it, Gun found three letters, all bills. The letters had been postmarked two days ago.

Gun knocked for a third time on the wooden door, which was painted the light green of early seventies American cars. "You wanna go in?" asked Jack. But Gun was already reaching for his wallet.

It was a cheap lock, the kind that offered little resistance to a credit card, and there was no dead bolt on the door to complicate things. Inside they found fresh milk and eggs in the fridge, a case of beer, plenty of frozen dinners. In the bedroom a closetful of clothes and an unmade bed, in the bathroom a medicine cabinet stocked with all of the usual over-the-counter stuff, plus one bottle of a prescription antibiotic, half used up, issued a week ago.

"Your average citizen and taxpayer," Jack said. "Gone for a day or so, that about right? Out recruiting."

They ate at the hotel before Jack left reluctantly for Stony. The guy running his bar in Jack's absence was a college student and had to get to school.

Back in the room, the phone was ringing.

"Pedersen, I'm glad you're home." It was Hanson, and he sounded all business.

"How'd you find me?"

"It's what I do for a living. I wake you guys up? You were probably dreaming about Dirty Harry."

"Nope."

"Thought it might've been a late one for you last night."

"Why's that?" Gun said.

"Pedersen, I gotta be straight with you here. You've got to watch yourself. Now understand, I might've given you a little nod. But I did not give you the go-ahead to terrorize anybody you please. Or bust people up, for that matter."

"You said you had to be straight, so be straight," Gun said.

"One of our guys on the street got a complaint this morning about you and that friend of yours."

"Jack."

"Whatever. I'm told you came pretty close to killing somebody down by the river last night. In a salvage yard. Either you tried and came up short, or else you just wanted to scare him to death."

"If we'd tried, we wouldn't have come up short," Gun said.

"And maybe you know something about a certain pimp

that got himself stomped in the mouth the other night. The guy who runs that missing whore. That was downright ugly, Pedersen, and I'm not laughing."

"Who's that?" Gun asked. "What other night?"

"I think you know the guy I'm talking about. And I'll just say, it's not the way you go about questioning folks, even if you don't take a liking to their personalities. Now, I don't know about that guy down by the river, where you came up with him, but you leave Isaiah Bittens alone. We've had an eye on him from the start, and I don't want anybody messing it up. I hope you're understanding this."

"I am," Gun said. "Now let me tell you something, Hanson. I've never heard the name Isaiah Bittens, and I've never gone looking for a pimp, for any reason." Gun reached for the pen lying on the phone stand and wrote Isaiah Bittens on the palm of his hand.

Hanson said, "What about that other one? Down by the river."

"Like I said, if we'd tried—"

"Okay." Hanson sighed. "But if I hear about anything else like this happening, and I'm a good listener, I'll be all over the both of you."

"I believe you, Detective."

"Don't Detective me, Pedersen." He was quiet a moment. "Ah, crap."

"What is it?"

"You know? I wish I hadn't given you that case of stuff my wife brewed up before she left."

"Should I bring it back?"

"No . . . it's just, I thought I'd feel better getting it out of the house. I figured it might help me think about her less."

"It's not working that way?"

"No. At least when I had that beer of hers, there was something for me to do when I *did* think about her. I could go to the fridge and pop one open, lie down on the couch, and have a long slow one on Libby. Somehow it helped."

CHAPTER THIRTY

Isaiah Bittens was listed in the Minneapolis white pages. Gun didn't know the neighborhood, but it was easy to find.

There were cats all over the front entrance of the apartment building: cats huddling together on the wide cement stairs, others striding carefully along the makeshift handrail of unfinished two-by-fours. Up the street Gun noted at least three buildings of identical design, all their steps catless as far as he could see. He went up the steps, gently boosting away anything that rubbed against his legs, and pressed buttons until someone buzzed the door in return.

Bittens lived on the first floor, Apartment 119, east end. The carpeting in the hall was the cheap orange favored by slumlords and Hardees. Cat hair all over it. Gun found 119 next to a dark open stairwell and knocked, hard.

Nobody answered.

The door was lightweight with a fake brass knob and it fit so casually in its frame that light showed along the sash. Gun could hear a stereo somewhere, rap music, but otherwise the floor seemed quiet and he opened his jackknife.

He had to force the blade between the sash and the strip of metal that was supposed to protect the lock from jimmying. He held his breath. Felt the blade come up against the tongue of the lock and at the same time heard the music stop. A door opened and slammed. Shoes slapped in the stairwell, coming down. Gun wrestled with the handle of the knife and as he tried to pull it out the lock popped free.

But the knife was hopelessly jammed and as the shoes accelerated in the stairwell he gave the smooth black handle a
sideways snap, leaving the blade buried as he slipped
through Bittens's door and shut it.

Feet paused in the hall, moved on.

The first thing he wondered was how Bittens saw anything in this place, just a little brown light coming in
though it was midday and sunny. He moved out of the
small entryway into the main room of the apartment, surprised at the space in here, three big sets of windows with
thick dark beach towels tacked up over the glass. Bittens
lived like a vampire, and the apartment smelled like a
neglected toilet. At the far end of the room was an arched
doorway through which Gun saw a stove, fridge, cheap
pans sticking up from a sink.

The second thing he wondered was whether that was
Bittens he could hear breathing someplace. He was halfway
to the kitchen when the sound reached his ears and froze
him to the carpet: long satisfied breaths like someone sleeping. Gun's eyes had adapted now and he saw a dark wood-
veneer coffee table, a wingback chair with guts bunching
out, a tweedy pull-out couch. The breathing continued:
quiet on the inhale, protracted happy sigh. It was coming
from the kitchen. Gun went to the balls of his feet and
reached the arch in four steps. He imagined Bittens dreaming on the linoleum, a strange picture. He stuck his head in.

An enormous fat tabby cat was conked out on the table.
Head on paws next to an empty Tony the Tiger cereal bowl
and sure enough a box of Frosted Flakes right there on the
table. The bowl was licked clean and the tabby was snoring.
Gun left it and checked the bedroom, which lacked a bed
but had a sleeping bag spread on the floor, and the bath-

room. Empty, too: a bottle of codeine tablets on the wide-topped sink, also a hairbrush and a Rexall Disposal Home Enema, still in the box. And a dirty shirt in the bathtub. Gun turned the light on. The shirt was all blood. The walls around the tub and the faucet and its porcelain handles had been bloodied too and wiped with the shirt. Gun shut his eyes, thinking this out: Hanson's witness, the whore, was missing. Likely dead, even more likely done right here in her own pimp's bathtub.

This girl had seen something. She'd probably been frightened by it, probably told Bittens about it even before she ended up telling Hanson. Gun saw Bittens pulling the girl to him saying, *Hey baby, we should spend some time together. Why don't you come to my place tonight, we'll relax, take a nice bath—*

Gun opened his eyes, suddenly sweaty, left the bathroom for the kitchen. He was careless about noise now and woke the cat which stepped slothfully down to a chair and curled its tail around itself and looked at him. He opened drawers, looking for anything that would give him Bittens, finding nothing but trash, a bag of Christmas-colored pills, a fingernail clipper, twine and Scotch tape, and a coupon for fifty cents off his next box of Frosted Flakes. He felt the big cat's round pale eyes watching. He opened a cupboard above the sink, saw a set of pink dishes and a toilet plunger, all on the same shelf, saw also a department-store beer stein that rattled in his hand when he lifted it down. The stein bore painted representations of two happy, round-faced Germans, toasting one another with a clock tower in the background. Inside were several dollars in silver. Replacing the stein on the shelf, Gun noticed a strip of tape across its bottom. Masking tape. The numbered brass head of a Weiser key showed beneath it.

The hall was empty when Gun opened the door. He pressed and rotated the spring-loaded knob, twisted hard to make sure it was locked, and inserted Bittens's key. It turned as if filled with frozen mud, but it turned. The lock clicked open. He shut the door again, put his back to it, and lowered himself to the floor. The cat appeared in the dimness, a gray balloon floating along the carpet toward him, and he allowed it to climb into his lap and peer seriously into his face.

If Bittens killed the prostitute—killed her here, in the apartment, in the bathtub—then where was she? Gun recalled the unnatural grin on the face of Bittens/Mood, the stretching bloody hole below the pimp's fine nose, and this made him think of horrible crimes, things evil enough to be committed by the face he remembered. His mind conjured body pieces wrapped in wax butcher paper and found in dumpsters by homeless men foraging in darkness; he thought of Diane, between worlds, her blood slowing in her veins and arteries, her heart flexing for air like a small animal trapped in a plastic bag.

He rubbed the cat's soft head, flattening its ears, the cat turning this way and that, wanting its chin scratched.

He could wait for Bittens. That was one possibility. Sit around a while, look through the pimp's window on life. Have a bowl of Frosted Flakes and grab the guy when he walked in.

Or he could come back later. Bittens might be gone all day, but Gun guessed he'd be back that night. Someone had to feed Tabby.

And after all, Gun had a key.

The cat had become attached to him, its deep furnace cooking audibly, and it tried darting out of the apartment as

he gently closed the door. In the hall he could smell marijua-
na, a gloomy sweet scent. Quickly he opened the short
remaining blade of his jackknife and worked it into the jam
where the long blade had snapped off. A cautious pry and
the broken blade fell free to the carpet. He stooped and
picked it up, hearing as he did so the cat's claws raking at
the door.

At the entrance Gun paused, looking at the columns of
hand-written names on the apartment registry. ISAIAH O.
BITTENS.

He hadn't noticed the O before. Oscar? Oswald?

Who gave a damn?

At that moment a scatter of voices drew his attention to
the sidewalk. Three young African-American women were
elbowing each other in fine humor and turning in here—
coming home, it looked like, all three with shiny paper
shopping bags over their shoulders. Not wishing to be seen,
Gun returned to the stairwell from which he'd come. Keys
tapped, the door scraped open and as the women rustled
into the building he retreated down the steps into a cellar
that was even darker than Bittens' sorry digs.

It didn't smell any worse, though.

The walls down here were poured concrete and wet as
moss. Going down, his palm encountered a switch that
ignited four bare yellow bulbs strung in a straight line down
a narrow hall. On each side of the hall were plain, yellow-
painted plywood doors. The doors were stenciled with
black numbers.

They were large room-sized storage lockers.

Gun felt a shift in his chest, his heart rushing ahead. He
felt for Bittens' key in his pocket, squeezed it, started down
the hall.

Another cat was seated in front of one of the lockers. Sitting upright, calm, this one a yellow cat with white forelegs and hungry-looking ribs. Gun approached, knowing somehow that this would be Bittens's locker, his neck hairs stiffening at the thought of the cat sitting motionless in the dark, patient as a bronze bust. It didn't move when he stopped and held the key in his fingers. Yes, the door was marked 119. When he pushed the key into the lock the animal opened its mouth in a noiseless mew full of needle teeth.

The key would not turn.

He grasped the knob and shook it, twisted it, remembering how tightly the mechanism on Bittens's door had worked, but the lock held against him.

The yellow cat watched him and licked its chin and its long white whiskers. It stayed by the locker while Gun withdrew the key and moved farther along the hall. He had an idea of what to look for but didn't find it right away. He went the distance to the end of the hall, saw nothing but locked yellow doors and black numbers, turned and headed back, past the starving cat at 119 to the stairwell.

And there it was, another locked door tucked in beneath the steps. This one was stenciled in brown: MANAGER

Gun stood listening, nothing moving on the stairs, the smell of thriving mold emanating from the walls and floor. He put his shoulder to the door and gave a slow heave, and the plyboard warped inward slightly. He backed off a step and turned his face away and took a half-serious charge at the door, wood squealing against itself and his shoulder surprised at the sudden ache as he bounced back from the impact. He put his hands against the door—it was looser in its frame now—and he stepped back and hit it once more and the dead bolt tore through the sash and he was inside, astonished at the noise one could make and not attract armed citizens.

He switched on the fluorescent ring overhead and looked around at the usual caretaker's tools: pipe wrenches haphazard on a masonite workbench, a socket set in a greasy red steel box, cardboard cartons full of light bulbs stacked in a corner. Mousetraps, screwdrivers, a hickory-handled ball-peen hammer, an unopened case of D-Con, a cylindrical shop vacuum with long coiled hose. Above the workbench a flat wooden case the size of a printer's drawer was bolted to the wall. The case was shut with a Master lock and a stainless steel hasp.

It took less than a minute for Gun to find the proper Phillips screwdriver. The hasp was a cheap one, two screws exposed, more formality than security. He removed the screws, leaving the lock dangling from the cover of the case, and opened it. Light glittered from seven rows of various-colored keys, each with an attached tag.

He brushed through the keys with his fingers, located number 119—and the stairs directly overhead suddenly filled with a rush of shoes coming down. Kids, from the laughing and the hard footfalls. Two or three kids. Boys. Gun snapped off the fluorescent and shut the door.

"You wanna see it? You don't believe me?"

"No way. You don't got it."

"Your old man better not come down."

Pre-adolescent voices, kids eight or nine.

"You got it? Prove it."

In the darkness Gun smiled as the voices went farther down the hall; some things didn't change. But he couldn't afford to wait around through whatever rite was taking place. He opened his door a crack and cleared his throat. "Boys! What're you up to?"

There was instant scuffling, then steps of forced calmness as the boys came trudging back. Gun heard whispers, a panicky giggle, and one of them said, "Nothin'. Nothin'." As they clumped up the stairs, it was impossible not to feel their hot faces, the little lies forming in their brains.

Gun took down the proper key and stepped back into the hall. The skinny cat had disappeared.

This time, the locker opened.

There was no overhead light inside. Gun propped the door open and the glow from the hall showed him the cramped mess of Bittens' belongings: cardboard boxes saying Jack Daniels, Christian Brothers, Washington Apples. A Schwinn bicycle, ten-speed, handlebars tilted way back like ram's horns. And along the left-hand wall an old humming Kenmore deep freeze. It rose from the floor like a presence from another era, enormous and chrome-handled, a great white Studebaker with a hood that begged lifting.

Gun laid his hand on the lid of the freezer. He shut his eyes as if to pray but no prayer came and he opened them again and flung back the lid.

She was in there. The prostitute. A short girl wrapped in a green vinyl tablecloth, her hair jet black, red at the roots. Her feet were bare and tiny and the skin of her toes was white and wrinkled as if she'd had a long soak. She lay among boxes of Hungry Man Dinners and pepperoni pizzas, Totinos. She lacked neither food nor company. Joe Sampler was in there with her.

CHAPTER THIRTY-ONE

When he got back to the Holiday Inn it was four in the afternoon and Carol's car was in the parking lot. He didn't want it to be her car but he got out of his truck and walked all around it, a little white Miata with her steno pads on the passenger seat, no doubt about it, four or five of them rubber-banded together with a Pilot Razorpoint pen on top. He had told Carol where he was staying, but he hadn't expected her to come after him; now here she was, waiting for him, in the lobby or maybe in his room, waiting with questions on her mind he couldn't even think about answering.

He had questions of his own to answer first. Like: Why hadn't he gone straight to a pay phone, called Hanson, and told him what he'd found in Bittens's freezer? Why had he instead spent the subsequent two hours sitting in his truck opposite that cat-infested building, waiting—without success—for the pimp to come home?

When Gun really thought about these things he had an inkling about the answers. He knew what he wanted from Isaiah Bittens, and he had an idea of how to get it; but he couldn't tell Carol this, couldn't confide to her what he wanted to do and what it might mean. And he would not stand in a hotel room and look in her face and tell her lies.

He stood by the Miata with exhaustion coming into his legs. They ached for sleep. He climbed back in the truck, leaned his head back and swallowed, a dusty feeling in his throat as if he stood at the lip of a deep and arid canyon, with Carol barely visible on the other side. He felt a widening space between them, unbridgeable, perhaps predestined, and pulling out of the lot he longed in advance for Carol's forgiveness. He did not expect it, and putting himself in her place he knew he did not deserve it. He thought: *When it's all done, I'm going to have to learn so much over again.*

He drove west from the hotel strip until he came into neighborhoods that predated the metropolitan spread: neat, mostly small houses, still well-cared for. Armistead had been a small town once and it still looked like one. It had a water tower with four spidery legs and a cylindrical tank and a lid like a pointed cap. Gun parked in front of a storefront that said Marlin's Drug and Counter.

The counter was really a small café that operated at the rear of the drugstore. He headed for it, the smell of coffee and clink of stoneware seeming as good as home right now. Passing a news rack he considered a paper, something to read with his coffee, but his eye was caught instead by a thick green paperback with the name Harper LaMont at the top in silver foil. *Pale Justice.* Gun picked it up, read the jacket copy, the story of an attorney who'd failed to get a conviction on a known child molester and what he did about it. There was a quote from Scott Turow—"Harper LaMont writes about the darkest places in the human heart," etc. etc. LaMont's picture was on the back cover. He looked pissed off.

Gun bought the book and carried it to a booth at the back of Marlin's and waited for coffee. A boy no more than fourteen brought it, poured it black. He told Gun he was a reader, too.

"Stephen King," the kid said.

"You'd recommend him?"

The boy blinked. "You've never read Stephen King? Allegory, man. Incredible. Good versus evil. We're reading Shakespeare in school and Stephen is better. Even my dad likes him. I left *Needful Things* in the bathroom once and my dad went in there and sat on the toilet for two and a half hours."

Gun held up *Pale Justice*. "How about this guy?"

"I read one of his. He's okay, but not as scary."

"All right."

The kid nodded, his judgment passed, and moved to the next booth. Gun smiled—*allegory, man*—and opened Harper LaMont's book.

It started:

Ethan was four years old and didn't understand why his mother wouldn't get off the bed. She had tucked him in last night, same as always, singing "You Are My Sunshine" and kissing him twice, once on the mouth and once on the forehead. But now it was morning and she wouldn't get up.

He said, "Please, Mom," remembering to be polite. He pulled at her hand. It was freezing cold and this scared him. Mom was never so cold. And she always answered him.

And someone was knocking at the door. Ethan didn't know what to do. His mom had told him, "You don't ever answer the door, not unless it's me. You leave it shut. You ever get scared you pick up the phone and you hit these numbers: nine, one, one. Do you understand? Like the TV show: nine one one. You're my sunshine, honey. Nothing bad's gonna happen."

She'd told him this and now he couldn't wake her up and somebody was knocking. Knocking real soft, not going away. Ethan looked at the phone. Nine, one, one. Something in the room smelled bad. He thought, maybe if I call on the phone I'll get in trouble. He walked toward the door. Maybe the person who was knocking would know what to do. Maybe they'd make the call for him.

Ethan reached for the lock.

Gun closed the book. He'd found that he liked Harper LaMont, a pleasant surprise, but he didn't need this. Maybe some day, when his own life didn't seem like something LaMont might have made up.

There was a movie theater across the street from Marlin's, the last matinee of the afternoon just beginning. Something with Mel Gibson; there were women in the lobby, most of them thirty-five and looking resigned. Also some kids. Gun bought a ticket. It was an old theater. Six steps led up to a balcony that was roped off with a scarlet ribbon, and Gun stepped over it as the music was starting.

He was alone up there. The movie spread itself across the screen, an ocean, bare blue sky and gulls tilting across the waves. An island with hard gray cliffs. A stone house atop the cliffs.

Gun shut his eyes before Mel Gibson even reached camera. The seat was old and soft and it leaned back with his weight. In his pocket his fingers encountered keys: for his own house, the hotel room, for Bittens's apartment. He felt himself going to sleep and thought it was maybe not a good idea, but the waves were a blanket to his tired mind and the music was so pretty.

CHAPTER THIRTY-TWO

At fifteen minutes to four A.M. Gun stood again at the front door to Bittens's apartment building. The two closest streetlights had been shot out and it was dark enough here that the stars showed, at least the brighter ones. Gun looked up through the steam of his own deep breaths and saw Sirius, the dog star, eight-point-seven light years away, an old dog still trotting nightly through the neighborhood. Doing its job, too: There were no cats in sight. Gun chose a fourth-floor number and rang the buzzer.

The speaker was silent. Gun rang again. There was quiet, then static and a tense woman's voice. "Who's that?"

Gun said, "I'm sorry, ma'am. Police."

"I never called the cops."

"No ma'am. One of your neighbors down the hall did. The elderly lady. She called 911 and we lost contact with her. Let us in, please."

It was that easy.

He found Bittens's door and put his ear to it for a minute before taking the key from his pocket. He couldn't hear much because someone was watching television down the hall; Perry Mason, loud and clear, the great attorney nailing another bastard. Gun turned Bittens's key and stepped through and closed himself into darkness.

There was breathing again, this time not a cat's.

A man sleeping, his thick adenoidal snores regular and unworried. Gun's confidence rose and he clicked on a small flashlight he'd bought back at Marlin's Drug and Counter and walked into the bedroom. Isaiah Bittens lay on his back in the sleeping bag. His mouth was open and his lips sunken over the teeth Gun had knocked out when Bittens was Danny Mood, Private Eye.

Gun crouched at the sleeping man's shoulder. Bittens's mouth was a collapsed cavity. His eyelids had no lashes and the left eye was open slightly, the white showing like pus in an incised boil. If not for the snoring Gun would have thought Bittens a corpse. He took the .357 from his jacket and turned off the flashlight and said in the darkness, "Wake up, Isaiah."

The snoring stopped cold.

"Isaiah," Gun said again.

Bittens snorted. "I can't see, man. Who's there? Who—" and Gun felt fingers touch his chest and yank away.

"Joe Sampler," Gun said, feeling perverse.

Bittens rolled away making noises like he was riding a nightmare and slammed against the bedroom wall. Something smashed to the floor and Gun could hear Bittens get to his feet and slither along the wall and at last a light came on showing Bittens wild-eyed and naked with his toothless mouth stretched. He'd held onto his pillow and was covering himself with it.

Gun said, "Remember me, Danny Mood?"

"You come to kill me?"

"Fair question. I have questions too. You answer first."

Bittens was shaking, standing bareass to the wallpaper. Gun reached down and gathered up the green sleeping bag and tossed it to him. "Cover up." He allowed Bittens to unzip the bag one-handed and drape it around himself, then used the revolver to point the way into the kitchen. Bittens quivered under the bag and he nudged a chair back from the table and sat, looking like an earthquake victim on the six o'clock news.

Gun said, "Are you the one that killed her?"

Bittens looked lost. Gun suddenly saw why.

"You're wondering which one I mean, aren't you?"

The pimp blinked and looked at the table. Gun said, "I know about the girl downstairs. I'm talking about Diane Apple."

"She saw us," Bittens said. "Samantha saw. I don't think she would've told."

"Samantha, from the freezer."

Bittens said: "She came out in the alley and saw."

"You killed her for seeing."

Bittens blinked again. "She was just a whore."

Gun slapped him hard twice, east and west. "No one's just a whore."

The pimp didn't reply. While his eyes watered the cat trotted into the kitchen and leapt into his lap.

"What about Sampler?"

"I didn't even know him. He came around saying things, it was like he'd been right there. He was lookin me up, man," Bittens said cautiously, moving his head out of slapping range.

"There were three of you," Gun said. "Who were the others?"

"Iron Sky. Sims."

"The cabbie? He was in on it?"

"What I said."

"Who's Sims?"

"No friend of mine, man. Just a guy."

"Where is he?"

Bittens watched Gun. Fear had swarmed in his eyes before the slap but they were calming fast. "I said, he's no friend. I don't keep track."

"Where's Iron Sky?"

Bittens almost smiled. "I told you straight about that, I was lookin for him. Sims showed up here, said, 'Find him.' So I looked."

"So Iron Sky took off, and Sims wants him back."

"Uh-huh." Bittens said cautiously, "What I think, they messed up. They left her someplace and she got found right off. Plus they picked a bitch people know about, she's a author or something. It ain't like with Samantha downstairs—there's all this heat. I think Sims wants to turn Iron Sky in."

"What do you mean, they left her? You were there too."

"I was there till those bastards opened the car door and kicked me out. Took me all night to get home."

Gun looked at Bittens who was warming up now, stroking the cat's head, a guy who saw his chances improving. He set the gun on the table before him, said, "I think you better back up. Tell me the whole thing."

"I tell you what I was doin. I was in the back office at the bookstore and I was lookin at resumes. You know what that is? A resume's a picture, sometimes two pictures. Of a woman, front and back. The guy owns the bookstore lets me back there on account we help each other sometimes. Referrals, see; we're in the same business, but I run strictly local. He does the occasional mail order. Out-of-towners got needs, too. The right guy calls, Ed will send him out a package. Three, four girls, more if the guy can handle it. Sometimes he'll do just one, a starter kit."

"Ed."

"The bookstore guy, Ed Fordrick."

Gun said, "You were in the back room."

"I was lookin at the resumes. They're horny pictures, some of 'em; it gave me the tickle. I started thinking I should go find Samantha. So I went out the back door into the alley and just as I'm coming out, guess who drives up in a taxi?

"Iron Sky was driving. Smiling bigger than any Indian I ever saw. Acting like he didn't know Sims: yessir, where to now sir? Sims was in the back with her and he was being a gentleman, not touching her at all. She was a looker, tight dress on, one of those nice ripe women like you could give a squeeze and the juice comes right out. Her coat was open and I could see how she'd look, under that dress, I get warm thinkin about it—"

Gun was out of his chair before Bittens could react, the pimp's throat between his thumb and index and the cat a gray scream out of the room. Gun squeezed until his hand felt the fibrous tremble of imminent collapse and Bittens' eyes rolled back like a compass, pointing north. He smelled the man's sweat and the rancid sleeping bag and he thought: There'd be no loss now. No loss at all. But he let up. He waited to see if Bittens would breathe. And Bittens did, and his eyes came back to Gun. They were hazed with hate. Bittens put his hand to his throat and breathed sore air. He said, "You want to know what happened? Or you want to end this now?" He leaned forward, squeezing the pillow into his gut.

Gun considered that, thought about what was in Bittens's memory to tell. He closed his eyes and saw a wide lake under a night sky and himself stepping down into it, not knowing its depth or its drop-offs. Bittens coughed and rubbed his throat, and Gun let him talk.

"Sims swung the backdoor open. Of the taxi. Said, 'Get in, Isaiah. We been driving all over and now we're gonna have a picnic and do you wanna partake?' I wanted to partake all right. And Albert says, 'Sir, the meter's running, where to?' Sims looks out the back window. The building next to the bookstore, it don't go all the way back to the alley. There's a parking place back there. Sims says, 'Turn off the meter, Albert. Park us.'

"I think she knew what was coming then. She had an idea. But it was like when he said 'Albert,' said his name like that—that's when she knew for sure. She clawed at the door and got it open but Sims was like a goddamn brick. He's a strong bastard, Sims. He got hold of her coat and pulled her back in. He peeled her like a banana." Bittens smiled with the ruins of his mouth, it was a good memory to him. "He got her first. I was holding her arms. It took him so long I wanted to kill him, I'm serious. Finally he's done—my turn, right?—but Sims says, 'Albert, dinner is served.' And Albert's outta that front seat like a big black bat outta hell, opens my door and throws me out. You know something, that woman could fight."

Gun listened, the shock of the story freezing all feeling in his nerves. He was unsure why Bittens would talk so freely. The pimp's fear had evaporated.

"Tell me who killed Diane."

"Wait," Bittens said, impatient. "I got in the front seat, turned around to watch. Banged my head on the damn glass. Albert was so quick I almost missed it. Next thing Sims is getting out the back, opens the front door and grabs me. I said he was strong. He put his face up to me—right here—told me he knew I could keep my mouth shut. 'I'm trusting you, Isaiah.' That's what he said. And he got in. Drove away."

Gun sat silent. His guts felt poisoned.

"You see, man? I didn't kill her. I didn't even touch her."

"You held her arms."

Bittens said, "They took her away and did it and dumped her off. But Albert's the one who killed her. I know that. Later that night, I was sleepin' in bed. Five in the morning. I woke up and Sims was in my room. Sitting on the floor looking at me, quiet-like, it was like waking up and there's a ghost. 'How'd you get in here?' He said, 'You gotta find Albert for me.' I said 'Why?' 'Well, cause Albert killed that girl and the cops already found her.' Sims said he had to talk to Albert."

"He couldn't find him?"

"Albert was already gone. I told you he's a reservation Indian. They get trouble down here, they head for the Rez." Bittens showed his gums. "Albert's used to this. He strangled a guy two years ago. Some homeless under a bridge, day before Christmas. He was gone four, five months."

Gun said, "You know a guy named Sergeant Hanson? At the Homicide unit. Let's go see him."

"Can I dress?" Bittens said. He was all smiles now.

"Yes."

Bittens let the sleeping bag go loose around his shoulders, but there was an excited twitch in the sinews of his neck and as he brought his right hand from beneath the pillow Gun saw a round black eye emerging. Gun grabbed for it and it blew fire once, his ears suddenly numb and his eyes full of Bittens's wild mouth shouting words he couldn't hear. He was standing over Bittens and he had something in his right hand, a heavy hot-barreled thing with a black eye smoking against his wrist. His fingers tightened on it and he saw Bittens's mouth working and felt his own hand traveling in a backhand arc. The handle of the gun took Bittens exactly in the temple and the struck-plaster sound of it was the first thing Gun heard after the shot. He crouched by Bittens who lay naked on his side with the green bag pooled around him. He watched Bittens's left pupil dilate until it was itself the size of the pistol bore and at that size it remained and Bittens was dead.

While Gun still crouched there he heard feet in the hall. A cough. Overhead an intermittent stream of plaster dust came from a new hole in the ceiling. The feet stopped at Bittens's door and there was a tentative knock.

"Isey?"

A woman's voice.

Gun stepped to the wall and shut off the light.

"Isey, you hear a shot?"

He hoped she didn't have a key. She knocked again, called him Isaiah this time, and at last went away.

When Gun turned the light back on the cat was sitting on the body, batting a paw at Bittens' left nipple as if it were a little brown mouse.

He knew what to do so automatically that he wondered if some part of his mind had planned it hours ago. He zipped Bittens back into the sleeping bag, shook it down, wiped off the gun and tossed it in. He put his own .357 back in his jacket, then found Bittens's greasy Levis in the bedroom and found a ring of keys. He went to the door. No one was waiting for him. He locked up, put the bag over his shoulder and went down the hall like Santa, finding the stairs and descending. After finding the bodies of Sampler and the prostitute, Samantha, Gun had replaced the key he'd found in the manager's office; had even replaced the lock and hasp. Now he used the key on Bittens's ring to get back into the storage locker. The drone of the monolithic Kenmore was loud and somehow threatening; Gun dreaded the prospect of lifting the lid, seeing what he'd seen. He considered doing exactly that, trying to pack Bittens inside with the others, but finally simply heaved the sleeping bag onto the freezer's wide lid. As he backed away from it, one hand held out behind him to find the door, he heard a long last moan of air come free of the man's body.

That sound laid sadness on Gun like an anvil. All this in the past five minutes he had done without contrition, almost without thought, but now a sorrow came which was worse than he'd felt on learning Diane was dead. He didn't regret killing Bittens. Not yet. He suspected there would be much to regret later and Bittens would be far down the list. What he regretted now as he walked from the building through the cold glassy night was that he had allowed Bittens to tell the story. He felt he would have it forever now, and its ownership was a thing he did not want.

CHAPTER THIRTY-THREE

The most pressing effect of having killed Bittens was that Gun wished for sleep. The sun was still an hour from doing anyone in this part of North America any good and he was driving through Minneapolis with his headlights on and his eyes mostly shut. Muscles in his back kept jerking. He set the radio to Seek and it sought out a public station, its somnolent announcer speaking gravely of Edvard Grieg, the Norwegian composer. The announcer spoke as if he had known Edvard personally, unhappy pleuritic fireball that he was. He talked about Edvard's parents, especially his mother, a fine pianist with delicate sensibilities. He said the words "of course" a lot. Half-sleeping Gun imagined the announcer, dressed as an organ-grinder's monkey—little cap on and a string under his chin—introducing the frail Norwegian at a party. *You all know my good friend Edvard, of course.*

He didn't want to go back to the Holiday Inn. He'd dodged Carol there once and was less prepared for her questions now than ever, but a cruise through the lot showed no Miata. Back in his room he ran a hot shower and turned off the light and stood in the dark with water belting him between the shoulder blades. He felt he might be able to sleep that way, upright in the shower. He thought again of Diane and the dream he'd had of her walking into his room. "I've brought you something," she'd said, and sure enough she had: She'd brought him Isaiah Bittens, the man who held her arms.

When he came out of the bathroom he noticed a piece of hotel stationery by the phone. Carol had written in fine-line black Flair:

What are you up to? Gorman is steamed, and what about Fordrick? Please come home. Call at least.

The sight of Carol's handwriting affected Gun more than the words themselves. It had the perfection of a high school girl's, flawless cursive letters sweeping into one another. Exhaustion stretched his sentiments to a maudlin distance: The smooth looping e's became not only perfect but guileless, naive. He had to sleep or else weep for Carol's penmanship. He lay on his back and shut his eyes and dreamed that the hours were a soundless black river and himself a bobbing traveler on it, the sun rising as a weak dab of yellow on the sky, too far for warmth.

Fordrick's bookstore opened for business at ten A.M. Gun was there early. He leaned against the bricks beside the wooden door until he heard the lock click and then pushed inside immediately, almost knocking Fordrick over.

"Shit," was all Fordrick said.

"Lock it back up. It's a holiday."

"I got customers, asshole."

"Only one today. Lock up."

"This is harassment," Fordrick said. He was eight inches shorter than Gun, not drunk this morning, a livid terrier. "You and me got no business together. You harass me and I'll drag your ass into court so fast—"

Gun hit him once. A straight right to the breastbone that blew Fordrick backward into a rack of videos and then to the floor, his arms wrapping around his chest and his mouth an airless O. Gun leaned down and took Fordrick's keys and locked the door. He said, "You remember Earl Battey? Old catcher for the Twins, a big fellow. I hit him like that one time, out on the field. We had a drink later and he told me that's the worst place to get hit. Said it made him feel like he wasn't even a man for a while, just an empty lung."

Fordrick's chest bucked suddenly and he began to breathe again, drawing furious wind.

Gun said, "I liked Earl. Felt bad about hitting him. But you're different, Fordrick. I'm aching to hit you again." He went to one knee and took the man's collar in a fist. "I had a bad night, Fordrick. I *feel* like harassing you. Now this is a new world for you, so listen: You have no rights. Do you hear? The courts don't exist for you. The only law you have is me. Tell me the truth and I won't kill you. Lie to me, and I will."

Fordrick looked up. His irises were a polluted green and Gun saw in their flat shine the void left by a long-departed conscience.

"Who'd you sell your daughter to?"

Fordrick shook his head. His cheeks were white and the whiskers on them black and badly shaved. "I didn't sell her."

Gun backhanded Fordrick, his knuckles feeling this one and Fordrick's right eye beginning immediately to close.

"Try again."

Fordrick put a palm to his eye, released a dry sob. "Guy at Hawk Lake Casino. He's running whores up there."

"Yes, and you have a little mail-order business. You sell him a whole package, or just your daughter? Did you even know she was thirteen? Little young for a starter kit, Fordrick."

"She wanted to go."

"I wonder why. Life must have been so good for her here. What's his name?"

Fordrick said, "What?"

"Your casino friend. I need the name."

"Please. Don't."

Gun grabbed Fordrick by the neck and lifted him to his feet. Marched him to the glass counter where the cash register was and forced his head down until Fordrick was looking at his own reflection from six inches away. Gun said, "Look at that. Do you think you have anything left to lose?"

And Fordrick looked at himself a long while without apparent judgment, his eyes staying with it while he told Gun in a monotone that it was Stanky he'd sold his daughter to, Ron Stanky at Hawk Lake, other women too, and wouldn't Gun go away now and call the cops or do whatever he was going to do.

What Gun did, after twice using the pay phone behind the counter, was to take Fordrick out to his truck and let him slump in the passenger seat. Fordrick didn't say anything but shrank into his corner of the cab, seeming to become physically smaller as the miles clicked away behind them. He smelled like a great dying fungus and Gun imagined tiny things living on inside the truck long after Fordrick's departure. Fordrick issued a snore.

"Hey," Gun said. He intended no comfort for the man and was annoyed at such easy sleep.

Fordrick woke and squinted. He said, "Do you believe in the devil?"

"Is this a joke?"

"Just a question."

Gun looked at him. "Yes."

"I met him," Fordrick said.

"We've all met him."

"I was nine years old. He came to my window one night in October. The devil." Fordrick's voice was calm. "You should of seen. He had a long black suit coat like a guy out of the old west. He had big pale eyes. No eyebrows. He scratched at my window one night."

"I'm not your shrink or your priest. Save it."

Fordrick was looking out the window. They were well out of the city now, taking 169 north past Princeton and Cambridge, little towns with ambitious names.

"I was watching my neighbors that summer," Fordrick said. "I had a telescope in the attic. I used to watch this guy across the back alley. Him and his wife. She had blond hair . . . I could see what they did."

"Shut up," Gun told him.

"The devil knew I was watching. He told me that. He was standing outside the window and talking and at first I couldn't hear him through the glass. Then he put his hand up and reached through the window—reached right through the pane and it didn't break and it didn't even seem strange. He pressed his hand right here, up by my shoulder. Then my ears opened and I could hear him talking. He said, 'Why have you been watching that man and his wife?'"

A blade of sun caught Fordrick across the eyes and Gun saw him wince and lift a forearm to his face. He kept it there and continued speaking.

"I told him I watched because it made me feel good, what they were doing. Except when they were done, then I felt bad. Really bad.

"The devil said, 'You hate them, don't you? They make you feel so bad and you just a little kid.' And he was right. I hated them. And then he disappeared. He was gone and my shoulder ached where he touched it and I went back to bed."

Gun said, "Fordrick. It took more than the devil to make a whore of your daughter. Blame yourself."

"I watched the neighbors some more," Fordrick said. "God, I really hated them. They had no guilt. Finally I was sleeping one night and the devil came again. He stood outside my window calling. When I answered he said, 'Do you hate those people back there?' I sure did. He said, 'Bring me your daddy's lighter then, son.'" Fordrick coughed, bringing his arm down from his face. "God it's bright in here," he said. "I loved that lighter. It was silver and it had Harley Davidson on it and those wings. My dad was passed out and the lighter was in his pants pocket. I had to reach in there. He'd of killed me if he woke up. But I got it. I went back in my room and looked out and the devil was standing in the yard holding out his hand. Not hands like ours: two long fingers and a thumb and that's all. He said, 'Throw me the lighter.' And I did, right through the window glass and it didn't break, just like before. He caught it. 'Go to bed now.' And I went to sleep, and in the night the sirens blew and the neighbors' house was burning down, and next day the cops came and grabbed my dad and put his face against the chimney."

Fordrick stopped. He was clawing at his shoulder, where the devil had put his hand.

"Is that it?" Gun said.

Fordrick nodded.

They turned west at the little tourist burg of Garrison on the edge of Lake Mille Lacs and north again at Brainerd, saying nothing while beside the road the trees changed from hardwood and aspen to conifer and birch. Two miles short of Stony Gun slowed and turned the truck into Jack Be Nimble's narrow drive. The tavern lay behind its screen of birches like a happy promise, green sign blinking.

"One thing," Gun said, "before we go in. When the devil came, that first time. Why'd you answer him? Why go to the window at all?"

Fordrick shrugged, and that was all the answer Gun got to what seemed to him a reasonable question.

They took one of Jack's rear booths though it was midafternoon and not a busy time. Fordrick took short shuffling steps and in his loose coat and pants looked like a man in pajamas. Jack brought coffee to the booth and nodded at Gun and went away without speaking.

They had made good time from the Cities and waited ten minutes before Carol arrived with her notebooks and her little Sony. Gun saw her pull into the lot and told Fordrick to stay put and went to the door to meet her.

She kissed him once and pulled back saying, "Well? Where's the surprise?" Expectancy in her eyes as if he'd brought her candy.

"It's over in the corner, having coffee."

Carol squinted into the dimness.

"He's got your story, Carol. He's ready to name customers."

She gave him a wondering look and he watched her shift suddenly to her daytime self and go briskly toward Fordrick in the booth. A song was playing on the juke, Bob Wills and the Playboys, so Gun couldn't hear what Carol said, but next thing she was sitting and arranging the Sony and taking notes while Fordrick spoke. Gun took a stool at the bar and accepted a beer from Jack.

"You want to tell me," Jack said, arms crossed over his

white apron, "how it is that Fordrick's fessing up to Carol? What kind of a bargain did you drive?"

"I told him I'd kill him if he didn't tell the truth."

That was forthright enough to make Jack look hard at him. It wasn't an easy look to bear. Jack said, "Gun, what happened down there? I came home too early, didn't I?"

"You came home at just the right time. Did you reach Durkins for me?"

"He'll be here in—let's see—twenty minutes."

"Should be enough."

"And what now? You got this pimp, that's great. You ready to let your friend Hanson take care of Diane?"

Gun said, "Look at her over there with Fordrick, getting the story. Can you imagine how the big boys at Hawk Lake are going to feel, reading this one over their cornflakes?"

"Maybe bringing her Fordrick, it wins you a little grace, huh?" Jack said. "Maybe you'll stay home a while now."

Gun sipped some beer and set the glass down. Dark and bitter on the swallow, it tasted too good, too much like a December fireside with all tasks completed. Too much like contentment.

"Guess I'll stay with coffee."

Jack nodded and tapped the counter and strode away in his compact fashion to draw beers for three men who'd just come in. The men were laughing about a mutual friend who'd gone out to poach a deer and shot off his own big toe and been too drunk to notice until a fat black crow landed near him and wouldn't leave, enticed by the smell of blood.

CHAPTER THIRTY-FOUR

Later in some kinds of silence Gun would remember the strangeness of that night: his discomfort in his own bed, even his own house, despite his exhaustion and need for familiar things. He'd remember how beneath the covers he was first too hot and then frozen and how the skin of his neck felt buttered each of the dozen times he woke. Carol did not come to bed. She was in the next room at the Macintosh with something of the same fever in her, striking keys and muttering. Twice in the night Gun heard her on the telephone, calm sounding, leaving messages on someone's voice mail.

He would remember too how Carol woke him next morning, not with whispers but with a full silence that preserved itself. She struck aside the curtain and undressed in the light and he knew watching her that her story was all but finished and she needed to get free of it. In bed she rose over him like a desperate new sun and he accepted her heat, stoked it, his own core running white at last so that he closed his eyes, not to watch what was coming to an end.

They didn't speak until later. Gun had carried the pine side table from the kitchen to the big front window facing the lake and Carol had laid it with breakfast. Butter-poached eggs, sear-sided ham, bread with blackberry preserves sent from Michigan by Gun's mother Madilyn. Strong coffee.

They ate watching the lake which this morning lay in blue unbroken ease, like a sea in Eden before Adam sinned and the gales began. A wood duck with its brilliant head stood on one leg at the end of the dock. When you had the lake, Gun had always felt, you didn't need conversation; still, talk was coming.

"Ed Fordrick is the worst man I have ever met," Carol said.

Gun smiled at her. "And I look pretty good, by contrast?"

"That's not why I pounced on you so hard this morning. I don't know. You were gone so long. I just—needed you."

"Did you finish the story?"

Carol refilled their cups, blue-glazed Nordics Dick Chandler had made for their wedding.

"Not quite. I drafted it out using most of what Fordrick told me. I have calls in to the other sources I'm going to need—Ron Stanky, Lou Gorman. They won't call this morning, you can bet they're conferring with their lawyers. And I called the attorney general's office. Deadline's not until tomorrow, so there's time."

"Well, you're nailing them. How does it feel?"

She turned to the lake and the light from it showed brown pockets of weariness under her eyes. "Did you know Dotty wasn't the first? Of his family, I mean. He sold a cousin of hers—his niece—almost two years ago. To a security man at a casino east of the Cities."

"I didn't know."

"They found her on the bank of the St. Croix River. A boy found her. He was fishing, I remember the wire story. It was put down as a stranger abduction."

Gun was quiet. He was feeling he'd been too easy on Fordrick, but what else could he have done? Hit him harder? He'd hit Bittens hard, but you couldn't kill everyone. He said, "You tell Durkins that part? He'll want to give the state whatever he can while he's transferring custody."

She nodded. "Sheriff Durkins showed up none too early. Gun—I thought we were done with Fordrick. How'd you turn up what he was doing?"

Gun let that settle a moment. He would not lie to Carol but the question filtered into some narrow places and he didn't want to go where he couldn't turn around.

"You knew that Jack came down," he said. "To the Cities."

"Yes." Her green eyes steady and not condemning.

"We talked to a number of people. One of them was a kid, Joe Sampler."

"Friend of Fordrick's?"

"A patron is more like it. I think he was a regular at Fordrick's bookstore. He seemed—harmless," Gun said, seeing Sampler again as he had seen him last, frozen with the whore among pizzas. The picture saddened him. "He mentioned Fordrick's side business. He didn't know it meant anything to us."

Carol measured out enough time to set the next question apart. "Did he know anything about what happened to Diane?"

"Very little."

"Can I ask you one more?"

He waited. He'd been dreading this, the one question that was really two or three: What next? Was he home to stay? Was he ready, as Jack had asked, to let the police take care of Diane? She would want him to say that he'd played this out far enough; that he'd spent all the resources he could on Diane Apple and that he was back in body and soul and that he was hers. He sensed forgiveness in her for his transgressions thus far. But in his mind Gun was already driving northward for the Red Lake Reservation and Albert Iron Sky.

Then Carol said, "How did you get Fordrick to talk?"

"Oh. Well, I hit him."

Sometimes you got off easy.

They watched the lake until Gun grew restive to be out there with it, walking the shore and breathing its smell. He stood. "You want to walk?"

"I'd better stay by the phone."

"All right." He crossed to the kitchen and shrugged on a zip-up sweater of charcoal wool. He took down the little Winchester lever-action .22, his plinking rifle. His hand was on the knob when Carol called to him.

"Gun? You know what Fordrick started telling me when he was done answering my questions?"

"I'd guess about meeting the devil."

Carol came into the kitchen. She said, "Most people, telling a story like that, I wouldn't believe them. I'd think they were trying to escape responsibility."

"Like, the devil made him do it. He couldn't help it."

"Like the insanity plea."

Gun opened the door. Sun poured in, and so did the songs of siskins and redpolls in glory at the feeder Carol had established, out by the woodpile. He said, "I'm finding I don't much care which way it is. Maybe he's insane, or maybe old Scratch really came out of the night and handpicked him. It doesn't matter to me. He sold his little girl and his niece and nothing that happens to him now can be bad enough."

He moved along the shore, taking its southeasterly course, for now shutting from his mind everything but rock and

water and pines leaning outward. There had been two or
three heavy storms in August, one with winds so strong
that a neighbor's johnboat had been lifted clean from its
grassy bed and bent around the trunk of a dignified elm.
The elm had shrugged it off, but Gun was always surprised
at the changes one good storm could make in an apparently
constant shoreline. He stepped across a driftwood log,
wave-driven so high onto the rocks that he doubted it
would ever drift free again. A little farther on, the same
waves had carved from a clay bank a hollow large enough
for a man to stand in, or a group of men. Tons of earth had
been washed away and a delicate white pine stood above
the hollow like a maiden over a volcano. The next storm
would swallow her.

The lake gave generously and seized in turn.

He followed the lake slowly, seeing nothing to shoot nor
wishing to but liking the weight of the little Winchester in
his hand, and then he heard the joyous yips of a dozen dogs
at feeding time and came onto the property of his nearest
neighbor, Dick Chandler.

Chandler made his living as a potter, a clay-colored man
who loved the solitude of the wheel but hated dealing with
the tourists who paid for his work. He'd become locally
famous because he shaped the pots with his feet, not his
hands. Years ago he'd been walking in from his fish house
after dark when a blizzard caught him, a classic January
blow that sneaked in from the west carrying snow and a
ripping wind that circled like wolves. His boy Babe was
along, six years old then, and Babe's hands were freezing in
their little knitted mittens; so Dick had taken off his own
mitts of heavy leather and knelt there with the feral snow
howling and pulled them over Babe's thin ones. They were

a quarter-mile from home but the walk took them six hours, Dick carrying Babe the better part of it. Afterward Dick had thawed his hands in a bucket of ice water but, as he'd told Gun, there was nothing there, not even much pain. The doctor took them just above the wrists.

Dick was feeding his dogs when Gun came up the slope from lakeside. Gun counted fourteen of them.

"Morning, Dick. You're stocking up."

"Training a few new pups this year." Dick owned a snow-mobile, an old red Rupp, but preferred his dogs and sled. The dogs were mostly huskies, bred for short thick legs and heavy coats. He was reaching into a white bucket and spearing each dog a frozen whitefish. On their chains the dogs were going insane.

"Dick, is Margaret still up on the Reservation?"

"Nossir."

Gun waited while Dick finished doling out fish.

"No, what I hear, her man up there got busted up in an accident. Driving along late and went off the road and got pinned in the wreck two days before somebody else came along. He lost a leg only, but you know Margaret." Dick held up his two steel hooks and grinned. "A whole man or no man at all."

"Well, she has terrible luck then."

Dick chuckled. "I think she's out in North Dakota now. Turtle Mountain Rez, they asked her to come teach. Why are you needing Margaret?"

"Not necessarily her. But I'm looking for a guy up at Red Lake, and it might help to know someone up there."

"Just go up, ask around. Somebody'll tell you."

"The guy doesn't want to be found. I doubt he's been showing himself much."

Dick shrugged. "Then you'd best forget about him." He walked past Gun to the lake and scooped up some water in the bucket and brought it back for the dogs. "The Rez is the best spot in this world to get lost if you're an Indian in trouble. A fellow like you, going up there by yourself, you don't have the words and you don't have the relatives. You're just a white man in the wrong place." Dick chuckled again. "A big white man, but that ain't enough."

"You're a white man," Gun said. "You get along."

"I was married to the Rez for eight years, of course I get along." Dick squinted at Gun. "I'm sorry, Gun, I can't help you. I've got a brother's getting married this week, the fool. Third time and he's still nervous. Gotta go hold his hand."

"All right. Thanks anyhow." Gun turned back to the lake, untroubled. He'd been a white man in the wrong place before and it had generally worked out, even on the reservation.

"Gun," Dick called. A clement breeze had sprung from the southwest and Gun at water's edge could just hear him over the easy wash of waves.

"There's a man up there, John Arnold. You talk to him, if you're going."

"Who is he?" Gun had heard the name before.

"He was a fighter. They called him Johnny Bear. You remember?"

Gun did. Johnny Bear had boxed middleweight out of the Cities in the late seventies. He'd compiled an impressive pro record, and then one clear day he'd vanished. His promoter just couldn't find him. It turned out he'd gone back to the rez and he didn't budge from it again. Johnny Bear never said why.

"He lives where?"

"East edge of Lower Red. Start with John, tell him you know me."

Gun waved the Winchester and started back toward home.

He entered his house and saw Carol standing at the sink and knew from the set of her shoulder blades that the peaceable mood had left her. She didn't turn to him immediately. It was as if she were counting time.

Then, her back still to him, "What did you say was the name of that boy? The one who told you and Jack about Fordrick?"

Gun felt a sudden stiffness take the fluid from his joints. "Joe Sampler."

She turned and plucked a newspaper off the kitchen counter, that morning's *Star Tribune*. She walked past him stuffing the paper into his arms and headed for the living room.

It was the state-metro section and it was folded to the headline: BODIES OF THREE FOUND IN STORAGE. The report had it all. A neighbor of the known drug dealer Isaiah Bittens had heard a single gunshot in Bittens's apartment two nights previous. She'd walked down the hall and knocked at his door, getting no response. She didn't call the police right away. When Bittens didn't answer the next day, she became frightened. She imagined him lying dead on the floor. She worried that the cat would starve. When the cops arrived they found the cat in good health and a bloody towel in the bathtub. They went downstairs and had the caretaker open Bittens's storage unit. They opened the sleeping bag and then the big Kenmore.

Also dead were Samantha Juliette Rhone, twenty-three, and Joseph Marcus Sampler, nineteen.

Gun laid the paper on the counter. The back of his neck was a taut shank of muscle and he felt vertebrae shift when he moved his head. He forced a long breath. For a time that morning he'd washed all deaths away in the cool sway of lake and birdcalls, but that seemed false now and undeserved and guilt rushed in the blood of his veins and in the meat of his chest and his arms. Guilt at having killed a man and having not dealt honestly with the consequences of the act. The storage locker seemed a coward's path, no matter his intentions. He felt guilt for Bittens. Still not regret, he realized. Regret only for Sampler and the girl; their unredeemed faces rode his memory.

He didn't follow Carol into the living room. Instead he went stiffly to the bedroom and reached a canvas duffle down from the closet shelf. He packed sparingly, a pair of wool trousers, two sweatshirts, a goose-down vest. There was a box of .357 ammunition in the back of his sock drawer and he tossed that in the duffle as well.

When he turned to go Carol was in the door. Her eyes sparkled with grief and her voice was without rage or impatience. "Can't you tell me anything?"

"What do you want me to tell you?"

"It was like you just dropped away. Like you went down a manhole. And here these people are dead and you knew about it, Gun, you knew or you wouldn't be taking off now."

He nodded. His throat was full and again he felt regret, this time for Carol. He owed her more than explanations but he wasn't sure how much he could give.

She said, "Please, what happened?"

"I killed Isaiah Bittens."

Carol waited. There were tears on her face.

"The other two, he'd already killed. But I might as well have. I caused it to happen."

Emotion worked at Carol's mouth but she caught it, held it away from him. "All for Diane."

He didn't answer. He zipped the miserable duffle shut and stood facing her, ready to leave.

She said, "You're not done yet, either."

"No." Walking past her now, Carol a hardening presence trailing him to the door.

"You know what I should do? I should call Durkins."

"I'm sorry," he told her. "Do what you have to."

CHAPTER THIRTY-FIVE

He drove under the distraction of his parting with Carol. The northern sky was high and lucid and geese ranged across it in strings which at such altitude and distance looked like long blue clouds. Gun barely saw them. Instead he saw himself leaving the house that morning, and Carol's face becoming stone as he moved, never slowing, through the door.

He shot at me, honey, from five feet away. All I did was hit back.

It's not just for Diane, it's the others too. Even Bittens. If I stop now they're dead for nothing.

He gave himself different lines as he drove. All were true but seemed not to explain what he was truly doing. As usual, words failed Gun. Still there were times, he felt, when you were at sea about exactly where your own actions were taking you, and at such times you were lost and little helped by stopping to say so. Better to keep moving while the light was good.

It's my case, that's all.

As he came northward the land flattened out around him in a huge glacial bed and trees receded from the road, becoming unimpressive humps of willow fighting for soil with the long brown grasses foretelling swamp. Gun hadn't met a car in forty miles. He sped impatiently and on the right a lump of black became a yearling bear that trotted into the road like a big blind mole. Gun braked and swerved, felt the bear whack the right rear hubcap, a small *innh!* inside the cab at fifty miles an hour. He pulled over and stepped out. The bear stood in the road shaking his head from side to side.

"Hey," Gun said.

The bear watched him without bitterness, his quizzical head shaking only mildly now. He looked a little like Ronald Reagan, Gun thought; a little confused but he'd be fine. Gun waited for the animal to mosey off into the ditch before getting back in the truck. He drove cautiously, wishing himself better luck with the next bear he saw, hopefully Johnny.

If you wanted proof that the Indians were a sovereign nation, a visit to the Red Lake Reservation did it. Many of the houses here had been left unsided, their roofs unshingled; many were old trailers angled into woods, propped on blocks or pieces of scrap lumber. Everywhere were dogs, some lying protectively on front steps, others with long ribs and scavenging faces loping by the road. The unpainted villages made Gun think of places where he'd played ball in the winter leagues: Guatemala, Costa Rica, sovereign nations where pride was mostly politicians' talk and visitors left quickly, shamed by their own prosperity.

Gun stopped at a gas station where the oval AMOCO sign had been painted over to say HENK'S OIL. He was starting the gas pump when Henk came out of the office smoking a cigarette.

"Full service," Henk said. He smiled; bad teeth and good humor.

"Thanks."

Henk pumped the gas, jiggling the nozzle intermittently

and drawing hard on the cigarette. He grinned at Gun. "You worried about something?"

"You always smoke on the pumps?"

"Nah, only for you." Henk's smiling mouth pushed his cheeks into high happy knobs. He seemed, Gun thought, like a man who knew something you didn't, and liked knowing it.

The gas pump was a slow one and Henk jiggled away.

"I'm looking for a guy name of Iron Sky," Gun said.

"No, I don't know Albert."

Gun looked at Henk who was absolutely shiny with grinning, looking back at him to see if he got the joke.

"Has he been here recently?"

"Let's see," Henk said. The pump clicked off and he goosed it to the nearest dollar. "I don't think so. I went down in my cellar this morning, looking for onions. He wasn't hiding down there. Then I came to work and cleaned the bathroom, and he wasn't in there either. Eleven bucks."

Gun paid. "If he comes in, tell him he won the lottery."

"Ha." Henk took a huge last draft from his cigarette and flicked it still alight to the gravel. "Only people who ever come looking for Albert want to cream his ass and put it on toast."

"His relatives live around here?"

"What are you, his big white cousin?"

Gun shook his head. He tried to remember the last time he'd been on an Indian reservation and not spent most of the time feeling like an idiot.

"Why you want Albert?" Henk said.

"The toast idea," Gun admitted.

"Ha. Well, he hasn't been here. I don't think he's been back for a few years now."

"Anything you say." Gun left Henk standing between two gas pumps, a knotted smile on his face, pulling a Camel Hard Pack and a green Bic lighter from his pocket.

Johnny Bear lived as Dick had said on the eastern edge of Lower Red. The cabin was small and yellow-sided with wood shingles and a yard full of box elders and willows going down to the lake. And blueberry bushes. Stepping from the truck Gun smelled clean water and fruit and also the barbed scent of smoking fish. A bicycle leaned against the cabin, an old single-speed with a wide leather seat.

Gun was still standing by the truck when Johnny Bear opened the door and stepped out. He looked good, a shade under six feet, his chest deep as a bathtub, as Gun remembered. His face was wide and he had the right kind of wrinkles at his eyes and a full ponytail with no gray in it at all. Johnny would be in his early forties, Gun guessed.

"Do I know you?"

"You don't. You know a friend of mine though, Dick Chandler."

Johnny smiled. Not like Henk; he didn't seem to have to work at it. "Dick still working the clay?"

"With both feet. He keeps getting better, you should see."

"I saw his boy last year, Babe. He's stronger than I am now."

"Good kid." Gun felt reluctant to say why he'd come; the place was so peaceful.

Johnny said, "Come in, there's coffee."

The cabin was bare and comfortable inside with a nicked pine floor and an iron wood stove. A framed *Pioneer Press* clipping was propped atop a wood desk: Johnny with the gloves on about to lay a potent right on the jaw of a nameless white fighter. There was an open bowl of tobacco on the table and a painting of Jesus at Gethsemane on the wall.

Johnny Bear lifted a blue-steel coffeepot from the stove and poured two cups. His voice was gentle. "Sit down. You come for the walleyes?"

"I wish it were like that. No, I'm trying to find someone."

"Yes?"

"His name is Albert Iron Sky."

Johnny Bear leaned back, clasping his hands behind his head. "Albert must have done something again."

Through a large paned window Gun could see light dotting the points of waves on Red Lake. A smokehouse was built on the sandy shore and a slow smoke rose from it, issuing from spaces between the planks.

"He killed a woman," Gun said.

Johnny nodded. "He could do it, I think."

"You know him, then."

"I know of him. I heard that he killed a man in the city, some time ago. Don't know if that was true, but it wouldn't surprise me. He came back here for a while."

"Didn't anyone come to arrest him then? If he killed someone?"

Johnny sipped coffee. The fingers of his left hand wandered to the bowl of tobacco and he pinched some up and rubbed it absently. "If he killed, he did it far away. I'm not defending him, but law here is strange. It's tribal law. There's BIA, but they're weak."

Gun said, "This woman was important to me."

"I see that." Johnny Bear studied Gun a moment. "It's strange we haven't met. Maybe I saw you somewhere."

"Maybe. I saw you once, at an arena in Detroit. You beat a guy, technical knockout, I don't remember his name."

"Mm, Detroit."

"I think Jerry Quarry was on the card too." Gun had been trying to remember that night. All he could bring back for sure was that he'd gone to the fights with the Tiger catcher Bill Freehan and that afterward Freehan had a nosebleed and told Gun, "Look at me, I'm Jerry Quarry."

"Quarry didn't have anything," Johnny said. "Are you a ball player?"

"Gun Pedersen."

Johnny laughed softly. "Ah. You quit, didn't you?"

"When my wife died."

"I didn't know that part. I just knew you quit. Middle of the season, right?"

"Why'd *you* quit? You had the sportswriters digging holes everywhere, looking for your corpse."

Johnny said, "I see you like the tobacco. I've got papers if you want to smoke."

Gun reached into his own pocket and fetched a paper. He laid it on the table and built the cigarette. Johnny Bear slid him a glass bowl for an ashtray.

"I didn't like my promoter. You know what he started wanting me to do? He went out and got this big Indian war bonnet, feathers down to my ankles. There was one Indian boxer used to dance around in the ring before his fights wearing one of those."

"Lopez," Gun said. The tobacco was strong and his first in days and it danced at the back of his brain.

"Yes, Danny Lopez. Little Red. My promoter said, 'Look, everybody knows Lopez now, he gets on TV all the time.' But I didn't want to wear the feathers."

"That's it? That's why you quit?"

"Other things too. I came home for a visit when my uncle was dying. This was his house and he asked if I would live in it after he went." Johnny got up and bent over the wood stove, checked the fire. "I was tired of hitting people. Also of getting hit. Then one morning I was up early, reading Genesis. The Garden of Eden, it sounded so great. And I thought, Hey, I know that place."

Gun felt a sudden ache for the sort of peace he'd once felt at his own house. He had the odd feeling that he couldn't stay longer at Johnny Bear's. Not on this errand. He snuffed the cigarette and looked at his coffee cup almost expecting to see his own filthy fingerprints on it. He said, "Can you tell me anything about Iron Sky?"

"Not very much. His family was originally from Lake of the Woods. They came down here I suppose in the fifties but his folks are dead now. There are a few cousins and I think his half brother is still around."

"Do you know where the half brother lives?"

"He's got a place outside of Redby, you came through on the way here. Used to be every year the family would go north a month or so in the fall, hunt deer and get a bunch of geese up at Lake of the Woods. The deer herd up there is unbelievable. They'd set up a camp and not come back until they had game."

Gun stood from the table, too abruptly he thought but Johnny only looked up at him mildly. "If you want to eat, I have smoked fish. Good walleye, just done yesterday."

"I better go," Gun told him, but he accepted a smoked walleye wrapped in waxed paper from Johnny Bear's cupboard and nodded at Johnny's invitation to come back some time and stay and go out on Red Lake when they were really hitting.

• • •

He found the half brother's place after two stops in the village of Redby. The half brother had four dogs that didn't bark when he pulled up and in fact paid him no mind at all except for one Border collie cross that trotted up languid as a hot afternoon and put both front feet on his belly as if reaching for a kiss. Gun told her she was a sweet dog and he scruffed her neck and ears a minute before knocking at the half brother's gray aluminum trailer. No one was home.

Back in Redby he walked into a small grocery called Trout Goods which sold iceberg lettuce that had been too long on the truck and Spam and an assortment of Shrade hunting knives at the front counter. The proprietor was a white man with a fat brown mole hanging under his lower lip like a wood tick. He knew the half brother, Charlie Kingbird, but he didn't know where he was.

"He goes to the Cities a lot, Charlie," he said. "Tell you who might know, though, is his brother, Albert. I saw Albert late last week and he usually stays at Charlie's when he's here."

That threw Gun a moment. "Albert was here? What's he up to?"

"Well, it's fall, and he bought one of these Shrades. Deer season's coming and I suppose he plans to hunt."

Gun thanked the man and left. He didn't bother going back to the half brother's. Deer season was coming and the herd at Lake of the Woods was unbelievable.

CHAPTER THIRTY-SIX

He'd been to the Northwest Angle several times for its autumn flights of ducks and once for a deer hunt with Jack LaSalle. The Angle, as it was called, occupied a relatively small area, about forty miles by fifteen, and on the map resembled a little rectangular hat sitting atop Minnesota's northern border and jutting into Canada. It lay farther north than any other point of land in the lower forty-eight, and was mostly covered with water, Lake of the Woods. The rest was heavily forested. You couldn't get there without gaining an appreciation of just how far it was from the rest of the world.

Leaving Redby, Gun had followed the southern and western shores of Lower Red Lake, then driven north through country that was low, treeless, and swampy, and marked here and there with empty, tilted shells of houses, barn roofs lying in their own rot. Across the road from one of these dead farms stood an unpainted church, and behind it, where the ground fell away to swamp grass and rushes, blackened tombstones leaning toward the south.

Twenty years ago, when Gun had first hunted the Angle, no roads had been cut through to it yet, and to get there you had to take a launch from Warroad at the southern tip of the lake, or hire a pilot in a single-engine plane. Now a motorist could reach the Angle by crossing the border above Warroad, driving northeast through Canada, then crossing back into Minnesota on the gravel road that wound through the forest and came to an end at the settlement of Angle Inlet.

Dusk rose early here. It was barely past seven o'clock, but the deep woods gloom of this hour had a lake-floor quality about it, a slow dark shimmer. Out of the ditch to his right a mother bear and two cubs appeared, and Gun touched the brakes. The bear family crossed the road quickly, heading for the dump ground to the north.

Gun pulled up to the grocery store that doubled as the office of McGovern's Resort. There were no lights on inside, and a hand-lettered sign on the door read CLOSED FOR THE NIGHT UNLESS I GET A WILD HAIR. Gun walked around to the back where the dozen or so cabins were clustered in a horseshoe arrangement. No cars back here, no lights. Midweek in mid-September and the place was empty.

He climbed back into his truck and headed for the other end of town—if you could call it a town. One of the reasons Gun liked it up here was that so few city folks had ever found it. For one thing it was too far away, and for another, Angle full-timers didn't cater to urban tastes. If you wanted a Minneapolis paper you were out of luck, you wouldn't find flavored coffee within an hour's drive, and the first telephones had arrived this year. As a place to hide, Gun thought, it had its strong and weak points. You were unlikely to cross paths with somebody who'd seen your name in the paper, but you were also unlikely to go unnoticed.

Gun pulled into the lot out front of the town's lone restaurant. Its windows were dark. He began to wish he'd stopped for supper in Warroad. The door, however, was open, so he stepped inside.

At first he could make out nothing, it was that black. He stood holding the door open behind him and waited for his eyes to give him something to move toward. Soon he could see the outline of booths along the far wall, a counter off to his right. "Hello?" he said.

"Can't a guy see we're closed?" The voice came from Gun's left, up close. "There's a switch there, by the door."

Gun found it. A man in a pair of striped coveralls got up from a table, squeezing an orange cap down on his wide graying head.

"You're Nate Overland," said Gun, putting out his hand.

"Well, Gun Pedersen." They shook hands. Nate nodded at the table where he'd been sitting and smiled apologetically. "I like the quiet," he said.

"You got anything to eat?" Gun asked.

A few years ago Nate had been running a small outfitting service in Warroad and doing some guiding as well. Gun had rented decoys from him several times, and once they'd gone shooting together. Nate was the real item, a local product, born and raised on the water.

He wasn't much of a cook, though, and he blackened both sides of the burger in the process of getting the middle done. The piece of meat was the size and shape of a beaten-up softball, and while it smoked and hissed above a gas flame set way too high, Nate griped and swore and fumbled through drawers and cupboards searching out a spatula, then pawed clumsily through a fridge for condiments. Gun sat on a stool at the counter, entertained.

"The goddamn cook has the flu and says he can't make it in, he's going down to Warroad, to the clinic. This is five days ago. And I say, 'Who's gonna cook?' I say, 'Listen here, I don't care if you got smallpox, get your ass in here.' And so he goes down to Warroad and the goddamn doctor puts him up in the goddamn hospital, and what happens? I gotta close down for the week."

When Nate finally managed to deliver the hamburger, Gun applied catsup and mustard liberally.

"Got any onions?" he asked.

"Umm . . ."

"It's all right. I'll be fine." And to Gun's surprise the hamburger wasn't bad.

"Well?" Nate asked.

"Good."

"That's on account of it's not hamburger."

"Venison?"

"About forty yards away, right out that back door." Nate aimed a finger toward the rear of the restaurant, then pulled an imaginary trigger. "I've gotta watch it, though. Got a new warden this year."

Gun ate slowly, savoring the rich dark gamy flavor. Nate pulled up a stool and watched.

"So," Gun asked, when he'd finished, "what happened to your place in Warroad?"

The question brought Nate upright on his stool. He shook his head. "I busted up my back in a storm, trying to get this dumb-ass kid out of a boat. Busted my back up good. He'd put the boat up against the rocks, see." Nate shrugged and looked around at his place. Above the booths along one wall were mounted a dozen deer and moose heads. Along another wall stood racks of picture postcards, paperback books, T-shirts, and baseball caps. Tables had been cleared away from the middle of the floor for a juke-box and piano. There was room enough for half a dozen couples to dance.

Nate said, "I had to find something slower. An old man's business."

"You're doing okay, it looks like."

Nate shrugged and with his thumbs he pulled against the straps of his coveralls. His eyes appraised Gun. He said, "You're too early for ducks, and too late for the good fishing."

"I know."

Nate waited, his hands resting patiently on the round shelf of his belly.

"I'm trying to find someone."

For a moment Nate held Gun's eyes, then he stepped backward and took hold of a rounded chrome coffeepot sitting on the oak countertop. He filled the pot with water and scooped coffee from a tin can into the top of the pot. When he'd plugged it in he turned back to Gun. "And the look on your face, you're trying mighty hard. What can I do to help?"

CHAPTER THIRTY-SEVEN

But Nate hadn't seen any Indians he didn't know, and though he did remember the Iron Sky name from years ago he hadn't run into one for a long while. He'd never heard of an Albert.

It was nine o'clock but felt more like midnight and they sat, both of them on counter stools now, drinking coffee and eating from a package of Oreos Nate sliced open with the big bloodstained knife he wore on his belt. From the distance came a high-pitched howl that stopped Gun's cookie hand halfway to his mouth, then sirened down an octave and a half and blinked out.

"Wolf maybe, or else one of them goddamn crosses of Butch Thelen's." Nate shook his head. "He had one of his Samoyed bitches bred to a wolf down in Baudette, and he kept a couple of the pups for his sled team. They give me the shakes, just hearing 'em. You oughta see their eyes."

Nate offered him the extra bedroom in the small apartment attached to the back of his restaurant. The bed was an old one with a worn-out flat spring that sagged like a hammock. Gun fell into it and lay there in the deep valley his body formed in the mattress. For what seemed most of the night he tried in his mind to slip past the wheeling chaos of thoughts and images brought on by caffeine and exhaustion. He saw Albert Iron Sky and the one named Sims as men with hyenas' bodies, their eyes black tunnels leading far underground to a city of flesh and of torn shredded flesh and violent laughter. For no good reason Gun's leg muscles ached like they hadn't since his playing days, and somewhere in the middle of the night a charley horse bit into the arch of his left foot. In the distance the wolf or dog-wolf, whatever it was, never stopped howling until the trees outside the bedroom window began to receive their daylight colors from the clean morning sky.

He ate breakfast with Nate then drove to McGovern's Resort and talked with Calvin McGovern, who told Gun pretty much what Nate had told him last night. Except for a few fishermen, white guys, he hadn't seen any strangers in weeks. He didn't know an Albert Iron Sky, but vaguely remembered the Iron Sky name.

From Calvin McGovern Gun bought a length of hard salami, some bread, a few cans of pork and beans, a can opener, a dozen apples, and a case of bottled water, then put in a polite minimum of small talk and drove a mile down a dead-end trail to the small resort he'd stayed at several times on his duck-hunting trips.

Porter's Post was owned by Dave and Faith Porter, former Missourians who'd been living on the Angle for thirty years. Gun didn't stop at their house but drove right on down to the store and walked inside. He found Dave and Faith at the back of the store in a spacious, open-beamed sitting room. They both looked up at once. They smiled in the controlled manner of those used to cold and solitude. They rose from the cedar couch which Dave had likely built himself and they stood, awkward for a moment, their arms half raised.

"What a life," Gun said.

"You know, we mostly just sit around," Dave said in his soft growl. He was in his sixties now but as thin and straight and bony-jawed as when Gun had first met him. Gun shook the strong hand he offered.

Faith came forward and put her arms around Gun's middle and squeezed, saying, "I always forget just how big you are." Her hair, which she had pulled back with a blue kerchief, had begun to gray, Gun noticed. She stepped back and her smile broadened now into the smile Gun remembered; and in the sway of its warmth he felt with sudden conviction that all would be well.

Dave pulled out a chair. "Sit down and tell us what the heck you're doing here."

Gun told them what he felt able to tell—who he was looking for but not why—and as it happened, Dave remembered not only the Iron Sky family but Albert, as well. Also, on a recent trip to Warroad for winter groceries he'd run across the name in the Minneapolis paper.

"Sort of grabbed me. It's not the kind of name you're gonna run into that often, and I thought, What's Albert come to? Remember, Faith? I got home and I said, 'Who do you think I read about in the paper?'"

Faith brought Gun coffee and sat down next to her husband. She said, "He wasn't a bad kid. Him and his brothers used to come in here for pop and stuff during hunting season. They camped off to the west a ways, on that land Nelson ended up buying. That's our neighbor. This is twenty-some years ago now, at least. I suppose we saw him every year for what, three, four years?"

Dave shook his head. "No, he wasn't a kid, Faith. He was grown up already, must've been twenty-five."

"What I'm saying, he wasn't bad."

"He wasn't a drunk, anyway. But we didn't really get to know him well. Probably the only reason we remember his name is he ended up working for us to pay off a bill. I was putting up number three that fall and needing some help on the rafters. He handled himself pretty good. He was big and strong."

"He ate a lot," said Faith.

"What did he look like?"

Dave shrugged. "Big. Six one, six two. Kind of husky."

"Beautiful skin," said Faith. "I remember how smooth it was, and dark too. And for his size he had these really short legs, remember, Dave? We said how he sort of walked like a sailor."

"He's bowlegged?"

"Well, it was like he rolled along, his body swaying a little. And he told jokes that never made any sense to me. Always with a straight face."

Dave took a pack of cigarettes from the chest pocket of his worn flannel shirt and lit one, and the line of smoke wound upward toward the high golden open-beam ceiling where a slowly revolving fan swirled it away. Holding his eyes on his own hands, Dave asked, "Did you know this woman that was killed?"

"Yes," Gun said, and set his fingers to work on a cigarette of his own.

"Do you know how Albert was involved?"

Gun said he wasn't sure.

"You want some help looking for him?"

"No, but I'd like to know where *you'd* look if you were the one looking."

Dave got up and walked to the front of the store. He

came back with a map, which he spread out on the table. "Have we got any pencils around here?" Faith reached over to a small desk and took a pencil from its top drawer.

"If it was me, I know exactly what I'd do," said Dave, "and it wouldn't be hard." He began to make small X marks on the map, mostly on the islands that dotted the northernmost waters of the lake. "See, a good share of the cabins are seasonal these days. Didn't used to be that way so much. But now, Labor Day comes and everybody takes off. The place stands empty for the next eight, nine months."

"And you think Albert could find himself one of those and make himself comfortable for a while."

"Why not? I mean, if he's up here at all. Of course, he'd have to get himself a boat, supplies. Hell, he could spend the winter, Gun. Some of these places I'm marking are pretty damned out-of-the-way. Get into one of them, and you're like Goldilocks. Except the three bears are in Florida, or Fargo, or someplace."

"I'll be needing a boat," Gun said.

Dave smiled and blew smoke. "We got plenty of those."

CHAPTER THIRTY-EIGHT

Gun spent that afternoon and all the next day on the water, going from X to X on the map Dave had marked, and by supper time of the following evening he'd run out of X's. He'd investigated some twenty cabins, most situated on the rocky islands. Not one of them had showed any sign of recent guests.

That night at the dining room table of the Porter house, over baked walleye and fried potatoes, Faith said to her husband, "You didn't have him try Bear River?"

"Umm, no." Dave scowled and blinked. "Yeah, that's a good idea."

Faith pushed the bowl of potatoes toward Gun and said, "It empties into the lake about a half a mile west of here. Not much of a river, if you want to know the truth. More like a glorified stream, but—"

"There's a couple of cabins up in there, along the Bear," Dave cut in. "Four, five miles upriver. And this time of year there's nobody in 'em."

"What got me thinking," said Faith, "was how the Iron Sky party used to go after the ducks up there, remember, Dave? They used to camp on this side of the bank, before—"

"That was before those cabins went up," Dave said. "Yeah, I'd say it's worth a look in the morning."

Gun sat back in his chair and glanced out the window at the moon, nearly full and resting on the sharp tops of the pine trees. "I'd rather look tonight," he said.

• • •

Dave set him up with a square-stern canoe powered by an electric trolling motor, a long-handled searchlight, and precise descriptions of the landmarks Gun would need to find the cabins at night. By nine o'clock Gun was guiding the canoe through a field of rushes that marked the channel of Bear River. The air was still, the temperature mild for the season. Gun wore a wool sweater and a canvas hunting jacket. In his jacket pocket was the .357 with a full clip, and for the first time since leaving Red Lake he began to think with purpose about how he might use it. In his mind a picture of Iron Sky clarified and grew large. He was heavy in the upper body, his face in shadow, sitting in a chair, leaning forward elbows on knees and breathing heavily through clogged lungs. Behind him, sitting crouched on the floor, was Diane Apple, her eyes covered by the long fingers of her beautiful hands. Her lips were torn and bleeding and they opened and closed without making a sound.

An urgent scrambling erupted from the heavy brush on the shoreline, then a high-pitched squeak like a small animal in distress. Up from the shallows flapped a blue heron, huge wings bruising the air. Aloft, the bird was silent and immediately gone. For reassurance, Gun's heart required several deep breaths. He coughed, quietly.

At ten-thirty—Gun figured he'd gone at least four miles upriver—he saw the first landmark: a pair of large aspens, both leaning far out across the water, their branches just grazing its surface. Gun maneuvered around the aspens, cut the soft-humming electric motor, and paddled carefully and quietly to the grassy left-hand bank. He pulled the canoe up on shore and stood for a moment studying the heavy woods, searching for the outline of a roof. What he saw instead—and he suddenly smelled it too—was a narrow trail of wood smoke, a vertical line of gray against the black trees.

Circling to the right, staying low, Gun moved quickly to the dense shade beneath an old fir tree's shaggy wings. The cabin, twenty yards away, was large with a steep roof, the three windows on this side dark. For several minutes Gun watched and listened, trying to decide how to coax the cabin's occupant outside. Then he heard a cough, followed by a quick scraping noise like chair legs on a wood floor. He crawled out from under the sagging branches of the fir and circled to the right until he could see the back of the cabin, where a dim glow leaked from a single window.

He closed the distance between himself and the cabin on all fours, then crouched beneath the window against the log wall, trying to keep his lungs from sucking too loudly. He palmed the .357 and waited for his breathing to even out. He straightened slowly and peered into the bottom right section of the four-paned window.

He saw a man in profile, sitting on a kitchen chair that was hiked back on its two rear legs. His feet were propped on the kitchen table and he was reading a magazine in the weak light of a kerosene lamp. He wore nothing but a white sleeveless underwear shirt and white boxers. He was thick through the body and upper arms, skinny in the legs. His feet were bare. His hair was black and shoulder length. He looked forty-five or fifty. At his right elbow was a wood stove, and as Gun watched, he took the cigarette from his mouth and tapped its ash on the stove top. Gun thought first of simply walking in through the front door, surprising him. Then thought better of it. What if the door was locked? Or suppose Iron Sky had a pistol there on his chair, or in the right hand which Gun couldn't see, or close by? So instead Gun took a firm grip on the big metal flashlight of Dave's, cocked his arm and swung the heavy light forward, demolishing the bottom half of the window and spraying glass into the cabin.

"Stay put!" Gun said. He brought up the .357 and leveled it on the man who had fallen backward in his chair and now lay quiet in the glittering sweep of broken glass that textured the wooden floor. Gun swung the flashlight again, finishing off the window, then scissored himself over the casing and inside.

"Albert Iron Sky?" Gun asked.

The man, still on his back on the floor, nodded—just the smallest tip of the head. He seemed relaxed, the fingers of his two hands linked together and resting on his chest. He said, "I wish you wouldn't of come. You're up here to kill me." He spoke with absolute certainty and disinterest.

"Get up," Gun told him.

"Waste of your time," said Iron Sky. He laughed quietly.

"Stand up," Gun told him, motioning with the pistol.

"All right, all right." Deliberately and with apparent stiffness he rose and tiptoed through glass back to the table. He bent to pick up the fallen chair, but Gun told him to leave it alone.

"Take the other side there," Gun said. "I want the stove for a while."

Iron Sky said okay and sat. The magazine he'd been reading was still in his hand, and now he tossed it to the center of the table. It was a copy of *People*, Clint Eastwood on the cover in a tux and an easy smile, his good face grizzlier than ever. The magazine lay next to a pack of generic cigarettes.

Gun crunched over glass to the fallen kitchen chair, right-ed it, shoved it to the table and sat down. The stove was turning out a mild radiation perfect for the night. A dozen or so lengths of split birch had been stacked against the wall, within arm's reach. Gun turned up the kerosene lamp and looked carefully across the table at Iron Sky, whose smooth dark skin lived up to the description Faith had offered. There were lines of white in his black hair, and Gun saw flat resignation in his eyes. Small pouches of skin sagged from his jawline. His large brown hands were folded one inside the other on the tabletop. "This about what you expected?" asked Iron Sky.

"I can't say. We haven't gotten started yet."

"Before we do, mind if I get something?" Iron Sky showed Gun the palms of his hands and slowly stood up. "In that cupboard there," he said.

"Sit down."

Iron Sky shrugged. Then sighed as he lowered himself back onto the chair. "Second door from the right. And glass-es in the next one over."

In the cupboard was a fifth of Johnny Walker Red Label, several pint bottles of flavored brandy, and half a dozen liters of cheap red wine.

"Which?" Gun asked.

"The Scotch. And a glass, if you don't mind."

Gun set the Johnny Walker on the table in front of Iron Sky and put two clear plastic water glasses down beside it. He watched Iron Sky open the bottle and fill one glass three-quarter's full and take a short swallow. He poured two fingers in the other glass.

"I talked to Isaiah Bittens," Gun said, sitting down. "The stuff he told me I don't want to hear again."

"I don't know what he told you."

"If necessary, I'll stop you," Gun said. "Just start talking."

Iron Sky took three swallows of Scotch, big ones, his throat pumping. He asked, "Did you kill Bittens?"

"Yes."

Iron Sky nodded at this, his eyebrows lifting pleasantly. "And I wanna know who you are."

Gun considered what to do with the question. He drank some Scotch.

"It don't matter, does it?" asked Iron Sky. "You're gonna kill me anyway. But I wanna know whether it was Sims put you here."

Gun shook his head. "I was a friend of Diane Apple."

"Mmm." Iron Sky lifted his fingers to his temples and rubbed. "Yeah, you're gonna have to kill me."

"Depends on what you tell me and how convincing you are."

"It's a waste of your time, coming way up here for me. Should've gone after Sims."

"A waste of my time?" Gun asked.

Iron Sky shook his head and started to rise from his chair. "It's getting cold. Let me fill the stove."

"Sit down," Gun said, "weather in here's fine," and keeping the eye of the .357 trained on Iron Sky, Gun leaned down and quickly popped the door of the wood stove and had a look inside. There were several big chunks, burning slow. Just right.

"Shit," said Iron Sky. He drank more Scotch, put the glass down, and hugged himself. Goose bumps covered his bare, fatty arms. "Just let me get some clothes on."

"You're fine," Gun said. "Now tell me what you did to Diane. I mean *you*, Albert, what you did. And what Sims did too. And why it happened in the first place."

"In the first place?" A big grin opened his face up, and Gun remembered what Bittens had said, "smiling bigger than any Indian I ever saw."

"What's funny?" Gun asked, blood rushing into his throat. He took a sharp breath to keep from throwing the table over.

"Nothing," said Iron Sky. "You said, in the first place, and I'm thinking how far back this goes, that's all. Nostalgia."

"Did you kill Diane?" Gun asked.

"No. Well, maybe I had a hand. Yeah, I had a hand."

"Bittens said you and Sims raped her. He said after that Sims threw him out of the car."

"Yeah, that's how it was. Except Sims took her first, not me, I was second. Bittens say that?"

"Yes." Gun was trying to pretend that he watched Iron Sky from a distance, that this conversation was a memory, that it was part of a past beyond immediate feeling. But the trick wasn't working. The man was sitting right here, right now, four feet away, his heavy face gleaming in the yellowish light from the kerosene lamp.

"Then you drove her out to the park. You killed her out there."

"By the time we got there she was gone . . . we thought. I mean, he knocked her around a little bit. But then after we got her unloaded she started coming to, so we twisted a shirt or something around her neck. Both of us, till she quit breathing. Then we went back downtown and I parked the car."

"That's it," Gun said.

"That's it." Iron Sky spoke without apparent regret.

"Why did you leave the car where you did, in that

garage? It's so close to where you picked her up."

"I dropped off Sims and then all of a sudden I just had to ditch it. I don't know. I wanted to be out of that car and out of that town, you understand? I knew about that empty garage, so I just left it there and walked out to I–94 and hitched a ride north."

"Sims live in the neighborhood?" Gun asked. "Close to the Service Center?"

"Not exactly." Iron Sky smiled again, slapped his arms and shivered. "Look here, if you want the shit on Sims, and I'd say you don't just want it, you gotta have it, then give me something to put on or let me sit by the stove, because it's not the kind of shit I can tell with my ass freezing off."

CHAPTER THIRTY-NINE

A rough woven rug lay just inside the door and Gun gathered it up and tossed it to Iron Sky. The Indian covered his shoulders, then lifted the glass of the kerosene lamp and lit a generic cigarette on the wick. He took a slow pull, closing his eyes. "So, a long-ago story for bedtime." He took a few quick breaths, as though trying not to hyper-ventilate. Sweat streamed from his hairline and down across his face.

"Sims moved up to Red Lake when I was fourteen and he was seventeen. His father was BIA, some sort of big man in the school system. I was a freshman, not old enough to quit, and Sims was a senior. We ran cross-country that year, numbers one and two. I was number one, a little faster. We shot some birds and just screwed around, you know, two boys. We got on."

"Sims is white?"

"His old man was BIA, didn't I say that? White as your ass, but he held his own pretty good. He had some balls and so he got left alone. Except for this one kid, Willy Whiteheart. Willy gave him shit all the time. Never let him forget who he was and where he was, who his father was. A few times they got into it at school, and Willy always got the best of him." Iron Sky picked up his glass of Scotch and held it up at eye level, peeked around the glass at Gun. "You with me so far? Good, now hold onto that part because I'll come back to it." He took half a dozen hard-blinking swallows from his water glass of Scotch and the glass was empty.

"Now it's Halloween night," Iron Sky said, "and Sims and me are drinking a little beer and horsin' around. This is out at my place. My folks are off to a party and I'm supposed to be watching my sister who's eleven years old. Anyway, me and Sims decide we're gonna go for a ride in this pickup camper sittin' in our yard which belongs to my dad's cousin from the Turtle Mountains. He's just here for a day or two, and tonight he's off at the party with my folks. So I put my sister in the back of the camper and lock her in so she doesn't fall out, and we're off, it's Halloween, and Sims and me've got these masks on, I don't know, werewolves I think. And drinking beer and just shootin' around, and then who do you suppose we stumble across, stalled out there in the road?"

"Willy Whiteheart," Gun said, seeing it coming.

"Hey, it sure was. And not only that, Willy Whiteheart's a halfback on the football team and the week before he broke his leg and now he's standing in the road on his crutches, trying to flag us down." Iron Sky finished another cigarette and he ground it out on the bare table and threw the butt on the top of the stove. He lifted a finger toward Gun's face and spoke in a lower voice. "I don't know what you people think, and I don't give a rat's ass, but me, I believe there's such a thing as evil. I don't mean bad luck or a psychoshithead personality stuff. I'm saying evil, all by itself and flying around out there in its own little body or whatever, and then just zipping into somebody and taking him the fuck over. You people and all your professors and doctors, you can say what you want about it, but I know. I've seen it happen, and I know."

"Tell me what you saw," Gun said.

Iron Sky poured himself another glass of Scotch, recapped the bottle, and looked outside through the window Gun had smashed coming in. A wind had come up and the pine trees made breathing sounds, rising, falling away. Sucking in, then blowing out long and slow. Iron Sky lit another cigarette from the wick of the lamp.

"I saw something going into him right then, as we're sitting there stopped in the road. And I couldn't even see his face behind that mask. But I saw him swell up, just puff up, and then I saw like a mouth opening in his eyes, and then he was saying to me, Just wait here a second, Albert, just wait right here. And he grabbed a wrench from the floor of the pickup, this pipe wrench as long as my forearm, and he hopped out of the truck and I heard him say to Willy Whiteheart, 'Can I help?' or something, in a voice I didn't know, and then he was beating the living hell out of Willy, moving so fast you couldn't follow it, a thousand miles an hour, it was almost funny. Really, I was just about laughing, watching that wrench go up and down and then his feet kicking, kicking. And when he got back in the truck he was breathing like a bull in the clench, and looking at me, those mouths in his eyes, and I couldn't look back at him."

Iron Sky, his fingers trembling, took a long draw on his cigarette. Blowing out the smoke he said, "Shit, and that was nothing. It's what happened next."

Gun felt himself prepare. He squeezed the muscles of his stomach. He tightened his grip on the .357. He knew what Iron Sky was going to say, then listened as he said it.

"What Sims did, he told me to give him the key to the rear camper door which I'd locked to keep my sister from falling out. Sims told me, 'Give me that key.' And I gave it. I gave it, you understand?" Iron Sky looked straight across the table into Gun's eyes and said, "You're wasting your time up here, white man. Because that bastard took the key and went back inside the camper with my sister. After that . . . well, after that, let's see. Willie Whiteheart was a tough bastard and pulled out of it, though he couldn't prove who it was that almost killed him and probably wouldn't have wanted to. My sister, she grew up somehow. And Sims and me, we were still buddies—even after he swallowed me whole that night and shit out somebody else. You understand that? I mean, what could we do besides kill each other? I had something on him, and he had it on me. What I'm saying is, now we *knew* each other, and that's the rarest thing there is."

Gun sat, working to absorb what he'd heard while at the same time trying to decipher a quiet signal he could feel almost like a pulse in the deepest part of his brain.

"He moved out of Red Lake, him and his family, after he graduated. Then he went on to college and a big life," said Iron Sky. "Real big, a lot of money, a lot of all the good shit. And every few years he'd get hold of me or I'd get hold of him. There was a stretch when we didn't, his wife didn't think I was good for him. After she died it started again: like last summer, he just called me up. Things were bad up on the Rez, and he helped me come down to the Cities and get started with that taxi. And all he wanted back was a free ride once in a while."

"How did you get her in the cab?" Gun asked. "Did she flag you down for a ride? How did you set her up?"

"No, no. I got the call from Sims, and I picked him up and took him over to the restaurant. He went inside and came back out and had this babe on his arm, that friend of yours. I mean, she was *with* him that night. He was showing her around town, showing her the parts most people don't want to look at. But she wanted to look. She was asking all the questions. She was full of them. Like about whores and pimps and peep shows and kiddy porn. Wanted to know everything. I thought it was weird, but then Sims said she was a writer and gonna write about this shit and had to get the details. And so he's giving them to her, telling her what he knows, and after a while he starts getting excited, I can see it. I can see him swelling up. Puffing out. I can see those black mouths growing in his eyes. Still, maybe nothing would've happened except this fruitcake named Rory, he comes up at a stoplight and knocks on the window, and says to Sims, 'I'm here for ya, babe, and I'm cheap tonight, half price, cause I liked you so well last time.' And that did it. I'm sure that's what did it."

"What do you mean?" Gun asked.

"I mean, the woman saw that Sims was *interested*. She saw that he wanted that little faggot, and wanted her at the same time. And I think Sims *saw* that she saw. I know he did, and that was it. No turning around, no hiding anymore behind anything. From that point on, I could see it all happening before it happened, and that friend of yours could see it all happening, too. She could."

"You let it happen," Gun said.

"I did more than let it happen."

"You're not sorry?"

Iron Sky shook his head and laughed, his voice a kind of high moan, his mouth all knotted up around the sound he made. "I'm someplace sorry don't reach," he said, and covered his face with his hands.

"How do I find Sims?" Gun asked. "Who the hell is he?"

Nothing from Iron Sky. The man just sat with his face

hidden behind his fingers, his shoulders trembling with cold or something else. Gun leaned across the table and slapped him once, hard, on the side of the head. "I said who the hell is he?"

Iron Sky smiled now, almost sweet. "Tell you one thing. You won't find him under Sims in the phone book. Because that's not his real name. Sims is what we called him in high school, to give him a hard time. That was his old man's name, see. Sims LaMont. His name is Harper. Heard of him?"

CHAPTER FORTY

There were surprises you couldn't get over, and there were surprises like this one that made you want to kick yourself for being so stupid. How, Gun wondered, could he have failed to give LaMont a harder look? LaMont, after all, was the one who Diane had come to Minneapolis to see. His office was a few short blocks from where she'd been raped. He was the acknowledged expert on the sewer she'd disappeared into. For God's sake, the man hung out in places like The Service Center, disguised.

"I guess you can find him, can't you?" asked Iron Sky. He was sitting up straight now, and he'd stopped shaking. His face had brightened and relaxed. He finished his current glass of Scotch and set it back down on the table. "It is cold in here. Now how about giving me the stove seat."

"Sure. But first get a pen and a piece of paper. There's something I need you to write. And an envelope."

Gun followed Iron Sky into the corner of the room, holding the .357 on his back. There were paper and pens and envelopes in a desk beneath a painting of a wolf on a hill in winter, a painting Gun had seen in a hundred northern homes. They walked back to the table in the kitchen, where Gun let Iron Sky sit by the stove. Then Gun dictated a letter and had Iron Sky sign it. He told Iron Sky how to address the envelope.

"There." Gun folded the letter into the envelope, which he slipped into the chest pocket of his shirt. "Thanks."

Iron Sky said he better put some more chunks of birch on the fire, and Gun told him, "Go ahead." Iron Sky went to his knees in front of the stove, pushed four lengths of split wood inside, and closed the cast-iron door.

"Damn it," he said, wiggling the handle of the door. "Thing won't close right." He bent way down to have a better look, slipped his arm quickly beneath the stove, and when he came up he had a revolver in his hand. It was aimed at the ceiling, and he was saying to Gun, "I don't want to shoot you, I don't wanna shoot you."

"Then put it down." Gun had all ten fingers on his .357, the sights lined up on the middle of Iron Sky's chest: third button from the top on his own canvas jacket, the barrel no more than eighteen inches from that button. "I'm not gonna wait," Gun said quietly. "Just take it slow. Bring it down, away from me. Real slow."

"Not putting it down," said Iron Sky. "I told you, it's a waste of your time, coming to kill me. You know why?"

"I'll shoot," Gun said.

Iron Sky was shaking his head back and forth, that sweet smile on his face, the same hollow eyes. He was crying. He started to bring the revolver down now, very slowly. "Because that night we killed your friend I saw the same thing come into Sims again, the thing that came into him when he beat up Willy, and did my sister. And *this*: I felt it come into me, too." The revolver descended to ear level and its barrel turned in toward Iron Sky's head. "Don't try to stop me. Please don't," he whispered, and at last there was more than nothing in the man's dark eyes.

Gun laid the .357 carefully on the table and rested his hands on either side of it. He looked off through the window he'd broken and thought for an instant that he saw an angel in the trees. The report was not as loud as he expected it would be.

CHAPTER FORTY-ONE

After a night's driving Gun arrived in Stony to a coming east wind that rounded the tops of the sentinel white pines edging town. The sun rose red and liquid and threw a chardonnay tint against the silver Stony water tower. The western bays of the lake churned with whitecaps the color of bloody milk. Though still September the mercury had slipped as if on ice; the digital sign at the local bank said seventeen degrees. The small-grain farmers to the south would be praying to God and the government. The inhabitants of Stony would wake with their quilts at their chins and gripes upon their lips. Back on Lake of the Woods blue geese would gain restlessness and then altitude and point away in long V's like arrowheads aimed at Mexico.

Gun didn't go straight home. He wanted breakfast before facing whatever awaited him with Carol. He had left after telling her the truth about the pimp Isaiah Bittens, after admitting responsibility for the other deaths as well. He had walked away and left Carol standing bitter in the doorway; she'd talked desperately of calling the law, of stopping Gun the only way she could, but no one had come after him. Or maybe they simply hadn't found him. Johnny Bear was right: Law was strange once you reached the reservation.

Jack Be Nimble's wouldn't be open for hours so Gun settled for the breakfast counter at the Walleye Cafe downtown. The waitress was a brisk black-haired girl whose eyes and minty smile and slender ankles showed a newness to the job.

"Enjoy your meal, Mr. Pedersen." She was there, and then she wasn't; such quickness, within half an hour of sunrise.

There was a copy of the *Stony Journal* on the counter beside the register and Gun picked it up and read it while drinking brewed coffee and eating French toast spread with smooth strawberry preserves. PORN DEALER ALLEGES CORRUPTION AT CASINO. He was momentarily surprised at the headline; he'd been so occupied with Diane's story he had almost forgotten Carol's. But here it was and she had done her usual thorough work:

> The owner of a Twin Cities adult bookstore said this week that he helped organize a network of prostitutes operated by one or more employees of the Hawk Lake Casino. Edward Girard Fordrick, 47, of Minneapolis, told authorities he "sold" six women to a high-placed casino official for purposes of prostitution.
>
> The official named is Ronald Stanky, 33, a media-relations specialist at Hawk Lake. Stanky would not be interviewed for this report.
>
> One of the women was Fordrick's 13-year-old daughter, who died by drowning in Stony Lake one week ago.

The article quoted a prostitute who said her boyfriend knew Fordrick and had arranged for her to move to the reservation shortly after the casino opened. There was a quote from another prostitute—her name not used—who'd been threatened with beating and had fled after it was learned she'd talked to a reporter. Gun smiled; somehow, Carol had managed to find Loreen. There was an indignant response from Lou Gorman, the silver lion of Club King Inc., who promised "a full and uncompromising investigation into this outrageous behavior." Equal outrage from tribal officials and the state attorney general. Stanky was closeted with his attorneys. Fordrick was being held without bail.

"One hell of a job, is how I see it," said Jason Durkins. The sheriff was standing at the counter with his trooper hat tilted back on his head and his stomach prominent at Gun's left elbow. His star was pinned to a black bomber jacket with a fur collar. Durkins looked pleasant and tired, like a man who had breakfasted on doughnuts in a warm well-lit kitchen. He said, "Carol ought to report on some big metro paper. This town's lucky to have her."

"Yes it is," Gun said. "Are you here to arrest me, Sheriff?"

Durkins laughed and took the high stool next to Gun's. "No sir, not so's I know it." He held one finger up for coffee. "You know, Carol made herself some enemies on this one."

"I'm sure of it."

"Nothing to worry about, though. It's got to feel good, for Carol I mean, putting the planks to a guy like Stanky. He's a shit, like anyone listening to him can tell. That Fordrick, he's even worse." Durkins sipped coffee and investigated a menu from the black-haired waitress. "Carol tells me you were the one who talked Fordrick into confessing."

"Sometimes a person needs to confess."

"Uh-huh."

Gun saw the sheriff looking at him over the menu, the man's eyes puffy and kind. It was like being watched by an aging, intuitive beagle. Durkins said, "I gotta say this, you look like an all-night drive."

"Yup."

"Anything I can do?"

Gun gave it a little thought. Not much. He rose and dropped a five on the counter. "Thanks, Sheriff. Stop out one day, have coffee."

"Count on it, Gun."

Carol's car was in the garage and this relieved Gun until he pulled the truck in next to it and saw suitcases crammed into the Miata's meager passenger space. He went to the house and it was quiet and neat. In the bedroom he opened the drawers of Carol's bureau and they slid out as if waxed, empty boxes that smelled of soap and cedar and barren months ahead.

She was standing at the lakeshore in her red-brown Chief Joseph coat, hands in her pockets and the easterly kicking the hair up off her shoulders. The sun had risen high enough to lose its redness for a winter white and Carol's cheeks showed white when she turned to him and her eyes dark green as early ice.

"Have you been in the house?" she asked.

He nodded but couldn't speak of it.

"I saw the paper," he said.

She watched him, hair blowing across her face.

"You're better than I ever knew."

"Better at what? Reporting?" Her voice was hard and louder than necessary and he couldn't tell which of them it mocked.

"Yes, that. Other things too."

She faced the lake. "What happened on the reservation?"

"I found Iron Sky. We had a conversation."

"And that's all there is to it."

"He committed suicide."

"He killed himself? You were there? What was he trying to do, beat you to it?"

He didn't answer. He felt the wind anesthetize his lips and face. Around them whitecaps smashed the rocky shore and rose sunlit to plumes of ice and flame.

"I'll tell you something about reporting," she said.

She waited so long to speak again Gun wondered if she would. "Stanky is probably going to prison. Certainly he'll come up on charges. Fordrick might go free."

"What?"

"I talked to an assistant in the attorney general's office. Late yesterday. Stanky's the one they really want. He's visible, it's good PR. Fordrick is a bastard but he's the best chance they've got for a conviction on Stanky."

"They'll bargain for his testimony? You can't be serious."

"You know what the assistant AG told me? He said, 'The casinos are too strong, they need a little body-check right now.' So they're willing to give up Fordrick, but at least they get to use cute hockey metaphors."

"What about Dotty, and the niece? That's child neglect, if nothing else—"

"And that's just what he'll be charged with, if anything. Not with running prostitutes, not with criminal abuse. Remember that day, after they found Dotty out there? Think about that. Fordrick won't do time."

Gun shut his eyes. The wind was stinging. "If it's testimony against Stanky they need, why not use the prostitutes?"

"Because the way it worked, they never saw Stanky." Carol's breath trembled audibly. "Remember the night we saw Loreen? She said she didn't have a pimp, no one took a cut. And that was true, in a way. But the trailer, and the car—she was paying rent, and a lot of it."

"You found Loreen."

"She called me. I'd already put the paper to bed and she called me at two in the morning from Seattle. She actually apologized to me for leaving without an explanation."

"So, she explained?"

Carol folded her arms and hunched against the wind. "Gun, I have to leave."

He caught her arm. "Tell me the rest."

"Stanky never met the women, he didn't have to. He was in close with the son of the tribal secretary. A kid in his twenties. He set up some old trailers on Indian trust land and collected the rent for Stanky."

"How much rent?"

"Several thousand a month. Loreen was paying twenty-five hundred. She said she could make that much in a good week, and no one ever bothered her."

Gun wanted details, but more than that he wanted Carol to keep talking. He felt if she would just keep talking, she wouldn't leave.

"Where's the secretary's kid?"

"Big surprise, no one knows. I don't know what his cut was, but I'm guessing it was enough to buy a few airline tickets."

"So Stanky wasn't risking his own neck. Fordrick was the last person he thought would sell him out."

"Right." Carol started past Gun to the house, rocks slipping under her boots. "I forgot, I never thanked you for shaking Fordrick loose. Well, thanks."

He followed her up the path noticing the pressed backs of her jeans, her bare white fingers holding the cuffs of her jacket, her black hair like liquid showing lines of roving light.

She said, "Since the paper came out I've been cleaning the old apartment above the *Journal*. They're hooking up the water later today." She stopped, her back to him, put a hand to her face. "God, the wallpaper's horrible."

"Can I convince you to stay?"

She stopped. "Do you want to?"

"Yes," Gun said, but Carol must have heard something in his answer that started her moving again.

"The thing about reporting," she said, gaining strength, "is that it's half-assed. It's weak. You write as much truth as you can find, try to cover it all. But they slide out the edges, Gun. Do you know what Lou Gorman told me, when he finally returned my call? He *thanked* me for digging this poison out of his company."

She reached the garage and entered it, unstoppable.

"This was in the afternoon, when I was working on the story. Then guess what Loreen said on the phone, late that night: that Gorman was one of her customers. She didn't even know who he was until she got out west. Club King is negotiating with a tribe out there to build a new casino. She saw his picture in the paper."

"You didn't name her in your story."

"Loreen won't go on record. She won't testify." Carol's voice was a saw blade. Car keys rattled in her hand. "It doesn't matter that I found her an attorney, a good one. Loreen's starting over now. Loreen's got a hot new job as a temp secretary. She doesn't need this crap in her life."

"You got her a lawyer?"

"Harper LaMont volunteered his services. He called me after the AP ran my piece—"

"LaMont called you? At home?" Hair rose on the backs of Gun's hands.

"He offered to help. It doesn't matter. Pimps, whores, the whole underage issue, I guess that's his thing."

"It sure is."

Then Carol was in the Miata and the double door was rising behind her and exhaust feathering out into cold sun and gusts. Her window came down. "I'm sorry, Gun. I'm just beat. I'm so tired I'm starting to see why you do the things you do. How's that for scary?" Her skin looked papery with grief. "When you left, I was going to call Durkins. I really was. But I didn't do it, and then when you stayed gone all day, all night, another day, I started thinking: Maybe Gun's right. Maybe your way is the only way things really get done." Carol slid on a pair of sunglasses and looked up at him. "But I can't let myself believe that. I don't know what that would do to me, Gun." She turned her face from him, said to the windshield: "And I can't live with you while you believe it, either."

The window zipped up then and she backed away, the white car receding under green pines and shadow. He stood a long while in an island of silence, shutting out thought, the frozen-souled master of all he surveyed.

CHAPTER FORTY-TWO

He waited four days. The east wind brought its promised rain, a patient insistent rain that lasted death-like through wind and night and one morning became a callous sleet freezing on the grass. Gun sat unshaven in his kitchen rolling tobacco in his fingers. He drank strong coffee. He unplugged the phone and ate minimal meals and slept little. He did agonizing push-ups and the agony was the best of what he felt during those four days.

In the hours before sunup of the last morning the wind moved around to the north. The rain was a soft cold trance in the dark and Gun, stepping slowly along the rocky shore, felt change on the skin of his face. He stopped. There were needles of sleet among the drops. He walked on. Not fifty yards farther snow had replaced rain and was sticking white against the shoreline. The stones grew slick under his boots and he moved up into the trees and watched the dawn come, hazy, the snow roiling in like smoke across the waves.

By the time he reached home it was light. An inch of snow lay on the ground and a stripe of blue on the horizon. Gun entered his kitchen and poured coffee. He spread an old newspaper on the table and sat down to clean the .357. There would be sun in an hour, the norther having rid the sky of rain and clouds, and the earth of anything less than white.

•••

He entered the city late. The highway was a wet hiss in the tires and he rode the sound through empty-looking suburbs toward the blinking white dot atop the IDS Tower standing over Minneapolis. He had the sensations of flight and unwanted swiftness. There was little traffic: a Chevette the color of stained teeth with a woman at the wheel and baby hands waving at the back window. A Toyota wagon was parked to the side, hazard lights flashing while its owner knelt sick in the ditch. A man stood hunched at an entrance ramp, his eyes shining wild and dumb as a doe's in the headlights. Cracking his window Gun smelled the weight of the impending city, repellent as an old bag lunch.

It was almost two in the morning.

He thought of the dream of Diane coming to his room. She hadn't returned to him since. Gun wanted to see her one more time, wanted Diane to appear and deliver him LaMont as she had delivered Isaiah Bittens. But Diane did not appear, and he flew forward without sanction.

At a downtown exit he pulled into a SuperAmerica. It was lit with fluorescents almost beyond tolerance. He dropped a quarter in the pay phone and dialed and counted sixteen rings before a young man answered.

"Charles Hotel."

"Has a Mr. Sims checked in?"

"Just a moment, sir. Sims. Yes, Mr. Sims checked in several hours ago. Should I transfer you up?"

Gun pictured LaMont in front of the TV, on edge. He said, "No, it's pretty late. It'll last until morning. Can you tell me which room he's in?"

"Six-fourteen."

"Thanks very much."

So Mr. Sims was waiting. One last time, Gun thought, Albert Iron Sky had summoned, and LaMont had responded in form.

The Charles Hotel was a faded edifice, an unsaved whale of a building so far ignored by the restoration crews. It wasn't a dive yet but it was on the board looking down. Gun street parked three blocks north and walked, feeling the .357 in the inside pocket of his dark wool jacket, its cylinder bumping his rib cage with every step.

He opened the front door an inch. The lobby was pink-carpeted and empty except for the night clerk, a man maybe twenty-five with a neat Washington ponytail and a mustache like two black matchsticks. He was watching a cable rerun of *Cheers* and laughing every time Norm opened his mouth. Gun watched through a set of commercials, wishing on the clerk an abrupt case of the runs, but the clerk stayed at his desk. Gun checked the street, saw a set of headlights growing in the west. On TV *Cheers* returned, Norm adjusting his tie and raising his eyebrows. Gun slipped into the lobby and through it. He reached the stairwell door just as Norm said, "I never thought of myself as *traditionally* handsome . . ."

The door closed softly on the laugh track.

He came out on the sixth floor. The carpeting here was teabag-brown and he walked it past seven occupied rooms, a vacancy, a door saying CUSTODIAN. He found six-fourteen. Put his back to the wall next to the door, avoiding the fisheye. The .357 was in his right hand. He knocked, five times.

Sounds came like the slowness of a dying clock: a chain slipping free, the squeal of gears turning in a hollow place, the deep chord of a voice close enough for secrets. "Albert, you always take your time—"

He led with the barrel. It pushed into Harper LaMont's cheek as if to penetrate it and Gun's other hand had LaMont's neck. LaMont backed up fast, tripping on his heels, his eyes not on Gun but on the Smith digging a hole in his face. He had on his Sims fedora and baggy brown pants and frayed braces over a white shirt. No weapon Gun could see. He drew back the revolver and struck LaMont once at the base of the neck, dropping him like a clubbed sheep across the double bed. Gun went to the door, shut it. On the bed LaMont rolled stiffly onto his gut, fists knotted back of his ears, breathing sharp snorts through his nostrils.

Gun sat back on the dresser top next to the television. He held the Smith on LaMont who was moaning into the bedspread, the flesh at his neck proud and rosy where the barrel had hit. At last the lawyer pushed himself slowly to kneeling. He breathed deeply, even now not rushing speech.

"Albert Iron Sky has distinctive handscript. Did you copy it, or was the letter his own?"

"Albert wrote it. I dictated."

"Ah." LaMont turned his head slowly right, left. "I really didn't expect anyone to find him up there, wherever it is he goes—God, ow, this lump. He must've told you something very bad about me."

"He wasn't easy on himself, either."

"A classic bad influence, Albert is." LaMont's tongue flicked out and wet his lips. His eyes lit on Gun, on the lamp, the door. "Did he tell you I told him not to kill Diane?"

"Don't bother, LaMont."

The lawyer met Gun's gaze. There were tiny darts of red

in the whites of his eyes, as if the blow to his neck had rup-
tured capillaries farther up. The eyes were wary and
remorseless, full of the strange optimism of evil. He said,
"All right. Say, I wonder if I'll be able to find a good attorney," smiling now as if to include Gun in the jest.

Gun stood up, the hard part of this still before him and
his desire for it gone. He crossed the room and pulled the
drapery open slightly. There were long cold stripes of rain
against the glass.

"I'd appreciate your telling them, down at Homicide, that
it's no emergency," LaMont said. "You'll spare me that, the
sirens and so forth?"

"Yes."

And then, Gun asked himself, What would happen?
Isaiah Bittens and Albert Iron Sky were dead. So was Joe
Sampler. So was Samantha Rhone, the hooker.

Who would testify against Harper LaMont?

Hanson and his officers could find trash on the man, they
could display him playing Sims, they could perhaps find
someone who knew that the New Master of the Legal
Thriller liked to wear the skin of a snake from time to time.
But proving he'd killed Diane—could they do that?

"I'll write a confession," LaMont said softly.

Gun looked at him. He saw pride in LaMont's eyes, and
limitless guile. No penitence. Diane came to his mind, in the
tattered dream-shirt, sorrow on her face as if she knew how
much she'd cost him. Anger rose in his blood—at LaMont,
yes, but also at Diane, and at his own betraying sense of
obligation. At the things it made necessary.

Of course LaMont would write a confession. It would be
the most eloquent confession ever penned, and every publisher in New York would bid for publication rights.

Gun remembered something LaMont himself had said: The animals always win.

LaMont stood from the bed. He was rubbing his neck, working up to a smile. He began to speak but Gun interrupted saying, "Hey, the rain," and when he turned to look Gun hit him in the lower jaw with every driving ounce. LaMont's head snapped halfway around compass, his jaw broken at the hinge and his spine at the third and fifth vertebrae, though Gun would be without these details until later. LaMont landed on the floor as if he were already dead. He wasn't. He breathed for twelve more minutes.

CHAPTER FORTY-THREE

Indian Summer took a sorry whack at the north country that autumn. The temperature rose to the high fifties, the snow sank away, and the walleye bed a quarter-mile out from Gun's dock became uncommonly active for a few days. But the sun stood off in a diffuse white haze that seemed to smell of smoke, as if from remote fires in the northwest of Canada, and the maples and birches and the pewter-bark aspen had turned weeks early and looked damp and grave without their leaves.

Carol did not call him. He saw her newspaper come out fresh each Thursday, saw her byline under stories about casinos and local gardeners and the city council; but he didn't read the stories, and Carol didn't call.

Hanson called twice from the city, the first time two days after Harper LaMont's body had been found in a sixth-floor room of the Charles Hotel. The Minneapolis *Star Tribune* had by that time printed three stories on the killing. The first was pure tragedy, equating LaMont with everyone from Keats to Kennedy and bemoaning the loss of a great Minnesotan, a man who had used his literary and legal talents to benefit the disadvantaged. The other two pieces were more cautious, focusing on the questions of why LaMont might have registered into a hometown hotel under an alias, and who might have wanted him dead. Hanson was interested in Gun's opinion.

"I've just read the papers," Gun said.

"The papers don't have everything. You know that Bittens guy that we found on his own freezer?"

"Yes."

"That freezer was in a storage compartment in the basement of Bittens's apartment building. The compartment has a lock on it. We found a key on Harper LaMont. It fits the lock."

Gun said, "No kidding."

"So, you were down here, checking out the potty district. You talked to LaMont. What, did he have some connections to these people?"

"Have you read any of his books? I suppose he had to do research."

"Uh-huh," Hanson said. "I suppose. Now, damn it, I'm going to have to read him."

Hanson's second call came the next day. He said, "You know anything about how Harper LaMont bit it?"

"The news said it was a broken neck."

"Yeah. Actually two vertebrae went, also his jaw was separated, back where it connects to the skull. It was one hell of a blow, Pedersen."

"Sounds like it."

"There are three spots on the left side of LaMont's jaw. Not abrasions exactly, more like dents. What they are, they're knuckle marks. I was trying to think how strong a man would have to be to break somebody's neck, and jaw, with his fist. One pop, it's done. That's a strong guy."

"Wasn't LaMont sort of a little fellow?"

"Sure, he was short," Hanson said. "What does short have to do with anything?"

"I'm sorry," Gun said. "Listen, drive up sometime. I owe you a beer."

"A beer? You owe me a boxful, Pedersen."

• • •

One morning Gun was smoking in his kitchen when the radio forecaster spoke of a cold front en route from the west, a wide slow-moving band of air that would arrive that night and unpack for a long stay. Gun flexed the fingers of his right hand. The knuckles hurt but were not as stiff as they'd been. He'd worn leather gloves the night he struck LaMont and they left no fingerprints but neither did they pad his knuckles from the impact. He went to his bedroom and picked a bat from the closet. Thirty-five inches, skinny-handled, bruises up on the sweet spot, the same Hillerich and Bradsby he'd hit with most of the summer, Carol watching from the kitchen window.

It didn't feel strange, though, to be hitting alone.

Out in the moist light, Gun loaded the magazine of his home-built iron arm with a dozen red-stitched baseballs. He switched it on and jogged to home plate with the bat in his hand. The machine hummed and the arm inching upward toward release made a ticking sound like warming steel. Gun stood waiting, the bat relaxed above his shoulder, eyes on the spot where the ball would suddenly come whole and growing like a planet flung from airless dark. He blinked and his concentration broke, the zone disappearing as the arm snapped forward and he stepped uncertainly into his swing. He missed and the ball bounded into the trees. He shook his head, set himself. The second pitch came in; this time he swung early and the ball hit the fat round tip of the bat and rolled feebly to the right.

He took ten more swings and never made the sort of contact he was used to. None of the baseballs reached the lake, a paced-off 380 feet distant. His knuckles ached, his palms stung. When it was over he unplugged the machine and rolled it into the garage. He coiled the long extension cord and hung it on a nail. He covered the machine with an oil-cloth tarp in the vacant place left by Carol's car. When he turned, Jack LaSalle was standing in the door.

"Hanging it up early this year?" Jack asked.

"That's right."

"World Series isn't even here yet."

"What do you want, Jack?"

Jack didn't hesitate. "I want to know what the hell's wrong with you, Gun. I want to know why Carol's living all of a sudden in that empty place above the paper."

"Jack," Gun said softly, "let me be a while."

"I kept waiting for you to come to the tavern, have a meal. Are you okay?"

"Thanks for driving out. But let me be."

Jack said, "You okay, Gun? Because I swear, if you're not okay, I'm going to come back out here and break your ass."

"Well, I appreciate that." Gun looked around himself at the great hollowness of the garage, the bare stud walls, the swept concrete. He said, "Go home now, Jack."

The front arrived ahead of schedule. By dark it was well below freezing and the wind smelled of December. The wood stove was choked with ashes and Gun scooped them into a lidded metal bucket and took them outside. He built a careful fire: a wad of pine tinder he'd shaved with a drawknife back in July, then a handful of hardwood twigs. By the time he reached for a chunk of split oak the flame was popping. He set the oak to burn, added a second heavy chunk and shut the steel doors. He listened a moment, spun the draft knob open until the fire fluttered and snarled inside, then stood and took his coat off the wall.

It was twenty degrees. The west wind bringing winter had arrived and slowed and the dark was a winter dark beneath which Stony Lake lay unsettled in its bed. Gun could hear the lake moving as he stood on the dock but the water tonight threw no light and was a wide black sheet of space before him.

He felt that he should pray, somehow. If there was ever a place you could be alone and call to God, it was on these icy ship-like planks. He wished for the mind of his father Gunsten Soren, who would know the things to say and how to say them.

When someone died, you prayed. So many had, lately.

He stood a long while in the quiet wind and the lake's hushed moaning. There were no stars, no moon, no shore lights burning across the bay. Behind him the house stood high and austere, bleak-windowed. Gun's knees were stiff as he knelt on the dock.

For Dotty Fordrick.

For Joe Sampler, and Samantha Rhone.

For Bittens and Albert Iron Sky.

For Harper LaMont, God help him.

Gun did not pray for himself. Not yet, though he had killed two men and owned some responsibility in the other deaths as well; he supposed he needed mercy as much as any man living. But Gun distrusted absolution sought too early on. He wanted time to exist with the things he'd done, to understand as much as possible the hurt and wreckage he'd dealt. He needed time and work and pain, and then at some undetermined moment he might lay down the whole bad mess, his lies and sorrows and yes his murders, and see what mercies there might be.

Gun did not question whether God lived. He sometimes questioned why He bothered.

For Diane Apple, who asked for none of it.

Slowly Gun reached forward. He let his hands come down until they gripped the end of the dock, then straightened his legs behind him. He took a long breath. The push-ups came as hard as if his joints were filled with grit. He'd get warm, though; the work would get easier. You could do it if you had to.

Below him the water turned uneasily. Gun pressed on, faster now, filling the empty places while the wind moved over him like spirits, and snow coming.